"Why aren't we married?"

Emily repeated Keith Roper's question silently. *Why aren't we married?* It didn't help.

"Are you one of those women who don't believe in marriage? Who refuse to be tied to a man?"

"Ah...no." She had no idea what he was talking about, but the truth seemed safe.

"Then...then it was me?"

"Mr. Roper—"

"Emily." His gaze was steady. "I'm sorry. I'm at a disadvantage here. I've forgotten a lifetime of information. Not only is my world filled with people I don't know, but I'm not even sure who *I* was. Was I the kind of man who'd carelessly get a woman pregnant, then leave her to fend for herself?"

Emily stared at him openmouthed, just beginning to understand what was happening.

He grasped her hand. "It doesn't matter how we came to this point. We're here. You're moving in with me, Emily."

For a woman alone in the world and only weeks away from giving birth, belonging to someone had incredible appeal....

Dear Reader,

I've always maintained that although every book isn't autobiographical, its inspiration and its emotional substance usually come from something personal in the author's life.

As a *mature* woman moving into my fifties with even more zest and excitement than I had as a girl, I am, however, plagued by the nemesis of middle age—memory lapses! It isn't severe, and if I don't belabor the elusive fact it will eventually come to me. But it annoys me a great deal, and is a source of amusement to my family and friends.

Still, a good writer can make use of everything that happens. The challenge was to make something *romantic* out of forgetfulness.

And then it came to me—amnesia! What could be more romantic than a man who's forgotten his past and a woman determined to convince him that she and the baby she carries belong in his present—and his future?

That's how *The Fraudulent Fiancée* came about.

Now all I have to do is find the romance in muscle twinges!

Sincerely,

Muriel Jensen

THE FRAUDULENT FIANCÉE
Muriel Jensen

Harlequin Books

TORONTO • NEW YORK • LONDON
AMSTERDAM • PARIS • SYDNEY • HAMBURG
STOCKHOLM • ATHENS • TOKYO • MILAN
MADRID • WARSAW • BUDAPEST • AUCKLAND

ISBN 0-373-70751-7

THE FRAUDULENT FIANCÉE

THE FRAUDULENT FIANCÉE

PROLOGUE

March

EMILY FRENCH looked into Greg Roper's evasive blue eyes and read in them all the things he wasn't saying.

"I want to set a wedding date," he insisted, bringing his hand to her cheek, "but it's distrustful and demeaning to make you sign a prenuptial agreement. Keith lost a lot in an ugly divorce, and now he thinks all women are out to fleece wealthy husbands. Anyway, I'm not telling the rest of the family about us until my brother and I have worked this out."

As a sous-chef at the Atlantic Eden, one of three hotel/convention-center complexes belonging to Roper Hotels, Emily was well aware of Keith Roper's reputation. President of the corporation and manager of the California Eden, Keith Roper handled labor disputes swiftly and fairly, was said to know every facet of the business and was purported to be ruthless in protecting his family's interests.

He'd been pointed out to her once when he visited the Atlantic Eden. He had the arrogant bearing to suit his reputation.

Emily took Greg's hand. "I told you I don't mind

signing a prenup,'' she said quietly. ''But that's not really the problem, is it?''

Greg smiled and wrapped his arms around her. ''My biggest problem has always been my brother. But I'm going to set him straight on this once and for all. If he won't change his mind, then he can just find a new manager for the Atlantic Eden and a new sous-chef, because you and I are out of here.''

Emily moved back a step. ''Greg, I don't want to be the cause of a rift between you and your family. If you don't want to get married, please be honest with me.''

She couldn't say precisely what had changed, but something had. Recently Greg seemed to have become someone else—someone less open, a little less spontaneous, much quieter than the warm and laughing man she'd fallen in love with.

Of course, two things had happened this week that could account for that. The first was her discovery that she was pregnant. The second was the sudden appearance of Greg's brother, Keith, and his parents, who ran the Northwest Eden, on the Oregon coast.

Greg pulled her back into his arms. ''Please, Emily, be patient. I want to marry you more than I've ever wanted anything. I just need a chance to talk to Keith. First we have to deal with business, then I'll get to us. He and the folks are here to find something wrong with my running of the Atlantic, I know it.''

Emily held him, waiting to feel the rush of warmth and excitement she used to feel in his arms. But the knowledge that she sheltered another life inside her made her less trusting than she'd been before.

"Greg." She pushed him away again and looked searchingly into his eyes. "I don't want a halfhearted father for this baby. If fatherhood isn't what you want, tell me. Then we just go our separate ways."

He met her gaze and held it. "I told you. I'm fine with it. We're going to be married, but on my terms, not Keith's." He glanced at his watch and gave her a brief kiss. "I've got to go. Keith's meeting me in my suite in ten minutes, then the family's getting together for dinner. I'll see you in the morning."

Emily watched from the doorway of her staff cabin as he walked to his Mercedes, waved and drove away. Then she pushed the door closed against the chilly March afternoon—Florida was unseasonably cold this month—and replayed their conversation in her mind.

I'm fine with it, he'd said about her pregnancy. Not the *I'm delighted* or *I'm thrilled* she'd hoped to hear. Disappointment joined her concern over the subtle changes in his behavior.

In fairness, she had to remember that Keith was here. Greg had told her how his parents had always favored Keith. They'd showered their affections on him when the brothers were children and now entrusted him with all the plum positions in the corporation while leaving everything that needed reorganizing or retooling to Greg—like the Atlantic Eden.

Greg had been sent here from the California Eden two years earlier because of the center's failing profits. Though the hotel and the dining room were generally full, expenses remained high, and Greg suspected that his family had arrived to express displeasure over his inability to put the center in the black.

Emily drew a deep breath, patted her still-flat stomach and went into the bedroom to dress for her shift. She would try not to worry about Greg tonight. The situation would be clearer after Greg had his conversation with Keith. He'd promised to share that with her in the morning.

In the meantime she would simply do her job and let her mind wander to the miracle of the life growing inside her.

KEITH ROPER poured scotch into a tumbler of ice and fought the anger he always experienced when he was forced to deal with his brother. It wasn't that he didn't care about Greg. In fact, fraternal instinct made him approach each encounter with the hope that this time it would be different, that this time he would find some glimmer of character at work in Greg.

But he was invariably disappointed.

"So you're telling me you're still operating like a tomcat despite what's going on in the world today?" He turned to face Greg and took a sip of his scotch.

"Her protection failed," Greg replied. He paced nervously, hands in his pants pockets. "She's a nice girl, but now she thinks she's my fiancée, and marriage is really not what I had in mind." Greg turned to Keith, his eyes both frightened and regretful. "I was going to call you about this, but now that you're here, you have to help me."

Keith couldn't count the number of times he'd heard those words. There'd been the cathedral's broken stained-glass window when Greg had been six and he'd been ten, the gate left open at the country house in Connecticut that had resulted in the loss of six purebred springer spaniel puppies, the joyride in a friend's father's Rolls that had ended with the car in the bottom of a river. Not to mention the girlfriends he'd wooed and conned into believing they had a future with him when nothing could have been further from the truth.

Greg's career, too, even though he worked for his own family, had been one disaster after another. And it wasn't that Greg didn't have a head for business. He simply didn't have the heart for work—of any kind.

Keith swirled the ice cubes in his glass. "You played out an adolescent fantasy and fooled around with...who? The aerobics instructor?"

"No." The reply was grim. "She works in the kitchen."

"A waitress?"

"A sous-chef."

Keith shook his head. "I'd have thought a woman experienced enough to be a chef would know better than to swallow the tripe you dish up."

"She likes *me*," Greg said defensively, jabbing a thumb at his own chest. "She isn't always on me for what I do wrong or what I don't do. And I like that about her."

"But not enough to follow through on what you've started."

Greg shrugged. It was a familiar gesture, one that usually followed a misdeed and preceded the excuse.

"I don't want to be tied to anyone." Greg looked around the elegant suite he occupied. "God knows being tied to the family business is bad enough."

Keith pointed to the door. "Freedom's just a few steps away."

Greg smiled crookedly. "I'd never make it on my own. We all know that. That's why I stay and that's why Dad keeps me. So are you going to help me or not?"

Keith squared his shoulders, accepting his brother's assessment of himself as the sad and simple truth. "What does *she* want?" he asked.

Greg studied him a moment, then sighed and turned away. Keith wondered if his brother was feeling pangs of conscience.

"She wants to get married," Greg said, looking out the window at the setting sun. "But I thought maybe you could buy her off and transfer her to one of the other Edens."

Keith swallowed the last of his scotch, hoping to drown the disgust that rose in him like nausea. Greg's character flaws couldn't be genetic. His father was as honest as the day was long, and his mother considered the most junior person in housekeeping before she thought of herself. It had to be some aberration individual to Greg that made him the selfish coward he was.

"I'll see that she has money," Keith said. "But I'm not getting you off the hook. You want out of her life, then have the decency to tell her the truth. Now come on. The folks are expecting us for dinner.''

Keith wandered into the hotel dining room's kitchen while Greg brought their parents up to date on the Atlantic Eden's spring conference schedule.

The Atlantic's chef had worked for the Ropers since Keith was in college. He was French, with a weakness for opera and women.

His kitchen ran like some sophisticated piece of machinery, parts moving smoothly, even humming—and that was literally. Edouard Chabot, in full chef's regalia, was pum-pum-pumming his way through some aria Keith didn't recognize, and a much smaller figure in a matching outfit was singing along in an exaggeratedly high falsetto while deftly chopping parsley.

The aria was completed at the same moment Edouard removed a pan of scampi from under the broiler and transferred it to a plate. After a sprinkle of chopped parsley, it was passed to still another figure in white who put on the designer garnish, then handed it to a waiter.

Edouard laughed and threw his arms around his small assistant in a quick hug. As they drew apart, Keith saw bright dark eyes under beautifully arched brows, a straight little nose and a warm open smile. A woman. There was only one woman on staff in the Atlantic's kitchen. The one carrying Greg's baby.

For an instant Keith simply stared, thinking how pretty she was, a considerable accomplishment in that formless outfit and with all her hair tucked up under a chef's hat.

Her hair, he was sure, would be as dark as those beautiful eyebrows.

Celine, his wife, had been blond and cool. She'd bowled him over with her beauty and led him, unresisting, to the altar. She'd made his life miserable for a year and a half and then taken him to the cleaners. She got the Ferrari, the place in the Hamptons and half his stock portfolio.

After Celine's cold indifference, he'd longed for a woman with fire in her eyes, passion in her soul, laughter in her voice. And here she was—about to be cast off by his brother.

As he watched her laugh and talk with Edouard, he wondered what had ever attracted her to Greg. He supposed it was possible she wasn't as smart as she looked. He'd been without a woman for a long time. Maybe he was seeing in her what he wanted to see.

He'd swear he could even tell she was pregnant. Though it didn't show at all in her body, he could see it in her face—in the delicate ivory complexion that ran to high color on her cheeks, in the glow of her eyes, in her manner that suggested magical forces at work.

A latent greed rose in him and he found himself wishing fervently she was his. Imagined what he would do with her if she was. Spoil her. Protect her. Love her often and well. His mind even conjured up an image of them wrapped together in the middle of his mahogany bed.

Then Edouard turned and saw him. He hurried over and enveloped Keith in a hug, too, one that probably would have rendered him unconscious had he been smaller.

"Keith!" Edouard exclaimed, holding him at arm's length, then embracing him again. "How good to see you!"

Keith noticed the young woman look up abruptly from her work. He caught her eye and watched the lively warmth there turn to animosity. *Ah,* he thought, *Greg has no doubt been telling her about his cruel older brother.*

Edouard began interrogating him about life in California, and the woman moved to the other side of the large kitchen.

That was the last he saw of her.

He brought Edouard out to join his parents, then watched the diners come and go while his parents caught up with their old friend.

From where he was, Keith could see through the dining room's open doors to the hotel desk. Either business had taken a sudden upward turn this particular weekend, or there was some kind of unidentified drain on the hotel's income. Activity was far livelier than profits indicated.

He was going to have to look into it.

And somehow he would have to get the pretty sous-chef out of his mind. She'd fallen for Greg, after all. A woman had to have more savvy than that to get by in this world.

THE FOLLOWING MORNING Emily had a clear picture of her situation before Greg even said a word.

He stood on the mat in front of her door, an air of impermanence about him, as though he was eager to be off.

"I'm sorry, Em," he said, turning a long white envelope in his hands. He glanced at her once, then went on, "Keith says he won't let us marry without the prenup, and if we do, I'm financially cut off. Then what would our baby have?"

As love shriveled and died inside her, she felt a terrible rage at herself for having been so deluded.

Under other circumstances, she might have been amused by the flimsiness of his story. But she understood it wasn't the story that was flimsy, it was the man. And that was sad.

She'd had only a quick glimpse last night of Keith Roper's handsome arrogant face, but the way he'd looked at her had stayed with her all night long. He'd obviously decided she wanted more from his brother than love, and was determined to protect his family's fortune.

But she didn't believe that any man with backbone would let another man dictate his future and whom he could love.

She nodded regretfully. "Our baby would have the love we give it. Still, what's that worth?"

Greg studied her suspiciously, as though he suspected sarcasm.

"He's sending me to California for a short while," Greg said, "so that you and I don't have to, uh, see each other every day."

"How generous," she said.

Greg frowned at her, then held out the envelope. "He wants you to have this."

"Is it a check?" she asked quietly.

"Yes."

"A big one?"

"Yes."

"Good." She took it from him, tore it in half and handed it back. "Put one-half in each ear and push. I'm sure they'll meet somewhere in the middle. Now get the hell out of my life." She slammed her door with great satisfaction.

It lasted about two minutes.

Then she sat at the kitchen table and cried her heart out. She cried for one hour for having been gullible and stupid enough to have fallen for a man everyone had warned her about.

Then she cried for another hour from sheer terror. She was having a baby alone.

Raised by a single mother who'd worked around the clock to keep food on the table and a roof over their heads, Emily had done many things in her life alone. But she'd hoped that when the day came she had her own child, she'd have a husband by her side and they'd walk into the future together.

Instead, she would have to do what her mother had, and her child would be faced with the same loneliness she'd known.

She spent the next hour drinking tea and convincing herself that didn't have to be the case. She would find a way out. There had to be a solution.

She was good enough to work in any five-star-hotel

dining room—Edouard told her so every day. But until the baby was born she would have to stay with the company that carried her health insurance.

Perhaps she would ask for a transfer to the Northwest Eden. Oregon was supposed to be beautiful, with clean air and clean water and a low crime rate. Yes. That was what she would do.

She rubbed her hand gently over her stomach. Her baby was going to have every chance she could give it.

CHAPTER ONE

September

"WHOA, WHOA! Will you slow down? Please! Have pity on a poor girl who uses her Nautilus for a clothes rack and smokes too much."

"What a wimp!" Emily patted her very large stomach and laughed at her cabin mate, who was bent double, gasping for breath. "I'm carrying this enormous front pack and I could run circles around you."

Vangie Bishop straightened and nodded, still breathing heavily. "Why don't you...do that?" she suggested. "Maybe it'll wear you out."

Emily pointed toward the staff cabins and slung an arm around Vangie's shoulders. "Come on. It's my night to cook and I have pork-roast leftovers in the freezer. Pedestrian, I know, but yummy."

Vangie put a hand to her heart and closed her eyes. "Pork roast. You do redeem yourself sometimes, Em I mean, usually you're such a disgustingly healthy and perfect little chef and mother-to-be that none of us can stand you. And don't think that shower the staff threw for you in the ballroom proves differently. It doesn't. They're just all afraid you'll stop baking cookies for the employees' lounge if they don't show their support.''

Emily thought of all the gifts safely packed away in the chest that had also been a gift and felt joy shaded by pain. Her baby, due in eight short weeks, would be born without a father.

Well, nobody had everything. She'd found good friends at the Northwest Eden, and that was a great blessing. Vangie, who worked on the front desk, was like a sister. Their backgrounds were very different, yet they had a lot in common—in particular, disillusionment with men. Vangie had found her fiancé in bed with her maid of honor the night before her wedding; she'd abandoned her job as a legal secretary and taken off for new adventures.

At their cabin in the woods behind the hotel, Emily gave Vangie a gentle shove toward the bathroom. ''You can have first go at the shower while I put dinner together.''

Turning on the television in the living room, Emily listened to the news while she worked. She made a salad to the sounds of strife in the Middle East, quarrels in Congress, distress over the economy and a seemingly endless litany of sports scores.

She was setting the table when she heard the name Roper very clearly on the local news. She went into the living room, two sets of silverware in her hand. There'd been talk of plans for a new Eden somewhere in the Southwest, and she wondered if the reporter had more details than the company grapevine had provided.

The picture on the screen froze her to the spot.

Vangie wandered out of the bathroom wrapped in a terry robe. "Did I hear—" she began, but Emily shushed her.

On the screen was a red Thunderbird upside down and off the road in what appeared to be a remote and hilly area.

"...apparently missed a curve," intoned the announcer, "went off the road and over a steep embankment. Both men were thrown from the vehicle. Gregory Daniel Roper, thirty-one, was declared dead at the scene, and Keith Cushman Roper, thirty-five, is in guarded condition at Santa Fe Memorial Hospital. Keith is the president of the famed Roper Hotels and Convention Centers, and Greg was manager of the Atlantic Eden. The men were scouting locations for a new hotel when the accident took place. It is not clear, according to Sheriff Peter Fuentes, which brother was driving."

Emily put a hand to her stomach in an unconsciously protective gesture. Vangie, the only one in Emily's life who knew the identity of her baby's father, put an arm around her and drew her to a chair.

Emily sat, feeling no personal loss, but only sadness in general for the loss of a life. And sadness for the parents, with whom she'd had little direct contact, but whom all the employees respected. She could only imagine the heartbreak of having one son dead and the other in the hospital.

"Are you all right?" Vangie asked anxiously, kneeling beside her. "What can I get you?"

Emily shook her head. "Nothing. I'm fine. The love I felt for Greg died the morning he handed me that check."

"I know." Vangie studied her worriedly. "I wish you *had* kept the check. Now that he's gone you'll never have the opportunity to get child support for this baby."

"I wouldn't have taken it. If he didn't want us, we didn't want him."

"Big talk. Wait'll the kid needs braces."

Emily smiled thinly at her friend. "I have a few years to prepare for that."

"Maybe you'll fall in love again."

Emily rolled her eyes. "Considering how poorly I did the first time, I think the baby and I are better on our own." She stood up and grasped Vangie's arm, then hauled her to her feet. "Come on. Let's go to the hotel. I'm sure there must be plans under way to do something for the Ropers. We'll eat later."

KEITH ROPER stared at the gray-haired bespectacled doctor and tried to take in what he was saying.

"You've lost all episodic memory, that is, memory of your circumstances, events in your life, the people you know."

Keith looked over at the older couple who'd been hovering by his bed since...since...he wasn't sure how long. They'd told him he'd been in an automobile accident and sustained a head injury. They'd looked horrified when he'd asked who they were. The woman had wept. He'd felt guilty and mean, and he'd searched his mind for some memory of them—but there'd been nothing there. And no one. His past was a startling terrifying nothingness.

Then he'd lost consciousness once more and drifted in and out of it with only brief periods of wakefulness.

"You don't remember being with Greg in the car?" the man had asked during one of these.

"No," he'd replied. "Who's Greg?"

The woman had wept again and the man had put his arms around her and held her close. Keith saw terrible pain on his face.

When he'd finally awakened—and remained awake—the doctor had conducted several tests.

"This type of memory lapse is fairly common after a serious head injury, though your physical recovery suggests that your memory should already be returning. Still—" the doctor smiled kindly "—every case is different and the brain is always surprising. Actually your case seems more like old-fashioned psychological amnesia to me. But of course, you're in no position to tell us whether you learned something shocking at the time of your accident, or if something shocking *caused* your accident."

Keith was holding panic at bay, but just. He could remember nothing.

"On the good side," the doctor went on as the couple watched worriedly from the foot of his bed, "your knowledge and skills memory is intact. You know all you need to know to get through a day. You can talk, form semantic thoughts, lay down and store new memories. You probably remember your multiplication tables, dance steps, hobbies. I suspect you'll even be able to work—you just won't know anybody there. But most important, this is temporary. You could begin reclaiming memory in a week, particularly if this condition is the result of your concussion. If it's psychological, it could take longer. The important thing is to remain calm and not try to force memory. That will only hold it back.''

Keith nodded. This nothingness could go on for months. Panic and anger were stirring deep inside him, but he drew a breath and tried to will them away. It wasn't his style to succumb to either of those emotions. He found a small measure of comfort in knowing that.

"If my problem is psychological," Keith said, "what does that mean exactly?"

"Probably that you've repressed something," the doctor replied calmly, "that you learned something you didn't like and decided to forget it. The brain set up a barrier between consciousness and what you've submerged beneath it. But you'll retrieve the memory eventually."

"This...Greg...was with me in the car."

"Yes. You remember Greg?" the doctor probed gently.

"No," Keith replied. "My...father told me." It was strange to say "father" and not feel the emotional attachment that should have backed up the word.

His father's name was Neil, he'd learned, and he was tall and solidly built, with thinning gray hair and kind blue eyes. He looked strong, steady. A good father, Keith guessed.

"Who is Greg?" Keith asked the doctor.

There was a moment's hesitation, then, "Greg was your brother."

Keith caught the note of...what? Grief? Condolence? He also caught the past tense.

"*Was* my brother?" he asked. His voice sounded strangled. "He...he died?"

The doctor put a hand on his arm. "Yes."

He'd had a brother. And that brother was dead. He should be experiencing deep emotion, a sense of loss, profound grief. But he felt nothing. And strangely *that* hurt.

"Was I driving?" he asked bluntly.

"We don't know," the doctor replied. "Neither of you was inside the vehicle when you were found. We don't know if you were thrown out, if you crawled out, or what happened."

Keith searched the emptiness that was his brain and realized that the only thing he knew for certain about his past was that he might have killed his brother. That hardly seemed like a foundation on which to start over.

"Darling." The woman—his mother, Barbara—came to sit on the edge of the bed beside him and took his hand. She was short and plump and looked as though she'd wept off all her makeup. Her eyes, dark brown and red-rimmed, were filled with love and sadness as they rested on him.

Strangely, although he didn't feel those same emotions, he could sense the depth of her devotion to him at that moment—and her grief for the brother he couldn't remember.

"Your physical injuries are so minor," she said, her voice raspy, "that the doctor agrees you can come home tomorrow. We have a place in the woods about half a mile from the hotel. You probably don't remember that."

He didn't. "No."

"Well. Dad's hired a plane to fly us all home—"

"All?" Keith asked.

"James, too." She indicated the doctor. "Of course, you don't remember him. James Stoneman, a neurosurgeon at Oregon Health Sciences Center. He was on a museum fund-raising drive with you and your father last spring. We sent for him when we realized you had amnesia." She dismissed that detail with a wave of her hand. "Anyway, we'd like you to stay with us in Oregon—your father and I manage the Northwest Eden..." At his confused look she stopped and gave him a brief explanation of the family-run business, including the fact that he used to manage the Northwest Eden, then switched with his father to manage the California Eden. "So we thought, until you're ready to go home to California, the Northwest Eden would be a good place for you to recuperate. Besides, you'll know everyone there—"

She stopped again as she realized what she'd said, then flashed him a quick reassuring smile. "Well, they'll remember *you*. We'll take you around town, show you where things are. And when you feel up to it, we'll take you to the hotel and help you get reacquainted.''

The suggestion appalled him, not because he didn't appreciate it, but because he felt a sense of desperation at the thought of being cared for, hovered over.

"I, ah…'' he began to protest.

She squeezed his hand and made a wry face that was still somehow warmly maternal. "You haven't forgotten that you hate being looked after, have you? When you were little you were one of those children who tied up baby-sitters or locked them in closets.''

A smile formed on his lips. The expression seemed natural. And though he didn't remember his parents, he felt sure he'd loved them very much.

But what if he'd killed their other son?

"I appreciate the offer,'' he said, "but I think it might be best if I…''

His father came around the opposite side of his bed and looked into his eyes. Keith had the feeling he was trying to communicate something. "What happened two days ago was an accident,'' he said. "You don't remember things, but I do. I know you as well as I know myself. And whether or not you were driving, you weren't responsible for the crash.''

He held Keith's gaze. There was a part of Keith that wouldn't be able to accept that assurance as truth until he knew for certain. But another part of him was apparently deeply connected to this man and took comfort in his words.

"Now,'' his father continued, his manner lightening just a little, "Your mother won't give me a moment's peace if you insist on going back to California alone. She won't give you any, either. She'll be calling you at all hours or we'll be flying down to see you. So do us all a favor and spend at least a few weeks with us. You like our pool. You used to swim competitively in college."

Keith relented. "Thank you," he said. "I'd like to go home with you. As long as you promise not to fuss."

His father looked at his wife. "Think you can do that, Babs?"

She shook her head, then smiled apologetically. "I know I can't, so why promise?"

His father turned to him, arms outspread. "Guess you'll have to come, anyway, and risk being fussed over."

Keith smiled and leaned back against the pillows, suddenly exhausted. "Guess I will."

EMILY FOLLOWED the chef into his office, dropping her apron into the laundry bin. It had been a long day and she was anxious to get home and put her feet up.

Usually she managed to maintain a cheerful outlook about her situation, but this morning she'd learned that her car needed extensive repairs she couldn't afford, and the news had put a major dint in her positive thinking.

Added to that, she felt ugly. Her face and ankles were swollen, and her stomach and breasts were huge. The baby, when she finally came, would probably be terrified of her.

"Guess what?" David asked brightly, yanking off his apron and tossing it after hers.

"What?" she asked, forcing herself to display some interest. David Ambrosio, the Northwest Eden's chef, had become a good friend over the past months, and he and his wife, Maria, had given her a crib and playpen that had been stored in their attic. Their youngest was five.

"The Ropers brought their son home about a week ago," David said. "He's doing very well, thank God. Keith's a good man. God forgive me, but if one had to be lost, I'm grateful it was the other one."

Emily found his words very distressing. Not David's brutal assessment of the man who'd fathered her baby—with the clarity of hindsight it was now easy to see that she'd imagined Greg's good qualities because she'd been lonely and had wanted them to be there. No, it was the prospect of coming face-to-face with Keith Roper that was terrifying. He knew she was carrying Greg's baby. He'd written the check she'd torn up. She couldn't help but wonder how long she'd remain on the Northwest Eden's payroll when he discovered she'd transferred here.

"Greg had so much potential," David said pensively. "He worked with me one summer, and I expected him to be like Keith had been four years earlier—intelligent, eager, hardworking. But he wasn't. He was intelligent, all right, and very charming. Everyone loved him at first. Then it became obvious he was selfish and self-serving. The guy always had an angle." David shook his head regretfully. "Just a bad seed, I guess."

The moody expression left his face and he gave Emily a broad smile. "Anyway, apparently Keith's getting restless at home, and Neil thought it would be a good idea to bring him through the hotel and the restaurant to see if it'll kick-start his memory."

Emily had been shrugging into her jacket, but now she paused. "Memory?"

"Yeah." David helped her with the jacket. "I thought everybody knew. The accident left him with amnesia. The doctor says it's only temporary, but it could last a week or a year. So Keith's decided not to sit around and wait. He's coming back to work here so that his family and their doctor can keep an eye on him."

"He's forgotten...everything?"

David folded his arms and leaned a hip on the counter. "Apparently not everything. It's a little quirky. The way Neil explained it to me, he remembers how things are done, but he doesn't remember people or episodes in his life. It's as though he's equipped with how to get by but has no memory of his relationships."

"Oh." Emily felt a rush of sympathy. Even considering what his loss of memory meant to her personally, that seemed like a very lonely sentence.

"Yeah. So the family's counting on the staff to help. You haven't seen much of the Ropers since you've been here, have you? Neil and Barbara have spent a lot of time scouting locations for the new Eden.''

"No, I haven't formally met them." But she'd seen them around on their breaks from traveling, and they'd often smiled at her.

"I'll introduce you," he said. "Wait up, and I'll drop you at the cabin on my way home. And until you get your car fixed I'll pick you up on my way in to work, too."

Emily knew it was futile to hope she'd be ill tomorrow. All through her pregnancy, she'd been healthy as a horse.

She just prayed that Greg's mother wouldn't look into her eyes and know her secret.

Impossible, she told herself as David drove her home. People couldn't read minds. And the only man who knew she carried Greg's baby had lost his memory.

CHAPTER TWO

IT WAS AN ELEGANT HOTEL. Keith wandered through the lobby with his father, who was greeted by everyone with the deference given a man both liked and respected. Keith was introduced to some members of the staff and prodded by others who asked good-naturedly if he was *sure* he didn't remember them.

But he didn't. And beautiful as the place was, he didn't recognize it. Still, his mind seemed able to retrieve a few facts.

"You know, it's strange," he said to his father, "but I know that five percent of bookings are expected to be no-shows, eight to ten percent are cancellations and overbooking is a gamble—but the only way to protect revenue." He laughed. "And I can hear a voice in my head telling me that a hotel room is a very perishable commodity. That if it isn't sold tonight, it won't be."

Neil put an arm around Keith's shoulders, and a smile brightened his usually worried expression. "That's *my* voice. And it's a good sign. You seem to have a handle on business facts."

Keith returned a waved greeting from a young woman behind the front desk. "That's probably because I grew up with them, didn't I? I mean…I don't remember growing up, but those facts and figures seem to be as much a part of me as language. Which is something else I haven't lost.''

Neil's smile dimmed fractionally, but he squeezed Keith's shoulder. ''It's more than your simply growing up in the business. You were rapidly becoming the heart of it because you were trying to help your mother and me ease toward retirement. I'm sure that spending some time here will help you recapture your memory—the Northwest Eden was always your favorite. You traded with me for the California Eden because that hotel generally has the most activity, the most influential and demanding clientele—and you're the best we've got. But you love the Northwest.''

Keith believed that without remembering it. In the few days since he'd been here, he'd felt himself relax just a little. He'd stood out on the balcony of his parents' house and stared for hours at the ocean, which seemed like a metaphor for his past. It appeared to stretch into infinity with no identifying marks on it, except for the occasional fishing boat or freighter in the distance, which might be likened to the bits of learned memory he'd retained.

Scruffy big-needled pines surrounded the house in a close embrace, and he hiked into them every morning and evening, listening to the sounds of life hidden in the undergrowth and high in the interwoven branches. There was something comforting, friendly, about the wild, and he usually ventured well past the guest house and deep into the woods before returning home.

"Come on." His father picked up their pace, led him through a dining room where just a few late risers were eating breakfast, then pushed his way through a pair of double doors behind a waiters' station where a small elderly man in a white jacket was making fresh coffee. Behind him were racks of glasses, an ice machine, tubs of silverware and flats of clean linen napkins.

The napkins would be folded into the bishop's-hat style. It startled and reassured Keith that he knew that.

The waiter looked up in pleased surprise. "Good morning, Mr. Roper. Mr. Keith, how are you doing?"

"Fine, thank you," Keith replied, offering his hand to the waiter. "And you are?"

"Roland, sir," the man replied with a friendly smile. "We had a bet on the Yankees-Orioles game and you lost." His smile widened. "But if you've forgotten that, I'll understand."

Keith wanted to remember that teasing grin, but he couldn't. He could only relate to the friendship extended.

"You sure you're not just scamming a man with a bad memory?" he asked, grinning. "My father tells me I was at the California Eden."

Roland nodded. "You were, but you call once a week to talk to David—that's David Ambrosio, our chef." He pointed toward the double doors apparently to indicate where the man could be found. "I always take the call and we talk baseball and make bets."

"What do I owe you, Roland?" Keith asked, reaching into the inside pocket of his jacket.

"Christmas week off," the waiter replied. "You promised to adjust my schedule." The man shrugged apologetically. "But please don't worry about it now. I'm so sorry for your loss." He glanced at Neil. "I'm sorry, Mr. Roper."

Keith saw the pain in his father's eyes and experienced a familiar sense of alienation. His brother had *died* and he felt nothing. Because he didn't remember him. It was as though he'd been an only child—except that he also couldn't remember his childhood.

Roland shifted uncomfortably, and before he could apologize again, Keith clapped his shoulder. "Thank you, Roland. And I'll take care of the schedule. You'll have Christmas week with your family."

His father began to lead him toward the double doors, but Keith hesitated, turning back to the waiter. "I'm the one who's the Yankees fan," he said with conviction.

Roland looked surprised, then pleased. "Yes, sir. You're remembering things!"

Neil raised an eyebrow. "I don't know. You've been a baseball fanatic since you were seven and used to memorize all the statistics. That could be learned memory, too, like your multiplication tables."

Keith grinned at Roland. "I'll bone up on my stats. You could probably use New Year's Eve off, as well, couldn't you?"

"Yes, sir!" Roland laughed. "But you've won as

many of our bets as you've lost. You could be in for a couple dozen of Arlette's date bars.''

''Arlette?''

''My wife, Mr. Keith. You sampled her bars on one of your visits, and since then your end of the bet is always three dozen of them.''

''Then I'll really study those stats. Have a good day, Roland.''

''You, too, sir.''

''So I have a weakness for sweets?'' Keith said to his father as they entered the kitchen.

Neil rolled his eyes. ''Yes, and good food in general. In fact, you should look like Marlon Brando, but you play tennis like a fiend, and in California, you can do that almost year round.''

Keith put a hand to his flat stomach. ''Good thing.''

''Keith!''

A man in a chef's hat stepped out from behind a wide chopping block in the middle of the room. A rack above it was hung with pots and pans and utensils.

''David Ambrosio,'' his father coached him. ''Finest chef west of Paris. Possibly even including Paris. And a good friend of yours. You started out together here.''

The man ignored Keith's proffered hand and grabbed him in a hug.

''Keith! We're so glad you're all right.''

David pushed him away to hold him at arm's length, and Keith took the moment to study the man. He was large, with twinkling dark eyes, a wide mouth and a booming voice. When he took hold of Keith's shoulders and gave him a friendly shake, Keith concluded that the man's feelings, as well as his gestures, were emphatic.

"I'm here," Keith conceded, "but my random-access memory needs a little work."

David dismissed that with a scornful snort. "It'll come back. You live and breathe Roper Hotels."

Keith nodded. "I seem to remember a lot about the business. I just don't remember the places or the people."

"What about food?" David pulled him toward a wok sizzling with vegetables and chunks of meat. "Chicken stir-fry, one of your favorite lunches. Sound familiar? Smell familiar?"

Keith inhaled the delicious aroma and felt his stomach growl in reaction. But it was in anticipation, not in memory. He looked at David warily. "If I don't remember it, can I have some, anyway?"

David gave the mixture a quick toss with a spatula and turned down the heat. "Still the wheeler-dealer," he observed, "despite the lost memory. Of course you can have it." He indicated a thick sandwich that had been dipped in egg batter and was now being turned on the grill. "And a Monte Carlo for you, Neil." He shook his head. "Not gourmet fare, but, hey. I can cook down for the little people."

Keith didn't hear his father's response to David's teasing. He'd turned to smile at David's assistant, wondering whether or not he knew him—when he realized the assistant was a woman—and very pregnant.

Suddenly an image flashed in his mind's eye. A

woman dressed just as this woman was dressed—in chef's pants and jacket, her hat covering every strand of hair. But in his image, the woman wasn't pregnant.

He could see her face clearly in his mind—dark eyes under beautifully arched dark eyebrows, pink cheeks, a straight little nose that gave her an air of innocence.

Then the image dissolved.

Disappointed, angry, he refused to let the first flash of memory in a dark ten days peter out so quickly. As though watching someone else perform the action, he took the woman's arm—the living breathing woman's arm—and turned her to face him.

Startled eyes framed by long sable lashes looked up at him. Lips the color of raspberries parted in surprise. He saw recognition on her face.

Well, that was nothing unusual. Most of the employees recognized him. But this was recognition that went deeper. This was knowledge that suggested... intimacy.

And as he had that thought, he experienced another flash of memory. He remembered wanting to spoil the woman, of wanting to protect her, of...

He chased the thought as it receded and this time he was successful. He saw them together in the middle of a bed, arms and legs entangled. She was telling him how much she loved him. He felt her warmth and her passion, and his own passionate response.

"Keith? Keith!" The sound of his father's anxious voice and the feel of fingers biting into his arm brought the curtain down on the memory.

Keith discovered that he was still holding the young woman's arm and that the expression on her face had a pleading quality.

Please don't tell them. Please don't say anything. He could read the thought in her eyes.

He released her arm and stared at her. No other face in the past ten days had triggered his memory. And why was it that he could read her mind when he couldn't even remember what had been on his own? Had they been lovers?

And if they'd been lovers... He looked at her advanced pregnancy and felt possession. This woman and her baby were his.

"Mr. Roper..." she said. Her voice was breathless and a little high. She pulled a stool from behind her and pushed him onto it.

Fascinated by the sound of her voice, struggling to remember it, he let himself be pushed. They were now eye-to-eye, and hers still held that urgent plea.

She reached for a cup of coffee near the stove and gave it to him. "Mr. Roper," she said again quietly, with a concerned glance at his father and at David, who hovered nearby, "you might not be as ready to leap back into things as you think you are."

Keith guessed she was trying to divert attention from herself to him. For some reason she didn't want anyone to know he'd recognized her.

And he wondered why, if he was so sure she was carrying his child, he hadn't married her. Or why they weren't living together. And also—on a very practical level—how they'd done it. He'd been in California, but she was…here?

"I'm calling his doctor," Neil said, turning to do just that.

Keith reached out and caught his father's arm in a grip that must have convinced him of his good health. "I'm fine," he insisted. "Don't call anyone. I just felt…weird for a minute. Shouldn't someone be watching my stir-fry?"

David swore and turned to the stove. His father studied him doubtfully for a moment, then went to rescue his sandwich.

Keith took hold of the young woman's arm again. With his free hand he brought his coffee to his lips and took a long swallow, feeling it warm him. Then he put the cup aside and gazed into her dark eyes.

"What's your name?" he asked quietly. Memory told him they'd been intimate, but not what he'd called her.

"Emily," she replied. Her arm was tense under his fingers. "French."

"You are?"

"Yes. I mean, no. I'm not French. I'm…" She fidgeted, looking around her as though hoping for rescue. "I'm Emily French. It's my name, not my nationality."

He nodded, pleased that she seemed unsettled. He was tired of being the only who didn't know what was going on. "And where are you from?"

She acted surprised by the question. "Why?"

He released her arm and shrugged, finding a certain

element of confidence coming to life within him now that he was out and around. "Because I'm trying to get reacquainted. To get back all the lost details of my past."

"But you don't know me," she said hurriedly. She glanced behind her to where David was transferring the stir-fry and Neil's Monte Carlo to plates. Then he put both on a tray, while Neil poured coffee. "That is, I worked at the Atlantic Eden. I saw you come through the hotel on one of your visits, but we've never spoken."

"I feel...like I know you," he insisted.

She looked confused. He'd expected her to look alarmed. "You don't, Mr. Roper," she replied, then smiled nervously. "Well...I guess you do now."

There'd been more to it than that; he could see it in her eyes.

But David was back to lead him after his father, who was carrying the tray with their lunches into the dining room.

"Thanks for looking after him, Emily," David called over his shoulder. "I'll be back in a few minutes."

FOR THE REMAINDER of the day Emily struggled against panic. Keith Roper, the ruthless head of Roper Hotels, who was supposed to have lost his memory, recognized her. She was sure of it. Greg had probably told him everything but turned the story around so that she had seduced him or blackmailed him or somehow forced him into being the father of her child.

And either he'd convinced his brother that she'd asked for money, or he'd suggested it himself as a way to buy her out of his life, because Keith Roper had offered her a check.

She wished now that she'd thought twice before tearing it up. At this moment she could be faraway from Roper Hotels—in a new car—with a nest egg for herself and the baby.

Instead, here she was right in the lion's den, probably about to be fired.

"WILL YOU PLEASE go home?" David said late that evening, taking the heavy saucepan she was drying out of her hands and pushing her toward the coatrack. "You've been here ten hours. I'm sure that isn't good for the baby or for you. Now, Maria left our old VW bug in your usual spot." As she opened her mouth to protest, he silenced her with a wave of his hand. "Just until you get yours repaired. So get in it and go home."

He pulled keys out of his pocket and handed them to her. "And if I see you back here in the next two days, I'll call the police."

She raised an eyebrow in amusement. "Isn't that a little extreme?"

"No," he said firmly. "What you do to yourself is criminal. I appreciate your covering half of Bernie's shift today, and I know you like the overtime, but do *not* show up tomorrow."

She hugged him fiercely. "Thank you, Ambrosio," she said as she pulled on a light canvas coat that no longer buttoned over her stomach. "But how will you cover tomorrow? Isn't there another conference coming in?"

"There is," he said, opening the back door for her, "and I've called in Mario."

"He'll put hard rock on the radio," she warned as she passed him.

He crossed himself. "I know. I'll put up with it knowing you're getting some rest. Now, good night. And go straight home."

After a minor altercation with the VW's gearshift, Emily drove home and let herself begin to hope she might have imagined Keith's reaction to her. She was very tired, and he was suffering from amnesia. All everyone in the kitchen had been able to talk about had been how good he looked, but how sad that he'd failed to recognize anyone.

She put the episode down to prenatal jitters—until she pulled into the driveway of her cabin and saw him in the beam of her headlights. He was sitting on her front porch steps, his back propped against a column, a forearm resting on a raised knee.

"Oh, no," she groaned as she pulled the car to a stop. She hadn't been wrong, after all. But she was too tired to defend her position with any dignity tonight. And the last thing she wanted to do was beg to keep her job, telling him how she needed the health insurance it provided her.

He loped down the steps and helped her out of the car.

She took the hand he offered, surprised by the courtesy.

"Why are you working a ten-hour shift?" he demanded before she could even say hello.

She explained about Bernie's daughter's piano recital.

"And there was no one else to cover for him?"

"I can use the overtime," she said simply.

He took her arm and led the way to the porch. "Yes. I imagine you can. I'd like to talk to you, Emily."

She dug in her heels. "Mr. Roper, I know what you—"

"There's no one around now, Emily," he interrupted, frowning down at her in the meager porch light. "You can call me Keith."

She blinked at him, confused. Why would she want to call him Keith? And what did it matter if anyone was around?

He placed a hand lightly at her back as she walked beside him up the few steps. Unlocking the door, she pushed it open. He waited for her to precede him, then came in and closed it behind him.

He looked around at the colorful eclectic furniture, the fireplace with an oak-slab mantel, the framed needlework that decorated the half-timbered walls.

"Your work?" Keith asked as he studied a cross-stitch sampler.

Emily tossed her jacket over a chair. "No, Vangie's, my roommate. She's on the front desk."

He turned to smile at her. "Tall blonde with a Vassar air?"

She had to smile back. He might not have a memory, but he certainly had perception. "That's her." She stopped smiling, knowing she had to put on a forceful front if she wanted to save her job.

But she wasn't forceful by nature. It wasn't that she was a pushover, but she generally liked everyone and had a particular soft spot for the abused, the misunderstood and the ill.

And right now Keith Roper was ill. Although if he'd recognized her, he was recovering faster than had been rumored.

He certainly was a handsome specimen. She remembered being so angry the one and only time they'd met that she'd only been aware of his arrogance. It remained now, despite his circumstances, but this time she noticed the ocean blue eyes, the strong straight nose, the well-shaped mouth set in an angular chin.

The features could have been Greg's, but something subtle in the eyes and jaw made him look completely different.

She squared her shoulders, pretending a command of the situation she didn't really feel. "I can offer you tea or hot chocolate."

He pointed her to the chair where she'd tossed her jacket. "No, thank you. But I would like some answers."

Here it comes, she thought, bracing herself. And to prove to him that it was her cabin even if the property it rested on was his, she sat in the rocker, instead.

"Very well," she replied in Vangie's Vassar voice. "Ask."

Though he'd wanted her to sit, he wandered across the room, hands in the pockets of an elegantly cut pair of trousers. The fabric pulled over taut hips and defined long lean legs.

Emily looked away, ashamed of herself for noticing. This man presented a threat to her baby's future, after all.

He finally turned, studied her a moment as though he'd reached a decision and moved to stand right in front of her.

"Why aren't we married?" he asked.

CHAPTER THREE

EMILY REPEATED the question silently to herself. *Why aren't we married?*

No. That didn't help.

He eased himself down on the raised stone hearth beside her. "Are you one of those women who don't believe in marriage? Who refuse to be tied to a man?"

"Ah…no," she replied. She still had no idea what he was talking about, but the truth seemed safe.

"Then…then it was me?"

"Mr. Roper—"

"Emily." She was rocking nervously and he put a hand on the arm of the chair to stop her. His gaze was steady. "I'm sorry. I'm at a disadvantage here. I've forgotten a lifetime of information. Not only is my world filled with people I don't know, but I'm not even sure who *I* was. Was I the kind of man who'd carelessly get a woman pregnant, then leave her to fend for herself?"

Emily stared at him openmouthed, just beginning to understand why he'd posed the question. But before she could even try to answer, he went on.

"When I saw you in the kitchen this afternoon," he said, his thumb running gently over her knuckles, "I recognized you. I remembered that I'd felt passionate and protective." He drew a breath and his voice fell an octave. "I remembered that we'd made love."

Emily could only stare.

"I checked your file this afternoon," he continued, "and discovered that you were working at the Atlantic Eden at a time when I spent a week there."

Emily remained speechless. She couldn't sort out what this all meant, much less what to do about it.

He closed his hand over hers. "I know this baby's mine," he said gravely. Then his voice filled with wry self-recrimination. "I'm sorry I don't remember the details. Did we have a relationship that extended beyond that week? Did we quarrel?"

Once more she tried to reply, but for the life of her she could neither accuse him of what he seemed to think he'd done, nor assure him that he'd done nothing. The moment seemed ripe with some undefined potential.

He sighed. "I can only imagine how upsetting it must be to carry the baby of a man who can't even remember the relationship." He squeezed her hand. "But as far as I'm concerned, it doesn't matter how we came to this point. We're here. And while I don't know what kind of man I was before, I know what I feel now, and that's what I have to go with. You're moving in with me, Emily."

Emily didn't even try to repeat that to herself. It had been terrifying enough the first time.

"Mr. Roper, you don't—" she began urgently.

He rolled his eyes. "Emily, you make me feel as

though we're colonial Calvinists. My name is Keith. *Keith.* Let me hear you say it.''

Oh, God, Emily thought, and that wasn't an irreverent exclamation—it was a prayer. What should she do? From the moment she'd grasped his mistake—though how he'd come to make it she had no idea—she saw what it could mean for her daughter. Security, protection, education, opportunity...

''Keith,'' she murmured, still debating the possibilities.

''That's better,'' he said, patting her hand. Then he stood and wandered around again, hands in his pockets. She made a point of looking away. ''The doctor isn't sure when my memory will return. It could be days, months, even years. And because I can't remember what I've done, how I thought, what I felt, even what we really had together, I think asking you to marry me now wouldn't be fair to you. But I want you and the baby taken care of and I intend to do it myself. If my memory returns and I'm someone you don't want to be with, we'll decide what to do then. If I'm someone you want for a lifetime, we'll get married.''

He crossed to the rocker as Emily pushed herself out of it. He caught her hands to steady her.

She looked into his eyes, trying to find the man Greg had described to her, the one who'd claimed all the glory and the praise and who'd criticized and belittled his brother. She found no evidence of him. This man seemed to be all kindness and consideration even in the midst of obvious anguish.

After having had a father she'd never known, a

mother who'd been too busy and too bitter to find time
for her, and a lover who'd come into her lonely life
only to prove himself a coward, Emily thought that
Keith Roper seemed like a gift from heaven. And for
a moment she thought of herself and not of her baby.

She didn't know what had happened in Keith's
damaged mind to make him think he was her baby's
father, but she knew he was truly convinced he was.
She could feel the sense of possession in the way he
looked at her and touched her. For a woman alone in
the world and only weeks away from giving birth, belonging to someone had incredible appeal.

But deceit went against everything she believed in.

She said firmly, "No. You have to concentrate on
recovering. Your memory has to be the priority—"

"Emily, look," he interrupted, his eyes painfully
earnest. "That's my point. I remember *you*. In the
huge dark nothingness of my world, *you* are all that's
familiar. You're the one flicker of light. If we made
some sophisticated agreement to go our separate ways,
I'm canceling it. I need you. Right now, you and the
baby are the only handholds I have. Stay with me.
Help me find my way. And I'll help you and the baby
make yours."

Emily saw the genuine plea in his eyes and stopped
wondering what faulty connection in his brain had
brought about this misunderstanding. He needed her.
And she needed him.

His warm supple fingers squeezed hers. "For now,"
he coaxed, "just come and stay with me. What ulti-

mately happens between us can be determined when my memory returns.''

No. She couldn't do this. Struggling against the appeal of the plan, she fought for reason. ''Keith, there's a baby involved here. If your memory returns and you...we decide we don't like being together...''

''My name will be on the birth certificate,'' he finished for her, ''and he'll have the full financial protection of that name.'' He smiled wryly. ''I don't really remember, but I'm told it's considerable.''

She shouldn't. She *couldn't*. But financial security for her child was a gift she couldn't ignore, and the guilt she felt over taking advantage of Keith Roper's confusion was assuaged by his own insistence that he needed her.

''OK,'' she said finally. ''Yes.''

He expelled his breath and ran a hand lightly up and down her arm. ''Good. Pack what you'll need for tonight and we'll come back for the rest tomorrow.''

''Tonight?'' she asked in astonishment. ''You want me to come with you now? It's almost midnight.''

He grinned. ''Apparently I'm impulsive.''

''But Vangie...''

He glanced at the clock. ''If you can be ready in ten minutes, we can catch her before she's off the desk. You can explain things to her then.''

Now that she'd taken action, fear was beginning to set in. ''I'm scheduled to work in the morning,'' she fibbed.

He shook his head. ''No, you're not. In fact, I'm going to have you taken off the schedule until after the baby's born. No more long hours on your feet for you.'' He looked at the clock again. "Come on. You're down to eight minutes if you want to catch Vangie.''

She folded her arms and tried to stand tall—a difficult feat for a woman who stood five foot three inches, and who appeared even shorter now that she was almost as wide.

She began to spin a little fiction, to create a past for them she could draw on.

"I can forgive you this," she said with a tolerant smile, "because of your condition. But you've forgotten that we have an agreement. You don't tell me what to do, and I don't…don't try to pin you down.''

He, too, folded his arms. "Well, like I said, since I don't remember, I have to go with how I'm inclined to deal with things now. And every impulse tells me that the best thing I can do for my baby is to take good care of his mother.''

She decided it was time to correct him. "*Her* mother.''

He looked puzzled. "Whose mother?''

She waved her hand. "*Her* mother not *his* mother. Your…the baby's a girl.''

A genuine smile brightened his face. "It is? All right! Does she have a name yet?''

"A first name," Emily replied, fascinated by his smile. For a moment she couldn't help wishing that it *was* his baby. "Rebecca. But I'm having trouble with a middle name.''

"Rebecca Roper." He said the name thoughtfully,

then nodded approval, that warm smile still in place. "I like it. Rebecca Roper."

Emily heard the name on his lips and felt a little shudder deep inside her that was half guilt, half excitement. Playing this role couldn't be wrong if it meant her baby would be born into a father's welcoming arms.

He turned her bodily toward the hallway that led to the bedrooms. "Go pack. We'll hang around and explain to Vangie when she gets here."

"But...aren't you staying with your parents?" she asked, still resistant about embarking on this dangerous scheme. "They won't want me intruding on their lives so soon after...I mean..."

He put a hand on her shoulder and walked her the few steps to the hallway. "I know what you mean. They have a guest house where we won't be intruding on anyone. Where you can rest and I can put my life back together. It's being prepared for me now."

Emily didn't know whether to be annoyed with his assumption that she'd fall in with his plan or impressed with his take-charge attitude. Greg had always been happy to let someone else work out problems and find solutions.

She placed her hands on her hips. "Women like to be consulted about major decisions. David tells me you've retained learned knowledge, despite your memory loss. I think that's something you shouldn't have forgotten."

He leaned a forearm on the door frame and smiled down at her. "I haven't. I thought, since we've obviously been involved, you'd want to be near me and help me reconstruct my life. And start preparing a nest for the baby.''

It would be hard to find fault with that assumption and let him continue his belief that they'd been lovers.

"Unless we've had a major quarrel," he asked, his gaze on her suddenly sharpening. "What precisely is our situation, anyway?"

She tried to think fast. "We...we fight a lot on the rare occasions when we do get to be together," she said, letting the story develop as she spoke. "You like things your way, and I've been alone for a long time, so I'm used to making plans without considering anyone else."

He lowered his arm and put his hands in his pockets. She had his full attention, and she felt an instant's guilt as she realized he was greedily absorbing what he thought were the details of their relationship.

Then she pushed the guilt aside, telling herself that most of what she said was true. Scuttlebutt was that he was a very decisive and demanding man, and she *was* used to making her own plans.

"How did we manage to get together?" he asked. "I thought we might have had only that week when I was in Florida."

Emily racked her brain for a solution that couldn't be contradicted by his parents or anyone else who knew his routine. "We...we've kept everything kind of quiet. You sent for me when you had free weekends."

"Why did we keep it quiet?"

That was a question she hadn't expected. "Well... I'm just a sous-chef and you're president of the company."

He raised an eyebrow. "And that mattered to me?"

This deceit was growing more and more entangled. It would have been expedient to simply say yes, but he obviously didn't like the suggestion that he'd been a snob. "No," she replied. "I wanted us to be discreet. I'm always teasing about wanting to be the next Julia Child, and I didn't want anyone to think our relationship was a political move on my part."

He considered her levelly. "And I let you get away with that?"

She frowned at him. "You didn't have a choice. I do pretty much what I like with my life."

"But this isn't just your life," he said quietly. "It's mine, too. And the baby's. It's a habit you'll have to change."

She supposed that sounded fair. If she was going to use him in this way, the least she could do was not make his life any more difficult than it already was. But if this charade of hers was to work, she couldn't risk being discovered.

"We can still be discreet," she proposed.

He shook his head. "Too late. I told my parents about the baby and that I wanted to move you into the guest house."

Oh, no. Emily closed her eyes. His parents had been away at the time of her shower, but a generous check had been sent to her in their name. "And what did they say?"

"They were surprised," he said. "I guess that's natural. They prefer having us take over the guest house, though, than setting up house elsewhere. This way my mother can hover over me, and my father can watch anxiously for signs of returning memory." His tone was teasing but tolerant of the parental concerns. "I hope that won't drive you crazy."

She knew it might, but not for the reason he thought. "You're lucky to be so loved," she said.

He looked into her eyes, obviously catching an unconsciously wistful note in her voice. "You sound jealous. Aren't you loved that way? I don't remember."

She shook her head. "My father left before I was born and my mother was overworked and bitter. There wasn't much time for me."

He took her face in his hands, his expression regretful. "I'm sorry. But what about me? Don't I love you that way?"

Emily groaned inwardly, wishing she'd never started this. But then he rubbed a thumb gently over her cheekbone and she knew she couldn't pass up this chance, however fleeting it might be.

"I think," she said in a small voice, "that you want to love me that way, but you're so consumed with the business. And I'm sure I'm not always easy to love."

"But I remember loving you," he insisted, frowning over his thoughts. "I do. It was my first real flash of memory since I woke up in the hospital."

Emily wondered how that could possibly be. Even in a mind in which a door had been closed between past and present, it didn't seem possible such strong emotion could have been created out of nothing. And yet it had.

She felt an urgent wish that there was some foundation for his feelings.

And then she realized she had to create that foundation for her baby's sake. At least until Keith regained his memory.

She put a hand on his chest, just over his heart. "I think sometimes you have difficulty telling me what you feel. But don't worry. It'll all come back to you in time."

Then she smiled and turned away before he could read in her eyes that his memory, when it did return, would tell him quite another story.

VANGIE STOOD in Emily's bedroom, her brown eyes enormous. "Why is Mr. Roper in our living room? And why did he tell me he's waiting for you?" She walked to the bed and frowned at the suitcase. "And why are you packing your things?"

Emily explained about that afternoon in the kitchen, about Keith's abrupt appearance at the cabin and his confusion about her pregnancy.

Her friend sank onto the bed while Emily walked into the bathroom for her few toiletries.

"He thinks *he's* the father of your baby?" Vangie asked in horrified disbelief.

Emily came back into the bedroom clutching shampoo, toothbrush and makeup. She made a shushing motion with her free hand. "Yes, he does. And keep your voice down."

"You didn't tell him it's Greg's?"

"He doesn't remember Greg."

"Emily, he will one day," Vangie warned. She held open a plastic bag so Emily could drop her things into it. "How come he remembers you?"

Emily closed the bag, tucked it into a corner of her case and zipped the case closed. "I don't know. He doesn't know. He says he walked into the kitchen and recognized me. He said he remembers loving me." She put a hand to her stomach and rubbed gently. "He's excited about Rebecca. How can I deprive her of that—a father who's anxious for her to arrive?"

Vangie stood and caught Emily by the shoulders. "Listen to me, Em. I see what's happening here. You thought when Greg walked away that your baby was going to have to grow up the same way you did— without a dad and with a mother who was so busy supporting you she didn't have time to love you."

"Except that I would find time for love."

"Of course you would. But that's not the point. The point is that you're walking into a lie and you're going to spend the time until his memory comes back building on it."

"He pleaded with me to stay with him. He thinks I can help him."

"Emily, please. What do you think his reaction will be when his memory *does* return and he realizes you tricked him?"

Emily sighed. "I imagine he'll hate me, but my

baby will have been welcomed into the world by a loving father, and he's promised to take care of her financially whatever happens. I can't say no to that."

"It's a dangerous game, Em."

"It's not a game, Vangie. It's…it's a role. He thinks I'm the woman he loves. And I will be until he remembers otherwise."

Vangie dropped her arms and studied Emily's face with new understanding. "Ah. This is as much for you as for the baby, isn't it?"

Emily looked away and picked up her case. "It's for all three of us—Keith and the baby and me. We're all tied together in this strange knot of false memory and creative fiction." She gave Vangie a quick hug. "Maybe there was a kink in my fate and I was supposed to meet Keith, not Greg."

Vangie looked skeptical. "Try explaining that to Keith when he's calling you a scheming liar."

Emily went to the bedroom door and stopped there, her hand on the knob. "I'll be back tomorrow for the rest of my things. I'll keep in touch. You're still on as my Lamaze coach?"

"Of course." Vangie gave her another hug. "With you for a mother, this baby will need someone to look after her—even while she's being born." Then she sighed. "Take care of yourself, Emily, and be careful."

Emily tried to reassure her. "He seems very kind," she said.

Vangie nodded. "I'm concerned for your emotional

well-being, not your physical safety. Losing a good man can be fatal, you know.''

Emily opened the door and walked into the living room where Keith was waiting. Presented with this surprising new beginning, she chose not to think about loss and death.

CHAPTER FOUR

KEITH GLANCED at Emily, seated beside him in the Lexus, and finally had a sense of reclaiming his life. She was all he could remember of his past, but he knew she'd been the center of it, so it stood to reason that he could build his future around her. Provided he turned out to be the kind of man she wanted.

What if he'd been responsible for his brother's death? He might have been the driver and guilty of recklessness or carelessness or some form of neglect that had caused the accident.

If that was true, would Emily still want to be with him? Would he be fit to live with even if she did?

"Did you know Greg?" he asked, pulling into the narrow lane that led to his parents' home and driving slowly forward. "He managed the Atlantic Eden while you were there."

"Yes." She turned to him, pale and quiet in the dark car. "A little."

"I don't remember him," he said. "I wondered what he was like. What you thought of him."

She shifted a little in her seat. "I think your parents would be better able to tell you about him."

He gave her a rueful glance as he drove past a beautiful brick-and-timber house partially lit by a coach lantern on the front lawn. "I don't want to bring up the subject of Greg around my parents because they've just lost him. And he didn't like the Northwest Eden, so no one around here really knew him. I thought you could help me."

"He looked a little like you," she said, before becoming distracted by the sudden appearance of the guest cottage, a smaller version of his parents' house. "How beautiful! Do you always stay here when you visit?"

Keith resigned himself to having to wait for information on his brother. "Got me," he replied. He noticed that the kitchen light was on as he pulled into the garage and turned off the engine. "I don't remember."

She groaned. "Sorry. That was stupid of me."

"No, it wasn't," he said, turning to her. The garage lights had gone on automatically, and she looked even paler, more wide-eyed, under them. "It was a perfectly normal question, I just happen to have a malfunctioning memory. Come on. Let's go in so you can get settled. You look exhausted."

He got her bag out of the trunk and came around to the passenger side in time to help her out of the car.

"I'm getting to the stage of feeling as though I'm ten months pregnant," she joked as she leaned heavily on his arm. "And I have all the grace of a Clydesdale on ice."

"I'm sure it isn't easy to carry all that extra weight in front."

She cast him a grin as he walked her to the door that led to the guest-house kitchen. "I don't think it's all in front. I'm becoming well padded everywhere."

He opened the door and ushered her through. It was impossible to detect body structure under the voluminous top she wore. He'd had that one swift mental image of her in his earlier flash of memory, but she'd been wearing kitchen whites then, and her figure had been almost as indeterminate.

It didn't even occur to him to fantasize about what she might look like when she wasn't pregnant. She was carrying his baby. She was his woman. And she anchored his whole world.

"Oh!" She stopped abruptly.

Over her head he could see his parents rising from the kitchen table. His father came forward, hand extended.

"Hello, Emily," he said, as she offered hers. "We met in the hotel earlier, remember? I'm Neil Roper, Keith's father."

"Yes." Her voice was breathless, nervous. Keith realized that meeting his parents under these circumstances might be uncomfortable for her. He dropped her case and put an arm around her shoulders. "This is all...a little surprising, isn't it?"

"It is," his father agreed with a quiet laugh. "And a little awkward, though that's not your fault. I thought we should wait until morning to come over because you were working late and we knew you'd be tired. But Barbara thought if we didn't come, you might think we...objected."

"Not *objected*." Keith's mother came forward, pushed his father out of the way and took Emily's hand in both of hers. "Who could object to a baby? But I thought you might think we didn't approve. Not that Keith would care if we didn't. But we do." She winced and asked, "Does that make any sense?"

"You're welcoming me?" Emily asked.

His mother's shoulders sagged with relief. "Yes! Trust another woman to read between the lines. Well. We'll get right out of here so you two can get to bed. We made up both bedrooms—" She paled. "Not that you have to occupy both rooms, but I thought—"

Neil caught her arm and tugged her toward the front door. "Let's go, Babs," he said.

"Isn't anyone going to say hello to *me*?" Keith called after them.

"Hello, son," his father said as he pulled the door open. "Good night."

"There're bacon and eggs in the fridge," his mother said over her shoulder, "and David's getting groceries for you when the food vendor comes...in the morning!" The last was added as his father literally dragged her onto the front porch. "Bye! Sleep well!" she shouted as he closed the door.

Emily put a hand to her breast and sighed. "I was afraid they'd hate me," she said. "Or at least be suspicious of me."

"Why?" he asked. "The baby isn't something you created by yourself."

She turned and looked up into his eyes then, her own softening as she studied him. "You're from a galaxy far far away, aren't you?"

He grinned. "Could be. I don't remember."

She giggled, then her expression sobered and for a moment he thought she leaned toward him as though she might touch him—or kiss him. The moment stretched, then she lowered her eyes and sighed again.

Although he had to admit to disappointment, he told himself she didn't know him. He wasn't the same man she'd made this baby with. He couldn't expect her touch or her kisses yet. But her presence beside him was like a lifeline.

He picked up her bag and led her toward a flight of stairs. "I'll give you the tour tomorrow. Right now we need to get you off your feet."

"You know, I'm really very healthy," she insisted, preceding him up the stairs. "I used to run before I got pregnant, and now I walk to keep fit."

"Good—left at the top of the stairs—but you still need more rest than you're getting. David agreed."

She turned at the top to confront him, her eyes disapproving. "You discussed me with David?"

He stopped, aware of her angry indignation.

"Yes. He told me he thought the father of your baby was out of the picture."

"He never said a word to me."

"I asked him not to."

"Well…" She looked sheepish for a moment, then turned left down the small hallway, chin in the air. "You and I decided not to get married. I'd intended to raise Rebecca by myself."

He caught up with her in the half-open doorway of the front bedroom. "I have a feeling," he said, "that *you* decided we weren't getting married. But, the situation's changed."

"Nothing's decided about it," she reminded him. "You said we'd leave the future open."

"True." He reached beyond her to push open the door. "But the past is a clean slate. We start from here. If you're used to dictating terms, you'll have to get over it."

She met his eyes, and though hers were tired, they still managed to threaten. "We are *not* going to get along well at all."

He shrugged. "According to what you've told me, that should be a familiar and maybe even comfortable situation for us. This is your room."

Emily stared at him as he placed her bag in the middle of the bed and proceeded to tell her about the room, clearly expecting her to accept that he'd assumed control of her life.

She resisted the admission that there'd been occasions in the past few months when she might have appreciated being able to let someone else take charge. Still, after a lifetime of being either abandoned or ignored, she'd met a man who not only intended to stay, but to care for her. That held a certain appeal.

"Think you'll be comfortable?" Keith asked. "Is there anything else you'll need?"

Emily turned her attention from the man to the room and saw a dark wood sleigh bed with cream-colored pillows banked against the headboard. There was a matching nightstand on which sat a tall slender lamp with a cutwork shade and several framed photographs.

An elegant chair upholstered in the same fabric and color as the pillows was against a bare window. A tall damask screen stood beside it, and Keith now moved it in front of the window. Framed botanical prints decorated the pale gold walls.

"I can't imagine lovelier surroundings," she said, suffering another stab of guilt.

He pointed her toward a doorway that led into a bathroom also decorated in creamy colors. There was a sunken tub, a shower stall and a deep walk-in closet with one wall of shelves and the other holding a clothes rod that must have been ten feet long.

"I can't fill a quarter of that closet," she said. "If *you* need more storage—"

"We'll use it to collect baby things." He walked back out into the bedroom and she followed, a little shocked by the elegant furnishings. "I understand the staff gave you a shower. David said that everyone came and you got a ton of things."

She nodded, remembering the gifts. "Even your parents sent a check, and I hadn't even really met them yet."

He smiled. "It's strange, but even though I don't

remember my past with them, I feel strongly connected to them already.''

''Of course,'' she said. ''I imagine love bridges even a memory gap.'' She gestured around the room. ''There's love in the way this room was put together.''

''My mother did it,'' he said. ''She told me when I asked her about moving us in here that she's a frustrated interior decorator.''

Emily nodded. ''Yes. The employee bulletin said she renovated the executive suites in the California Eden.''

''Really?'' His tone was rueful. ''I didn't know that—or I guess I don't remember it.''

A rush of sympathy made her walk over to him. But she stopped short of touching him, though she wanted to. This was all too new, too fragile. ''I'm sure it'll start coming back soon. I'll try to help you remember.''

She heard the words come out of her mouth and wondered what on earth she was doing. To compound the problem, she knew the words had been heartfelt and sincere.

For all his autocratic tendencies, she liked this man. She *wanted* him to have his life back. She just prayed that it wouldn't happen until her baby was born bearing his name.

She closed her eyes, realizing there had to be some special place in the depths of hell reserved for the likes of her.

''You get some sleep,'' he said, backing out of the

room. "I'm right at the other end of the hall. If you need anything, just shout or press one-one on your bedside phone. It's connected to my parents' house."

She moved to the door, her eyes widening. "Did you remember that?"

He laughed. "No. I was here with my mother before I went to pick you up. She told me. So far, all I remember is you."

Emily felt drawn to him despite all the cautions that should be flagging her actions. She knew that physical contact was dangerous, that if she truly was some trigger for his memory, she could be undercutting her own agenda, but she didn't seem able to stop herself.

She leaned toward him, one hand on the door frame. He looked surprised for an instant, then lowered his head. Their lips met in a swift chaste kiss. She had to have one, but that was all she dared.

His mouth was warm on hers, supple, tender. The contact was so brief she could analyze no more than that.

"Anything?" she asked, drawing back.

He concentrated on her a moment, obviously deliberating. "No," he said finally, then smiled wickedly. "But that was hardly serious enough to affirm the present much less resurrect the past. When you're not so tired, we'll try this again. Good night, Emily."

"Good night, Keith."

She closed her door and leaned against it, her heart rocketing. The baby stirred restlessly. She allowed herself a moment to regain perspective as she rubbed her stomach comfortingly. "It's OK," she crooned. "It was just a small kiss. I'm not sure why it felt so...big. But it's all right. I have everything under control. This is going to work out just fine for you, Rebecca."

But Emily couldn't help wondering just how this was going to work out for *her*.

KEITH WALKED into his bedroom and wondered if his feelings were so strong because there was more room for them with his memory gone.

Dear God. His body was rampaging as though he'd taken Emily to bed rather than exchanged a modest kiss with her. Desire that was more than simple lust thrummed through him.

Enough! She was a few weeks away from having their baby, and once Rebecca was born, it would be some time before Emily could make love with him—even if she was so inclined.

At the very least, he was looking at two and a half months of celibacy.

He lay on his bed in the dark, fully clothed, and let desire prowl through him. He couldn't remember, of course, but he had a strong feeling that whatever qualities defined the man he'd been, celibacy wasn't one of them.

KEITH AWOKE to the smell of breakfast—coffee, bacon, toast. He showered quickly, dressed and went down to the kitchen to find Emily.

She was poking through a drawer beside the sink,

apparently looking for something she couldn't find. She glanced up with a smile when she heard him. "Turner?" she asked.

He raised an eyebrow. "Ted? Tina?"

She groaned. "An egg turner."

"Ah. I don't remember. Did you try over here?" He went to the island in the middle of the kitchen as she opened another drawer.

"Got it!" She held one up triumphantly, then pointed with it to the sunny nook at the far end of the kitchen. A small oak table stood there, set for two with juice and silverware.

"I was hoping you'd sleep in," he said, walking toward her.

"Rick, one of the busboys, came by with groceries at seven." Her smile was teasing. "You didn't hear him but I did, so I came down to let him in and put the things away."

Keith hadn't heard a thing. Some guardian of her rest he was. "So it's my fault you're up."

She took a carton of eggs from the refrigerator and, as she closed the door, asked, "Do you always blame yourself for everything?"

He wasn't sure. "Don't you know?"

She opened the carton and seemed to be inspecting the eggs. "You...aren't usually very forthcoming. We don't share feelings very much."

That made sense. "Well, that'll change this time around," he replied. "Without memory, feelings are all I have. And I suppose assuming responsibility is the price one pays for being heir to a company. I feel responsible for guests, for jobs, for quality control.''

She carried the eggs to the counter near the stove. ''You remember feeling responsible?'' she asked as she broke two into the pan.

''No.'' He went over to the toaster. ''I feel responsible now. Want one or two slices?''

''One please,'' she replied as he opened the refrigerator for the butter. ''Can you cook?''

He waited for some learned memory to surface. It didn't. He looked around the kitchen and felt no response within himself. Again he turned the question on her. ''Have I ever cooked for you?''

She concentrated on blotting the bacon and putting it on the plates. ''No, you're spoiled. Room service caters to your every whim.''

''Well, I think you can trust me with toast. I do seem to remember that all I have to do is push a lever down, then wait for the toast to reappear.''

''Very good. If only the rest of life could be handled with the push of a lever. There'd be so much less to learn. So much less to remember.'' She pointed to the coffeemaker. ''Pour yourself a cup. It's David's special dark roast. He keeps a pot on in the kitchen at all times to make sure the staff stays awake. How do you like your eggs? Or do you know?''

He turned to her, an eyebrow raised. ''Yes, but don't *you* know?''

She mentally kicked herself for not thinking before she spoke. ''You're changeable,'' she said quickly, easily. "Sometimes you like them scrambled, sometimes over."

He seemed to accept that. "Over easy, then."

"You got it." She reached into the oven for a plate that had been warming with three slices of bacon on it, turned the eggs, waited for just a few seconds, then slid them onto the plate.

The toast popped up. He removed the slices and put another one in.

"You go eat." She handed him the plate. "I'll have mine done in an instant."

He sat at the table and watched her prepare her own breakfast, marveling that she was sitting across from him eating it before he'd finished his juice.

"Did you sleep well?" he asked, pushing the pot of jam toward her.

She hadn't, but not because her room wasn't comfortable. She'd been too excited about the sudden and complete change in her circumstances, too worried about the delicate balance of behavior required on her part to keep everything intact. She was certainly going to have to do better with casual remarks and questions than she'd done this morning.

"No," she admitted, "but it was because the baby was restless. I think she's going to be a mountain climber. Her feet always seem to be groping for footholds."

He frowned at her. "You're sure everything's all right?"

"Absolutely." She grinned. "*You* must have slept well."

He laughed. "I certainly did. Remembering you was the first sign of recovery I've had. And having you near has made me feel less...alien. That was the first good night's sleep I've had since I left the hospital."

Her heart went out to him. She understood the feeling of alienation. She'd experienced it often as a child—every time her mother had a day off and Emily waited eagerly for her company, only to find herself at a baby-sitter's again or packed off to a friend's so her mother could sleep, or do whatever she had to do, without Emily's chattering interference.

"We could drive into Beaver Bay today," she suggested, "and look in the shops and galleries."

Sensory input would stimulate his mind and possibly his memory—but since he usually worked in California and the accident happened in New Mexico, she couldn't imagine that Beaver Bay would bring back memories that would endanger her situation.

Fresh air would be good for both of them, however, and an excursion would remove them from the too-cozy atmosphere of this guest house. She found that smiling across the table at him was comfortable and had a sense of rightness about it that would be dangerous to entertain.

He thought about her suggestion, then asked doubtfully, "I like to do that?"

She was beginning to enjoy creating a little fictional

past for them. She laughed. "No, but I do, and you usually indulge me."

"Really." He sipped at his coffee, watching her lazily. "So I'm a sensitive nineties kind of guy even though I can't share my feelings?"

"Something like that." She nibbled on a piece of bacon and realized what he'd just said. "That nineties remark might be memory. It shows awareness of the times."

He frowned, then brightened fractionally. "Maybe. It's pretty unspecific, but it is something."

"I'll think of it as progress," she declared.

"You're an optimist, then?"

She'd better be. Her situation required one. "Yes." She leapt into her fiction with both feet. "And you tease me about it all the time."

"I'm a pessimist?"

She couldn't believe that of him. "A realist," she corrected.

"That might be why we quarrel." He took a bite of toast. "But if we learned to listen to each other, we might put our lives in balance. That would be a good environment for the baby."

"It would," she agreed. "We...we're always trying to do that, but it's harder than it sounds."

He raised his coffee cup to her. "Then I'll try harder," he said.

Emily lifted her cup in response, thinking for the second time that he had to be an intergalactic visitor.

AFTER BREAKFAST, Keith borrowed the hotel's airport shuttle and took her back to the cabin to pack the rest of her stuff. He carried plants and baby things out while Vangie helped her pack her clothes.

"What's he like?" Vangie asked when Keith made a trip to the van.

"You wouldn't believe me if I told you," Emily said, holding a cluster of hangers together while Vangie pulled a giant plastic bag over the garments that hung from them.

Vangie smoothed the bag, then tied a string around the tops of the hangers. "What does that mean? Good or bad?"

"It's hard to believe he's Greg's brother," Emily said, remembering the desperate and lonely state of mind she'd been in when Greg had walked into her life. She could only hope she'd have seen through him if she'd felt more secure, more at peace. "He makes Greg seem like the evil twin. He's kind and understanding and funny." Her voice caught and she took a moment to clear her throat. She could feel Vangie's eyes on her. "He seems to want so much to make our relationship work."

Vangie put a hand on her shoulder and said, "Em, you don't *have* a relationship."

Emily looked at her levelly. "We do, Van. It's been less than twenty-four hours, and we've hardly even touched, but there's something there. Something that already goes deeper than what I had with Greg."

"Honey, you just *want* this to work…"

"I do," she admitted, clearing her throat again. "But that isn't it. There's something there. Maybe that's why he remembers me."

"He doesn't *remember* you," Vangie reminded her. "His mind's confused. He never *knew* you."

Emily sighed, grim reality threatening her storybook morning. She let the homemade suitbag collapse over her arm as Vangie finished tying it. "I know. I can't explain it. I'm just telling you it's there."

"That ready to go?" Keith asked from the doorway.

Emily could see by his ready smile that he hadn't overheard the discussion. "Yes," she said, handing him the bag.

When he had gone back out to the van, Vangie said, "He sure is gorgeous. And he seems sweet. But hotel scuttlebutt has always been that he's a tough cookie. I guess your strategy should be to do nothing to make him reveal that side of himself. Though how you'll be able to stick to that when he starts remembering things—"

"Stop it!" Emily said with quiet firmness.

Vangie, in the act of packing a box of books, looked up in surprise.

Emily hugged her to soften the command. "I'm doing this for Rebecca and it seems to have a few perks for me, so I'm going to enjoy them. I'm not going to let what could happen in a couple of weeks or months or a year take any of the pleasure out of it. And neither are you. Is that clear?"

Vangie curtsied. "Yes, Your Majesty." Then she

added seriously, "Just remember that you're welcome to this room again if you ever need it." She smiled, obviously choosing to cooperate with Emily's dictum. "This is the last box. Come on. I'll carry it out for you." She added wistfully, "If only he had a twin for me!"

CHAPTER FIVE

DOWNTOWN BEAVER BAY comprised six blocks of shops tucked between pine-covered hills on one side and the ocean on the other. In the summer it was filled with tourists and driving down the two-lane street was almost impossible.

In mid-September, the crowds had thinned, but a resort atmosphere still prevailed. On the beach colorful kites flew against a blue sky and waves crashed vigorously against the shore—a portent of the coming change of season. On the street couples wobbled by on tandem bicycles and a group of laughing young men pedaled a surrey cart through a quiet intersection.

As Keith and Emily stood on a corner watching the boisterous group, Keith said, "I'd better tell you now—we're not doing that."

She took his arm as they crossed the street. "It looks like entirely too much work. There's a gallery we haven't explored." She indicated a colorful sandwich board on the sidewalk and the giant hand on it that pointed to a little corner shop, The Genie Gallery.

The scent of sandalwood filled the air as Emily and Keith walked in. Bright pottery took up one corner, and Emily paused before a tall glass case of handmade jewelry.

Keith walked past her to a shelf that held small sculpted figures trapped inside bottles that appeared to be handblown. He picked up one tall slender bottle that contained the figure of a man in a three-piece suit. The figure carried a briefcase, a rolled-up newspaper caught under his arm, and seemed oblivious to his confinement.

Keith found himself smiling. He liked it. He couldn't decide if he related to it because he'd been that kind of man before the accident—tightly enclosed by the responsibilities and pressures of his work—or if he identified with it in his present situation. Caught in a prison through which he could see but not escape.

Emily took the bottle out of his hands and replaced it on the shelf. "You don't want that," she whispered, hooking her arm in his and leading him into another room.

He pretended to resist. Actually, when she took his arm with that casually possessive ease, he would have let her lead him anywhere. Still, he felt called upon to put up at least a token resistance.

"I happen to like the guy in the bottle," he said.

She tugged a little harder. "I can see how you'd relate to him, but he's too depressing."

He held his ground. "Losing your memory *is* depressing."

She was very close to him, both her arms now hooked in his one. When he felt her stomach against his hipbone, a sensation like an electrical impulse shot through his body, ricocheting off everything it touched.

He saw that she was speaking, and he had to force his attention to what she was saying.

"That's why you can't have him. You aren't trapped forever like he is, but if you take him home and concentrate on him, you'll think you are and it'll take longer for you to remember things."

He bit back a smile. "And how many years have you been in practice as a psychiatrist?"

"I've been in practice as a woman for twenty-six years," she said with obvious pride. "And I'm carrying a baby. My natural intuition is at its sharpest just now. I'm right about this."

He was completely charmed by her and decided that he didn't want to fight it. "You're pretty bossy, aren't you?" he asked good-naturedly.

She laughed. "You don't remember?"

"No."

"Then I'm *sometimes* bossy, though always in your best interests. Usually, though, you find me endlessly delightful and diverting."

He ran his free hand along the side of her face, every bit as delighted and diverted as she claimed. "I thought you said we fought all the time."

"Well...between fights," she said softly, color brimming in her cheeks, "we enjoy being together." Then she pulled him insistently toward a display of clothing. "Come on. We'll find something more cheerful for you to relate to."

She had to keep moving! It was that or collapse, given the bone-deep weakness she felt when he touched her. She remembered their brief kiss last night and how the memory of it had kept her awake for hours. She had to learn to control her reactions toward him.

She held up a T-shirt with familiar sepia-toned illustrations of heroic profiles and muscular bodies on the unbleached cotton. "Recognize these?"

He nodded. "Of course. Leonardo da Vinci. But he was an artist and an engineer, neither of which feels like me."

"OK. Is this familiar?" She held up another shirt with vibrant colors and modern-art images.

"Ah...not sure."

"Joan Miró," she supplied.

"Interesting," he said, "but not me, either. I think I'm more...traditional. Are you an artist at heart?"

"Only in that I enjoy looking at it. I took an art-history class in night school and loved it."

"I don't seem to remember much about art. Either I wasn't interested in it or chose to spend my time on more practical pursuits."

"Art is practical," she argued, replacing the shirt and moving to inspect a display of ties. "It feeds the soul, and some of us can't function with hungry souls."

She ran her fingertips through the ties, then suddenly snatched one out and held it up for his inspection. "This is it!"

"What?" He studied a silhouetted figure that appeared to be free-falling in a field of stars.

"It's Matisse," she said. "This is called *Icarus.*"

"The boy in Greek mythology who flew too close to the sun?"

"Right." She seemed pleased that he knew.

"And fell because the sun melted the wax that held his wings together."

"Yes!"

He put an arm around her shoulders and shook his head. "Emily, I think you've strayed from your point of trying to give me a positive image to focus on."

She turned her attention from the tie to him, her expression victorious. He felt his pulse double its speed. "No, I haven't," she said. "This is one of Matisse's cutout images from later in his life when he couldn't stand up to paint. He began painting paper in bed, then cutting images out of it and creating some of the most memorable work of his career. He took a debilitation that should have ended his art and turned it into victory."

Her excitement over the subject and how she thought it applied to him was so genuine he couldn't help responding—at least to her.

"So, I'll buy the tie," he said, liking the warm softness of her in his arm and continuing to hold her close. "Did you see anything in the jewelry case you'd like?"

"Thanks, but my fingers and wrists are so swollen now, I can't wear rings or bracelets."

"What about a pin?"

"Thank you, but—"

He pulled her toward the case in the other room. "No, you found something for me, and now I'll find something for you." He peered into the case. "OK, what says mother-to-be and memory maker?"

She studied the pieces, then Keith jabbed his finger at the glass where a graceful silver swan was followed by three cygnets, all connected on a slender silver ripple of water. "What about that?"

It was beautiful. "You don't think three cygnets would be tempting fate?"

He laughed and hailed the clerk.

Keith stowed their purchases in the car. They walked hand in hand from one end of town to the other, then back again on the other side of the street. He waited patiently while she explored the shops that interested her, looking over her shoulder while she perused the window of a maternity shop.

One mannequin wore a blue denim jumper over a white long-sleeved jersey, and hiking boots with big socks. The other wore a sparkling berry-colored evening top over matching silk pants. Flowered cotton and plaid flannel shirts were tossed around the bottom of the case.

Keith pointed to the boots. "Are those in fashion?"

He'd leaned close to be heard above the street traffic. She could see their reflections in the window and thought they looked like an ad for insurance, sort of planning for the future.

Before the gloomy thought could form that she'd probably only have a month or two worth of future with him tops, she answered him. "Yes. But what's really important is how comfortable the boots are." She put a hand to the small of her back. "And you 'need good support at this stage of the game—for your feet, your back, your stomach, your chest.''

He moved her hand aside and pressed gently where she'd been rubbing. The pressure hurt for an instant, then soothed away a knot of discomfort. His hand still rubbing, he looked down at her feet. She was in running shoes.

''Let's get you some boots,'' he suggested.

''No.'' She grabbed his hand and tried to pull him away from the shop. ''I've only got six more weeks to go.''

''During which time you'll probably grow more uncomfortable.''

''I'll sit down more.''

''The boots will still fit you after you have the baby.''

''Then I probably won't even have time to leave the house.''

''Sure you will,'' he insisted. ''We're going to take this baby everywhere. Come on. Let's get the boots.''

''Keith,'' she said, planting her feet when he tried to pull her. ''You're not listening to me.''

He smiled. ''You have that wrong. It's you who isn't listening to me. You're probably causing the baby all kinds of unnecessary stress. And what are you going to wear to my father's surprise party?''

She stopped resisting. ''What surprise party?''

''He's going to be sixty-five a week from Sunday, and the employees are throwing a bash. My mother's helping. It'll be in the Crystal Room.''

The big ballroom with the chandelier that had been purchased from a French castle.

He pointed to the berry-colored evening outfit. "You like that?"

"It's beautiful, but it probably costs a fortune."

"Lucky for you," he said, drawing her firmly into the shop, "I have a fortune."

She left an hour later with the evening outfit, the boots, the denim jumper and the white jersey, and several of the flannel shirts from the window.

"I'd have to be pregnant for the next ten years to make buying all this economical," she protested as he helped her into the car.

He slipped in behind the wheel, then pinned the swan and cygnets on the collar of her pink shirt. "We do have two more cygnets to go."

EMILY COULDN'T quite believe the fairy-tale ease of her life. As one day rolled quietly into the next, she couldn't remember ever having been so happy—or so terrified.

Keith rose early to go to the hotel and try to recapture his life. Emily always got up then, too, prepared his breakfast and sent him on his way with a sense of their being some reincarnation of Ozzie and Harriet.

David had taken her off the dining room's schedule, and no amount of whining or cajoling changed his mind. "It's orders from the top," he'd said.

Forced to find something else to do with her time, she played with new recipes in the guest-house kitchen, met Vangie for coffee, drove herself to town and bought fabric to make a quilt for the baby. She swam in the hotel pool and walked with Vangie every afternoon.

She discovered there was more to life than work. It made her feel decadent.

And while she loved to cook for Keith, sometimes David prepared something special for Keith to take home for dinner, and sometimes Keith took her out.

Occasionally he worked in his room while she watched television and made stitches in the quilt. Other times he sat with her, insisting on getting up to bring her tea and an evening snack while she sewed.

She experienced guilt at such times, but it was far outweighed by the thrill of being so cosseted. It was a new experience for her, and her happiness was further heightened by his pleasure at the prospect of the baby's arrival. She'd been so alone with her anticipation for so long.

If there was one less-than-perfect aspect of their relationship, it was that at the end of their warm and cozy evenings, they walked upstairs together—and turned in opposite directions.

She lay alone in her comfortable but cold bed and imagined him beside her. They would lie in a spoon position, their bodies curved as though she was sitting in his lap. His arm would curl around her—and around Rebecca—and she would lean backward into him and hold his arm in place with her hand. His warmth would surround her and she would finally feel at peace.

But there was a good chance that would never happen. If his memory returned before the baby was born, they might never even sleep in the same bed—but she chose not to consider that.

Still, they'd undoubtedly sleep apart until the baby was born. And after that, Emily imagined there'd be little sleep for anyone, anyway. But somewhere in the third month of her baby's life, she decided, if his memory had not yet returned, she would think about seduction.

THE NIGHT BEFORE Neil's party, Emily heard Keith tossing and turning in bed. Then she heard him get up and go downstairs. She didn't hear him return.

She remembered that he'd seemed a little remote at dinner—unusual for him. He'd gone upstairs to work and come down only briefly before they both went up to bed.

An alarming thought struck her. He *knew* something! He'd remembered something—maybe that he wasn't engaged at all. That his brother had asked him for money to get her out of his life.

No. That couldn't be. His mother had come over after supper with plans for getting Neil to the ballroom the following evening, and she'd behaved as she always did—no suggestion of distrust or hostility.

Of course, he might not have told her.

A loud crash brought Emily bolt upright in bed. The baby protested, squirming and gaining purchase for her feet in Emily's ribs. Emily patted the mound of her stomach reassuringly and stood to pull on her robe.

She found Keith sweeping up glass from the kitchen floor. He wore pajama bottoms and a T-shirt, and looked as if he was in pain. She felt traitorous hoping it was physical pain—and not the emotional anguish of betrayal.

"Are you all right?" she asked, taking the broom from him as he bent to get the last fragments of glass.

He got down on his haunches and held the dustpan in place. "Yeah, just clumsy," he said. "I'm sorry I woke you."

"You didn't," she denied, putting the broom aside as he deposited the last of the glass in the garbage. "At least not when you dropped the glass. I heard you thrashing around upstairs. Did you have too many of David's enchiladas?"

He smiled thinly, took the broom from her and replaced it and the dustpan in the closet. "No. I'm all right. But I've had headaches since the crash, and I was groping around for a glass in the dark because light makes the pain worse, then I knocked one over and had to put the light on, anyway."

"Are you taking any painkillers?" she asked.

He held up a prescription bottle and reached for another glass. He filled it with water, then tossed a pill into his mouth and drank it down.

She crossed to the switch on the wall and flipped off the light. "Is that better?"

"Yeah." She heard the glass make safe contact with the countertop. "I'll be fine now. Why don't you go back to bed?"

"I have a better idea." She homed in on his voice and walked toward him.

He was silent for a heartbeat. "What's that?"

"Massage is good for headaches. You're always spoiling me, so let me return the favor." She made contact with a warm hair-roughened forearm and pulled it gently.

"Where are you taking me?"

"To the table so you can sit and I can massage the pain away."

He had little doubt she could do that. Just the touch of her hand on his arm turned his mind instantly from the pain in his head to the uncomfortable tightness in his groin that he'd been dealing with nightly.

He wanted to tell her he didn't think this was a good idea, but he didn't want her to have any concern about demands of intimacy on his part—at least not now. And he wanted desperately for her to touch him—wherever and for whatever reason she could find an excuse.

"All right." He brought her close to him and began to move slowly toward the table. "Watch it. You don't want to fall."

"I'm extremely surefooted. I may look like a rhinoceros, but I move like a gazelle."

"Not a rhinoceros," he corrected. "A nice little lioness after a big meal."

"Mmm." As she thought over that comparison, her hand made contact with a chair and she pulled it out. "That would make me queen of the jungle, wouldn't it? Sit please."

She took his hand and placed it on the back of the chair. He walked around it and sat down.

"Only if you're married to the lion who's king,"

he said. "If you're hooked up with one of the other males, you could lose your position at court."

"Well, you sort of are, aren't you?"

"I sort of am what?"

"The king. At least around here."

"I suppose. In a way. But we're not married."

She placed her fingertips on the nape of his neck and worked up to the base of his skull, searching for knots of stress. "I don't think—" she concentrated on the warm muscle under her fingers "—that the lion and his mate usually call in a minister. Drop your head and relax as much as you can."

He complied, then groaned a little when she ran her fingers up through his hair to the top of his head.

"Sorry," she said. "Vangie gets headaches and I can usually help her—at least a little."

"It's all right. I imagine the lion keeps his mate if she hunts well for him."

"I bring bacon and eggs to your table every morning—does that count? I mean, if you consider the difference in circumstances..."

"I think that would be fair. And you are providing me with an heiress to the throne. You've complied with all the rules of the wild. Oh, Emily..." His groan trailed off as she brought her fingers down and worked her way from the base of his neck to his shoulders and back again.

His head lolled against her breast, resting on the curve of her stomach.

"I can't tell you," he said in a hoarse whisper, "how good that feels."

"Are you sure you should be working full days?" she asked, continuing to massage his shoulders. "And bringing work home at night? That can be exhausting even when you aren't suffering from amnesia and haven't added a pregnant woman to your life."

"I'm fine," he said as she pushed his head forward. She inched her thumbs up his taut neck muscles. "According to my mother, I've always been very…in tense. I had headaches before the accident. They're just more frequent now."

"Well, you're going to have to stop being so intense," she said, beginning to work her thumbs down his spine. "There are lots of people to take care of the hotels, and I have charge of myself and this baby."

"No," he corrected mildly, "we share charge of the baby."

"Have you failed to notice who's carrying her?"

"Have you forgotten who gave her to you?"

The question lingered in the darkness, threatening the role she was assuming so easily.

Her hands moved up his spine to his shoulders, thumbs working at the base of his neck.

"Do you remember that?" she whispered.

He sighed. "I'm sorry to say I don't. Where were we?"

She'd been in Greg's rooms on the Atlantic Eden's top floor, and it had been the first week of February. He'd invited her to dinner, told her he loved her. And because she couldn't remember ever having heard those words spoken with such sincerity, she believed him. She went to him as though he were water and she'd been thirsting for years.

But in the past week and a half, she'd disassociated Greg from what was happening. Greg had nothing to do with this. This was her world and Keith's, and soon they would bring Rebecca into it.

So she thought about how she would have liked it to be and told Keith, "There's a beautiful little cove a short distance from the Atlantic Eden. You have to scramble down a rocky slope, so few people go there. But we braved it for the privacy. And you'd charmed the chef out of pâté and champagne."

"Clever me."

"I thought so. We talked for hours. The sun set and the moon rose and we…stopped talking."

He pulled her hands from his shoulders and drew her down into his lap. One hand rested lightly at her back, the other on her thigh. "And then what?"

She let her mind wander for a moment and experienced a little shudder deep inside her at how it would be with him. Slow, intense, life-altering.

"We…went there the next four nights, then you started talking about transferring me to the California Eden, and I got upset because…" She was really having to invent here. "Because I wasn't sure it would work between us, and you were angry at me because I wouldn't just drop everything and fall in with your plans."

In truth, she thought if such a fiction had ever really happened, she'd have moved to California in a minute. She was discovering there was an enormous difference between a man who simply wanted his own way and one who applied his will in the interest of a woman's comfort and security—and because something in him demanded he have her near. The behavior was still autocratic, but it was motivated by a purpose she could live with.

"But we continued to see each other." His voice came quietly out of the dark, just at her ear. She could feel his breath on her cheek and the brush of the stubble on his jaw when she shifted her weight, certain she must be crushing him.

"Yes," she said. "You were always changing my schedule so I could be free when you were. Then we'd meet somewhere, or I'd fly out to California."

"And you resented my manipulations."

Even though she was making all this up, she couldn't admit to that. "I pretended to," she corrected. "But I was always ecstatic to see you. Now, how's your headache?"

"Better. You seem to be magic for me." His hand moved in gentle circles on her back, and she felt as though she could melt into it—if it wasn't for the baby's toes curled into her ribs.

She tried to stretch. It helped to put an arm around Keith's neck and lift her torso.

"A pain?" Keith asked.

She felt every part of his body that touched hers go tense, and she laid a hand on his chest. "Yes, but not a contraction. Rebecca's quarters are getting a little cramped and she's having trouble getting comfortable.

She solves the problem by finding a niche for her feet between my ribs.''

Keith put his hand on her stomach and stroked gently from side to side, his fingertips exploring.

"Maybe she has a headache, too, and she's using her gravity boots," he teased.

"Oh." Emily gave a start as the baby moved. It felt as though one little foot made a clear arc across her stomach.

"Did you feel that?" she asked, reaching for Keith's hand to place it where the foot was still wiggling.

His hand was already there. "Yes," he said, his tone hushed, enthralled. "Her foot crossed right under my hand. God. How amazing."

The baby stilled and he moved his hand up to Emily's cheek. She sensed him studying her for a moment in the darkness, then in the most tender of gestures, he tipped her slightly back in his arm and kissed her.

This time he seemed to enfold her and she felt his touch everywhere. His muscled arms surrounded her, his strong thighs supported her, and his shoulders were a warm supple anchor she held on to as he leaned over her.

And this time the kiss wasn't chaste. His mouth opened over hers and his tongue dipped in to explore, to speak without sound of all the things he thought he remembered.

Emily responded, pressing her breasts to him, sparring with his tongue, returning kiss for kiss. His reality, she accepted without struggle, was rapidly becoming hers.

He planted kisses along her throat, then crushed her to him. Rebecca wriggled.

He laughed and placed a hand on the baby.

"I'm afraid there's something between us," Emily said.

"Not between us," Keith corrected. "Connecting us." He gave a sigh that was half groan. "Come on, I'll get you back to bed before I lose all good sense and do what Rebecca seems to know is on my mind." He lifted her into his arms.

It was on Emily's mind, too, but she didn't have the guts to encourage him. What if he made love to her, then remembered that he never had before? He was a very sensitive man; lovemaking required just the kind of emotional involvement that might bring the past back to him. And she had to make herself remember that, as charming as her fiction had been, it was just that. Fiction. Not reality.

"Keith, you're going to break your back," she protested as he carried her through the dark house. "I weigh a ton."

"Hardly a ton," he demurred gallantly. He carried her up the stairs and she felt a pinch of disappointment when he turned left at the top, instead of right.

He placed her on her feet beside her bed, helped her off with her robe, then provided a hand for balance as she climbed in. He pulled the blankets up, leaning over to kiss her cheek. "Good night, Emmie," he said.

"Good night, Keith."

He half closed the door behind him, and she listened to his footsteps as he went down the hall and into his room.

She smiled into the darkness as her mind replayed the sound of his voice saying, "Emmie."

CHAPTER SIX

"BUT I DON'T SEE why you want to eat in the dining room of the hotel," Neil complained as he and Barbara, and Emily and Keith stood in a little knot near the hood of his Mercedes arguing about where to go for dinner. "You've spent almost every day at the hotel since we brought you home."

Barbara cast a worried glance at Emily.

"I'm president of the company, Dad," Keith said reasonably. "I'm supposed to be there."

"But you're not on duty now. I thought we'd go down the coast for seafood at D'Onofrio's."

"Actually Keith is humoring me," Emily said, doing her best to look like the pregnant woman in need of indulgence. "I love the dining room's food."

Neil's manner softened, but he still seemed puzzled. "But, Emily, you used to help prepare it yourself every day."

She smiled widely. "That's why it's such a treat to eat there when I'm not on duty." She hooked her arm in his and began to lead him toward the passenger side of the car. "Can I sit in the front with you? I'd have the devil's own time getting out of the back seat."

She caught the gleam of admiration in Keith's eyes

as Neil helped her into the car. Barbara winked and let Keith hand her into the back.

Fifteen minutes later they were in the hotel lobby. "I may as well check my messages while I'm here," Neil said, urging Keith and the women toward the dining room. "You take care of the ladies—"

"Whoa." Keith caught his arm and pulled him back. Vangie, at the desk, caught his high sign and picked up the telephone. "And you're grumbling about me working too long. You're off tonight, Dad."

"That," Neil said pointedly, "is why I thought I might find myself somewhere else for dinner."

"We're indulging the mother-to-be, remember?" Barbara took Neil's other arm. "Do you want to starve your very first grandchild while you argue over where to feed her?"

As Barbara led him away, Neil turned to his son. "Have you noticed that executive positions in the world of commerce mean squat at home?"

Keith patted him on the back and fell into line with Emily. "The caveman probably noticed that, Dad. He probably killed the triceratops with his bare hands, but was clubbed by his woman because he was late for dinner."

Neil frowned. Bertrand, the maître d', was waving to them from the doorway of the ballroom.

"What's he doing there?" Neil asked, changing direction.

"I don't know," Keith replied. "Maybe there's a problem."

Neil walked into the room and it erupted with

shouts and applause while a small orchestra played "Happy Birthday."

The white-and-silver ballroom was aglow with candlelight, gleaming china, silverware polished to perfection and guests sparkling in their finery.

Neil stopped in his tracks and turned to Keith and Emily, a laughing accusation on his lips. But Barbara was hauling him toward the middle of the room where employees and friends crowded around him.

"Well done," Keith said, leading Emily through the tables toward an empty one in a corner of the room. "He certainly fell for your helpless-pregnant-lady routine."

She put a wrist to her forehead like a tragic stage heroine. "I had difficulty choosing between the kitchen and the theater." She dropped her hand. "Then an actress friend of mine told me most actors spend at least half their time waiting tables in a restaurant to support themselves, so I thought I'd save myself the aggravation and just stay in the restaurant."

He held a chair out for her. "Too bad. You show real talent. Do you know my cousins?"

Emily looked up and saw a gorgeous blonde and a bespectacled young man coming toward them. She recognized them as familiar faces around the Northwest Eden.

"You remember them?" she asked Keith, not sure whether to be pleased or concerned. If his memory came back now...

"No, but I've been recently reintroduced." He remained standing and waited for the couple to join them.

The blonde moved into his arms on a cloud of heady fragrance. She wore a white halter-top dress that showed off a curvaceous body, and Emily wondered if the likeness to Marilyn Monroe was accidental or deliberate.

Her voice, however, was not the soft sultry voice familiar to moviegoers, but had a more strident quality.

"So, how are you?" she asked Keith, taking a step back and running her gaze over him. "You look fine to me. I understand you even arbitrated a row between housekeeping and security, and made everybody happy. That's usually impossible."

He dismissed her praise with a shrug. "Apparently they've been shouting at each other for months, but no one was listening. I just sat down with them so they'd be forced to talk it through. It worked." Keith reached around her to shake hands with the man in glasses. "Hello, Jack. Do you two know Emily French?"

The blonde seemed to study Emily thoughtfully, but the man smiled and said, "Sure. She makes the best Bismarcks in the entire world and personally delivers them to board meetings." He offered his hand. "Hi, Emily."

Emily shook it. "Hi, Mr. Roper. You're the one who always asks for double jelly, aren't you?"

He nodded guiltily. "That's me. Always had a weakness for the sweet stuff."

"You know Jack's my cousin and vice president in charge of purchasing," Keith said. "But do you know Jack's sister, Janice? She's in charge of making the Edens beautiful."

Jack pulled out a chair for Janice opposite Emily's.

"I've seen you around," Emily said to her, "but we've never been formally introduced." The hotel staff liked Janice, Emily knew. She was a woman with a reputation for speaking frankly and behaving outrageously.

"Then, formally—" Keith smiled from woman to woman "—Emily, my cousin Janice. Janice, my fiancée, Emily."

Emily reacted with the same surprise Keith's cousins did, though she managed to hide it.

Janice smiled warmly and with obvious interest. "Hi," she said, eyeing Emily's stomach. "I can see why, but how? He was in California and you were here."

Jack rolled his eyes. "You can see why she's in hotel work and not international diplomacy. I think the right response to that is 'Congratulations!' And 'Welcome to the family.'"

Janice reached out to pat Emily's hand. "Of course, congratulations. I'm delighted for you. Everyone despaired of Keith's ever getting serious about another woman. Good work, Emily."

Another woman? Emily remembered Greg's mentioning that Keith's rigid attitude had something to do with a bad marriage and worse divorce. She'd forgotten that—probably because the man she now knew didn't seem rigid at all.

She looked at Keith to see him watching her speculatively. Was he wondering if he'd told her about his previous marriage? Or was he remembering it?

"We met while I worked at the Atlantic Eden," Emily said in answer to Janice's question about how. "Keith came for a week or so and we…fell in love."

That was both easy and hard to say. Easy because she so wished it had been the case, and hard because the falling-in-love part was true. It just hadn't happened there. And it wouldn't last forever.

"Is it a boy?" Jack asked, hailing a waiter passing by with hors d'oeuvres. "I'm looking for a replacement."

"It's a girl," Keith replied. "And where are you going? Retirement's a good thirty-five years away for you."

Jack sighed. "I don't know. Wherever the women are plentiful and energetic."

Keith laughed. "The roller derby?"

"I see you haven't forgotten your ability to irritate. No, I was thinking of somewhere tropical and rich in native warmth."

"You mean where the women don't wear clothes," Janice said.

Jack turned to her. "You know a place?"

"No," she replied heartlessly. "And I wouldn't tell you if I did. We're committed to the family biz, brother mine, and no amount of whining is going to get you out of it, so just buck up."

Jack faked a sob. "But I have the soul of a poet."

"Jack, you have the soul of a sidewalk entertainer. If you could make money sitting on a street corner and slapping a tambourine, you would."

Jack looked at his sister with bland innocence. "And that's bad how?"

She shook her head at him and turned to Keith and Emily. "Have you set a date?"

Emily searched frantically for a diplomatic answer, but Keith handled it with ease. "We're taking time to get reacquainted," he said, giving Emily a smile. "I remember so little and I imagine I'm different from the man she fell in love with."

Janice looked from one to the other. "That's probably wise. When's the baby due?"

"End of October," Emily answered.

Their conversation was interrupted by Bertrand, the designated master of ceremonies. He announced that the buffet table was open, that everyone should eat heartily but not try to escape before the after-dinner festivities.

Jack pushed away from the table. "Well, I'm part of the festivities, so I'd better go make sure I know what I'm supposed to do."

"Me, too," Janice said, then leaned over to hug Emily. "I'm happy you've joined the family. Keith's always been the charmed one. I'm glad to see he hasn't lost his touch—" she moved over to Keith and kissed his cheek "—even though he's lost his memory. Enjoy the evening. I'll try to find you later."

Keith leaned toward Emily. "I'll fix a plate for you if you want to wait here."

She got to her feet. "Thanks, but I don't mind standing in line. Of course, I'll take up two places."

He laughed and came around to take her arm. "I don't see a problem. You can get twice as much food."

Everyone stopped to greet them and offer congratulations. Judging by the number of employees who stopped them to express pleasure and offer good wishes, their news had already reached every corner of the hotel down to maintenance and housekeeping. Quite an efficient grapevine.

Emily noticed a few whispers and several suspicious glances, but for the most part everyone seemed happy for them. It was obvious that Keith was liked and respected, with or without a memory, and her friends had already shown their affection for her at her shower.

As she stood in line with Keith, his hands on her shoulders as they chatted with the people in front of them, she felt a warm sense of belonging—both to him and to the hotel. It was heady stuff for a woman who'd spent so much of her life relegated to the edges of other people's lives.

After dinner Neil was "roasted" by his friends and teased by the staff, who had enlarged photos of the early days of the business when he and his brother—Jack and Janice's father—had started Roper Hotels, first in Florida, then California, then the Northwest.

They had photos of the brothers working the desk

of their first hotel wearing gaudy silk shirts, later ones of them hosting in suits with wide ties and lapels, and still later, shots of them in Nehru jackets.

While Bertrand flashed pictures with Barbara reading the accompanying narrative, Keith watched, laughing with everyone else, feeling more relaxed and comfortable than he had since the accident.

Emily had turned her chair to face the dais and he'd pulled up his chair right beside hers so he could hold her hand.

Then, without warning, an image flashed in his mind. Faces in black and white, papers flying, someone laughing. He tried to make sense of it and couldn't. He pursued the memory as it tried to escape him.

Anger. He felt anger. Deep, very personal anger. And one of the faces he'd seen—a face that somewhat resembled his appeared frightened and desperate.

Then the memory was gone.

He was left staring into Emily's anxious dark eyes. "What is it?" she asked, squeezing his hand. "Are you all right?"

He wasn't sure he was. The anger had been so hot, so elemental. What did it mean? Had he been driving in that state? Had he...killed his brother?

As he contemplated that awful question, he heard his name called from the microphone. He looked toward his father.

Emily was prodding him. "Your father's calling for you, Keith," she whispered.

Keith pulled himself together. As far as he could

remember, his history with his father was only three weeks long, but he loved him, anyway. Neil had been as kind, as patient, as tenaciously watchful for any small sign of memory recovery as one could expect a loving father to be.

So if Neil wanted to drag him out in front of hundreds of people at the very moment when Keith was beginning to think it was possible that he'd killed someone—his brother, at that!—the least he could do was smile and obey.

So he did. Keith went to the dais, thinking that if his memory failed *after* this, he might appreciate it.

Neil put an arm around him and pulled him close. The room went absolutely still.

"You all know what's happened to the Roper family in the past month," Neil said, his voice emotional but strong. "You've shared our burden of grief, and we thank you for that. The gift out of all of this tragedy is that Keith was restored to us when we were afraid we'd lost him, too. He has no memory of us— a situation the doctor says will right itself in time.

"Though we tease him about it, I'm sure it isn't easy for him to function. But he comes in every day and does his best for all of us. And he told me that while he doesn't remember the hotel or his relationships with staff, he remembers the satisfaction the work gave him, and he thanks every one of you for that.

"So..." Neil's voice broke, and though Keith was wilting under the complete attention of four hundred people, he gave his father a bracing pat on the back.

"You can stop now," he whispered.

But Neil ignored him. "So," he repeated, "when you see this guy in the hall or the restaurant or the parking lot, don't be afraid to speak to him. Introduce yourself, and remember that he cares about each one of you, even if he doesn't remember who you are." Neil drew a steadying breath and went on. "Having him beside me, and you out there helping me celebrate, is the best birthday present a man could ever ask for. Thank you." Then he crushed Keith in a hug while his staff and friends hooted and applauded.

The evening seemed to go on forever. Keith smiled and talked and shook hands, thinking all the while that what he wanted most was to go back to the haven of the guest house with Emily and close out the rest of the world.

His father's tribute to him was generous. Keith would do his best to give his parents all the love and support he was capable of until he could reclaim his past, but the confusion over that past was beginning to wear on him.

Had he taken the life of their other son? He'd recognized the face in his memory flash. It had been Greg's. There was a photograph of the two of them on the grand piano in his parents' living room. His mother told him it had been taken at Greg's graduation from Dartmouth. Greg, in cap and gown, and Keith, in a suit, were arm in arm and smiling for the camera.

Had something happened to kill the camaraderie he'd seen there? Had they quarreled the afternoon of the accident? Had he driven angrily or carelessly because of it?

The possibility that he'd killed his brother—Neil and Barbara's youngest son—was burning a hole in his new life, which was otherwise close to perfect.

He had to find out, but there didn't seem to be a way to accomplish that. If he strained his memory too hard, he risked pushing it back even farther. He simply had to live with not knowing—at least for now.

Just after midnight he used Emily as an excuse to leave the party. His parents disengaged themselves from a table of friends to walk Keith and Emily to the ballroom doors.

Neil shook his finger at Emily. "I owe you big time, young lady. You lied to me with such expertise!"

She hugged him, thinking he didn't know the half of it. "You can't blame only me. Barbara planned it, Keith saw to most of the details, and your friends were more than happy to go along with the surprise."

Neil fixed a teasing frown on each of them in turn. "Collusion all around me. I feel like a Central American dictator." He dug into his pockets for car keys. "You want to take the Mercedes home? Mom and I'll take the shuttle."

Keith pushed the keys away. "Thanks, but Jack's going to run us home. He has an early tee-off time tomorrow. He just ran to make a phone call."

Barbara hugged Emily. "Thanks for your help. Are you feeling all right? You look a little pale."

"I'm fine," Emily assured her. "The baby has her

toes between my ribs and I can't seem to dislodge her. Maybe when I lie down, she'll change positions, too.''

"Neil!" someone shouted. "A toast!"

Neil waved toward the ballroom. "Harvey Whitstone about to toast me again," he said, giving Emily a hug, then Keith. "Truth is, I think *he's* toasted, but his birthday gift to me was a new putter. I have to be sociable."

Keith pointed his father back toward the party. "Go on. I'll see you in the morning."

Barbara walked them to the front door where Jack waited, swinging a ring of keys on his index finger. He smiled as they approached. "Nice party, Aunt Babs."

She hugged him. "Thank you, Jack. And thanks for coming. Is Janice staying?"

"Last I saw she was doing the Macarena with the bellmen. One of the women in her office promised to take her home."

"All right. Well—" she took one of Keith's hands and one of Emily's, her eyes grave "—thank you both for helping make this so special. Neil's tried to be the strong one through this, but it's been every bit as hard for him. You know how it was with him and Greg." She seemed to catch herself, then smiled thinly at Keith. "No, I guess you *don't* know. Your father loved both of you so much, but Greg was a terrible disappointment to him because underneath all Greg's charm and intelligence was a man who never really seemed to care about anyone, only what they could do for him. In the way of parents we blamed ourselves, instead of him. After all, *you* were wonderful, Keith. Where did we go wrong with Greg? And now, because he's gone, the loss goes even deeper because we feel as though we never really connected with him.''

As her eyes pooled with tears, Keith pulled her into his arms and held her for a moment. "I'm sorry, Mom," he whispered.

She pushed away and drew a breath. "No need for you to be sorry. Your father and I have to think about how much we have left. Thanks for helping us see that." She patted Emily's stomach affectionately. "And as much of a surprise as you and the baby were, it's been the best thing in the world for Neil. Good night, you two. Rest well." Barbara blew them a kiss and hurried back toward the ballroom.

Jack led Keith and Emily out to a glossy black pickup.

"Quite a rig," Keith said, a glimpse of memory stopping him as Jack opened the passenger door. He was aware of wind and speed and a very bumpy ride. But he wasn't sure in what or with whom. The thought dissolved before he could even try to pursue it.

"What?" Jack asked.

Keith refocused to find Jack and Emily watching him.

"Did you remember something?" Emily asked, a hand on his arm.

"Ah—" he frowned, wondering if an impression of speed could be considered a memory "—not quite," he replied.

"Was it my old truck maybe?" Jack asked, taking

Emily's hand and trying to assist her into the seat. "You used to tease me about it all the time."

The step was too high for her. Keith lifted her in his arms and deposited her on the seat.

"Whoa," he said. "Custom red leather seats."

"And a camper and tow package," Jack added. "Come on, you can get into the jump seat on my side."

"Do you camp?" Keith asked, following him.

"No," Jack replied with a grin. "I just like to look studly."

Emily watched with amusement as Keith wedged his long body into the minuscule space between the front seat and the truck bed, which contained two small seats that folded down from the side.

"Can you breathe?" She smiled at him.

Keith returned it. "Barely. Hurry up, Jack," he urged his cousin, "before I cramp up. Then you'll have to get me out through the sunroof."

Jack chuckled. "On my way."

He deposited them at their doorstep, helped Keith pry himself out of the back, then held the door open while Keith lifted Emily off the front seat.

Keith turned to shake his hand. "Thanks, Jack."

His cousin clapped his shoulder. "Sure. See you tomorrow."

The house was quiet and cool. Emily had left the light on in the kitchen and turned the heat down before they'd left the house, a habit she always followed. Keith had noticed it right along with an awareness of his growing affection for her.

"Want me to turn the heat up?" he asked.

She shook her head. "I'm going right to bed. Unless you're staying up?"

"No." He turned off the kitchen light and switched on the one that lit the top of the stairs. "I'm going up, too. You still have baby toes in your ribs?"

"Yes," she complained, rubbing at her side.

As she said good-night at the top of the stairs, Keith watched her study his features. He wondered what she was thinking, and so he asked.

"You look," she replied cautiously, "as though something is causing you an ache. Is it your stolen memories or something else?"

He didn't want to talk about it, particularly when she looked so tired. So he framed her face with his hands and kissed her cheek, then turned her toward her room. "Nothing you have to worry about. Thanks again for helping with Dad. Good night."

He went to his room, pulled off his coat and tossed it on the chair near the foot of the bed. Then he emptied his pockets of wallet, keys and change and pulled off his tie.

He was unbuttoning his shirt when he turned and noticed that the chair he'd just thrown his jacket on was empty. He raised his eyes. Emily stood at the sliding closet door, the jacket in one hand and a hanger in the other.

She'd never been in his room. He experienced a sudden and strong reaction to her presence.

"And this has always been the problem between us," she said. She sensed that Keith needed to talk and wasn't sure how else to draw him into doing so other than by luring him with details of their past relationship. The one that didn't exist.

"You make *me* tell *you* everything," she said, putting the jacket on the hanger, then the hanger on the rod, "but you keep everything to yourself." She faced him, arms folded over her stomach, gaze judicious. "Well, that's no way to treat a pregnant woman who already has all kinds of *imagined* problems without having to worry about what's worrying you."

He took a moment to ponder that, then shifted his weight and said gently, "If I don't tell you what's worrying me, how can you worry about it?"

She made an impatient sound. "What a male question! If I know you're worrying and you don't tell me why you're worrying, then I try to figure out for myself why, and that's usually worse than knowing."

He was trying not to smile. She wasn't sure whether to be pleased or annoyed about that. "If I tell you I'm not worried, can't you just believe me?"

"Not when I can see in your eyes that you are worried." She took his tie off the bed and draped it over a spoked rack inside the closet. "I begin to think—is he regretting his decision to take on a woman and a child? Has he suddenly remembered someone else who—"

He closed the small distance between them and put a fingertip to her lips. "I don't regret a moment of having you with me," he said gravely. "Not a moment. And all I remember is you."

She expelled a sigh and took his hand in her two.

"When we were getting into Jack's truck, you remembered something upsetting, didn't you?"

He hesitated a moment, frowning, and she experienced an instant of panic. Had he remembered something about his past that suggested it hadn't included her?

He finally shook his head, his expression bleak. "Not someone. But something—speed, wind, bumps and turns like an amusement-park ride. Only I don't think it was that. I think I was in...a car."

She reached out, running her hand gently from his shoulder to his elbow. "You remembered the accident?"

His eyes remained focused on the fragment of memory. "I'm not sure. But I remember I was angry."

"Maybe it was...fear?"

He shook his head, then drew a breath and turned his gaze on hers. "It was anger. I wanted to hit someone, hurt them."

"Who?"

"I don't know." He pulled her close and she wrapped her arms around him and leaned into his shoulder. "Ever since the accident," he went on quietly, his cheek resting on her hair, "I've been wondering if I was driving, if I killed my brother."

"The sheriff who investigated said it wasn't clear who was driving." She tipped her head back to look at him. "There's as much chance it was Greg. And even if you *had* been driving, it was an accident."

"Yes. But someone's always responsible for accidents."

"But most people don't try to assume blame when they don't have the facts."

"True," he admitted, kissing the top of her head, "they just worry about whether or not they were responsible."

Pushing Keith onto the edge of his bed, Emily sat beside him. "You don't remember your brother, but you heard what your mother said tonight. If the accident was a result of carelessness, it's far more likely Greg was to blame than you." She spoke the words firmly and let them sink in.

"Mother's trying to make me feel better," he said.

She shook her head. "Anyone who ever spent time around Greg knew he looked out for himself first."

Keith listened, his eyes reflecting surprise, then suspicion. She tensed.

"You said you didn't know him all that well," Keith challenged.

She sidestepped another direct lie. "Everyone talks about the boss. It was common knowledge that Greg Roper delegated everything and personally did as little as possible, and if anything went wrong, he was very good at pointing the finger."

Keith's frown deepened. "But he ran the Atlantic Eden."

"In theory, yes," she said, "but actually his assistant ran the place. Greg was charming and wonderful with guests—as long as they required nothing more from him than a greeting. He talked a good game and managed to convince people that he knew what he was doing—until they needed something from him. Then everything changed.''

Keith stood and paced to the doorway, then turned, still frowning. "Even if that's true, my parents loved him. His death is a great loss for them."

"Yes. But they both made it pretty clear how grateful they are to still have you. So if you have to think about something, think about that."

Keith sighed and ran a hand over his face, and she wondered if she'd gone too far by telling him his brother was a wastrel. He didn't know she spoke from experience.

Suddenly he smiled and walked slowly back to her. He took her hands and pulled her to her feet. Then he kissed first one hand, then the other. "Thank you for trying to ease my mind."

"Did it work?" she asked.

"Can't you tell? Or can you read only my worries and not the good stuff?"

She examined the quiet darkness of his eyes, the more relaxed set of his jaw. "I think it worked a little," she concluded. "But not completely."

"Well." He still held her hands. Now he laced his fingers with hers. It seemed to charge the atmosphere around them, as though some powerful connection had been made. His eyes roamed lazily over her face. "Is there anything else you can do?"

His meaning was clear. But at almost nine months pregnant she wasn't sure just which options were available to her. Or if he understood that. Maybe she was only hearing what she wanted to hear and his mind wasn't on physical contact at all. How could it be when she had the lines and grace of a buffalo?

She opened her mouth to launch into a complicated explanation of the Ninth Month chapter in her book on pregnancy when he pinched her chin between thumb and forefinger. Amusement wiped his concern about Greg from his eyes.

"I think I'm learning to read your mind, too," he said. "You're wondering how to tell me that making love in your condition might not be a good idea."

She sighed, half embarrassed, half relieved. "Yes."

"While I'd be ecstatic if that *was* an option—" he turned her around and unfastened the little jeweled button and loop at the back of her top "—I was just thinking how nice it would be to fall asleep with you in my arms."

He turned her to him again and tried to tug her top off.

She crossed her arms in sudden distress.

He raised an eyebrow, looking more surprised than angry or hurt.

"I'd love that," she assured him hurriedly. "I'll run into my room to change into my nightgown. Be right back." She spun toward the door, intent on a quick if graceless retreat, but found her feet working as though on a treadmill. She got nowhere.

"Pardon me," he said, pulling her back to him, "but weren't you just complaining about how you're forced to share everything with me while I keep everything to myself?"

Foiled by her own complaints.

"Yes," she admitted.

"And who's withholding now?"

"Me," she said wryly, "but it's in your best interests, believe me. The sight of what's under this outfit could affect you for the rest of your life."

"I'm sure it will," he said feelingly.

"I meant adversely."

"Not a chance."

"I'm telling you," she pleaded, "that I'm veiny and enormous and can hardly stand to look at myself. Your first sight of me—" her heart thudded against her ribs at the slip "—I mean, your first sight that you'll remember should not be of me at this point in time."

Folding his arms, he considered her with exasperation. Then he nodded.

"OK," he said, beginning to unbutton his shirt. "Good night, then. You go back to your bed and I'll sleep in mine. I'll see you in the morning."

She groaned. "You're angry."

"Not at all." He pulled off his shirt and kissed her cheek as he walked past her to toss it at the hamper in his bathroom. "I understand how you feel."

"But you don't want to sleep with me now?"

He sat on the edge of the bed and took off his shoes and socks. "There seems little point," he said. "If you don't want me to see you until you're centerfold perfect, then I can only presume that you don't want to be with me until I'm perfect."

She let her eyes explore his shoulders and chest, then met his gaze skeptically. "And you're not?"

Shrugging, he unbuckled his belt. "The body's all

right, but I have no clear memories, except of loving you, and all kinds of emotional problems you probably wouldn't want to deal with. And lying together tends to bring those out, you know? Confidences shared in the middle of the night. Secrets revealed as the sun rises.''

"Keith." The word was rife with frustration. "This is blackmail, pure and simple!"

He stepped out of his pants and tossed them at the chair. Then he faced her, a perfect specimen in snug T-shirt and briefs. Rounded pecs and flat stomach. The rest of him was long and muscled. There was another well-defined shape she allowed her eyes to dart over before she quickly looked away.

"It's not blackmail, it's honesty, Emmie," he said, leaning his weight on one foot, looking for all the world like the statue of *David* clothed by Joe Boxer. "You said you wanted me to tell you what I feel."

"Fine." She marched out of his room.

Well, he'd blown it. Keith remained where he stood, listening to the rustle of her silk pants as she strode down the hall. He was grasping at straws, but he took it as a good sign that she hadn't slammed any doors between them.

And then she was back, a fistful of white-and-pink flannel crushed in her hand. She shoved it at him. A flannel nightgown.

"All right," she said, tossing her head. She pointed to the nightgown. "I want you to give me that back the minute I ask for it. And I'm doing this not because

I'm wrong about my body, but because you're so damned...right.''

Then she yanked up the sequined top, folded it in half lengthwise and placed it carefully over the back of the chair.

Keith noticed her actions absently. His eyes were on the lacy bra that controlled but didn't conceal her full breasts.

Her cheeks were pink now, her eyes avoiding his.

Her stomach swelled large and round.

After a moment's hesitation she pushed her silk pants down, reaching for the support of his hand as she toed her way out of them.

"Would you put those on the chair for me, please?" she asked with dignity.

He tore his eyes away from her to comply.

"Thank you," she said. She unhooked her bra, then she lowered her white cotton briefs, holding his hand as she kicked them aside.

Her swollen breasts and stomach were big and blue-veined as she'd warned, but to him she couldn't have been more beautiful.

"Now can I have my gown?" she asked, looking very uncomfortable.

"In a minute." He took her hands and pulled her to him, wrapping his arms around her, loving the feel of her. "Did I never admire your body before?" he asked, puzzled by her self-consciousness. "You're carrying the life we made. I can't believe I've made you feel so uncomfortable about it.''

"It isn't you," she said quickly. "It's me. I just feel so huge."

"I think you're gorgeous," he insisted.

Then he freed her and reached behind him for the gown. She raised her arms obligingly as he pulled it over her head, and emerged from the high round neckline looking like someone from the last century.

He tossed the blankets back for her, then flipped the light off as she climbed in. At last he crawled in beside her.

She turned her back to him and he wrapped his arms around her, tucking his knees up to shape their bodies into a tighter warmer form.

"Do I tell you often," he asked, his lips at her ear, "that I love you?"

With his arms around her, he felt her deep intake of breath. It seemed an eternity before she answered. "Not often enough," she admitted, her voice fragile.

"I'll do better," he promised, then rested his head behind hers on the pillow. "I love you, Emily," he said.

She leaned into him with a broken little sigh. "I love you, too, Keith."

CHAPTER SEVEN

KEITH WALKED into his office a little later than usual the following morning, feeling mellow and curiously content for a man without a past.

"Good morning, Mr. Roper." The greeting came from a young woman from his father's office whose secretarial services had been lent to him for the duration of his stay. "You look cheerful," she remarked.

He picked up the newspaper on the corner of her desk and studied the headline. "That's because it's a beautiful day."

"Ah...sir, it's raining buckets."

He folded the paper and tucked it under his arm. "You don't judge the beauty of a day by the weather."

She nodded. "I know. You judge it by how many gorgeous guys ask you out, but I didn't think that applied to you, Mr. Roper."

He raised his brows. "You're incorrigible, Moneypenny," he said, pushing his door open.

"I keep telling you, sir." She followed him with a coffeepot and a cup. "It's just Penny. And you're not 007. Please remember that you do not have a license to kill."

"Pity," he said, dropping the paper on his desk beside a large squarish package wrapped in brown paper. "It'd be so much easier to deal with employees. What's this?"

"Your father brought it in," she said, pouring coffee into the cup and handing it to him. "He said the police finally relinquished it. It's your briefcase that was in...the car."

The car in which the accident had taken place. A sudden pall fell over his beautiful day.

He studied the package while Penny took the thermal carafe on his desk and filled it, too, with coffee.

"You OK, sir?" she asked, studying him uncertainly.

He made himself smile. It was his theory that Penny had been personally trained by his mother to watch his every move and change of mood and report back to her.

"Fine, Moneypenny. Thanks for the coffee."

"Want a doughnut or a muffin?"

"No, thanks."

"A fruit cup from the kitchen?"

"Nope. I'm fine."

"Want me to call Mr. Neil so he can help you open it?"

"Do you want to end up delivering for Pizzarama?"

She feigned hurt. "That's hostile, sir."

"I do have a license to fire, Moneypenny."

She frowned at him over her shoulder as she went to the door. "I could have moved to Los Angeles and worked at Universal Studios where the *real* James

Bond is, but I chose to stay near my widowed mother and work for the Northwest Eden. And what do I get in return?''

"Great tolerance of your eccentricities," he replied. "Bye, Moneypenny."

The door closed behind her.

Keith studied the package, took a sip of coffee, then put his cup aside and removed the brown wrapper.

The briefcase was the traditional box style in ox-blood leather. It bore the initials KCR and there seemed nothing particularly remarkable about it. He stared at the case, waiting for it to prompt memories.

It didn't. It simply lay on his desktop, looking like any other briefcase in the world, except for his initials. He tried to flip the snaps and open it, but it was locked.

In the two weeks he'd been back to work, using the new briefcase his mother had given him, he'd never once locked it. Had he been more careful in his un-remembered past? More paranoid?

When he dug his keys out of his pocket, he noticed a small key on the ring. He tried it in the lock and sure enough it fit. He slid the snaps and lifted the lid.

Again he waited for a flash of memory, but nothing happened. The case contained a number of paid invoices from the Atlantic Eden. He sorted through them, wondering why he had them. There were invoices for everything from paper products to furniture.

He looked through the papers for a worksheet he might have started or some notes that might explain why he had them. Had he been checking the Atlantic Eden's books? And if so, why?

He found nothing, but he knew if he *had* been checking the books, it was because there was something wrong with them. But what?

He punched up Atlantic's Accounts Payable report on the computer. He was in the midst of checking the invoices in his case against those listed on the program when his private line rang.

It was his father. "Good morning," Neil said cheerfully. "Any morning-after side effects?"

"No, I feel great," Keith replied. "You?"

"Me, too. How's your briefcase?"

"In perfect condition." He kept his voice level, but it was ironic that an automobile accident could take one life and leave another suspended between past and future, while not even scratching a twelve-by-eighteen-inch leather case.

"It doesn't happen to contain the missing Trailblazer season tickets, does it?"

Keith smiled. His father was diplomatically asking if the contents had brought back any memories.

"I'm afraid not," he said. "Nothing but the usual weekend paperwork."

He wasn't sure why he thought it best to keep the mysterious Atlantic Eden invoices from his father, but he did. At least until he could figure out why he had them.

"Are you...OK?" Neil asked.

"Of course," Keith said. "It didn't bring back any great revelations. It was just work, Dad. I'm fine."

"All right." Neil sounded relieved. "Good. You up for golf on Thursday afternoon?"

"It's supposed to rain all week."

Neil hesitated. "Keith, I've known you to golf with an umbrella handle hooked in the front of your jacket."

Keith laughed, the whole incident of the strange invoices lightening in significance. "Then I guess I'm up for it."

"How's Emily this morning?"

"She's great." And she had been. He'd awoken with her in his arms, only she'd turned to face him and was watching him when he opened his eyes. Hers had been filled with love, and he'd felt as though his heart might burst.

"Your mother's knitting booties."

Keith smiled. "Really."

"But at the rate she's tearing out and starting over, they're going to have to fit an eight-year-old by the time she's done. She's never been long on domesticity. But I guess you don't remember that."

"I don't," he admitted. "I just know that as mothers go, I couldn't imagine wanting anybody else."

There was a moment's silence on the other end of the line. "You'll have to tell her that one day. You and she were very close."

"*Are* very close," Keith corrected.

"Well—" Neil cleared his throat "—if you don't need me for emotional support this morning, I suppose I've little choice but to answer my messages and do something productive. Talk to you later, son."

"Bye, Dad."

As Keith went back to the computer screen, his private line rang again.

"Keith Roper," he said, trying to match the hefty invoice from Grayson Hotel Supplies with the appropriate account on the screen.

"It's me." Emily's voice sounded high and breathless.

He gave her his full attention. In the two weeks they'd shared the guest house, she'd never called him at the hotel.

"Hi," he said. "What's wrong?"

"Um…I'm not sure anything is, but I've been having some…" Her voice faded away, and in the background he heard, "Ow, ow, ow, ow!"

He was on his feet. "Emily!"

"Keith?" she asked, her voice a little fainter. "Are you there?"

"No," he said, shutting down the computer and closing the old briefcase. "I'm on my way home."

"But it might just be those phony contractions, you know? I mean, it's almost three weeks too early. I don't want to rush to the doctor's and discover that it's false labor."

"Yeah, well, I've heard babies don't always come when they're expected, and I don't want to *not* go now and end up delivering our baby in the back seat of the car. Have you called the doctor?"

"He said I'm supposed to go to the hospital when my contractions are at regular intervals. And they're really not."

"Hang up," he said, "and I'll call you on the cell

phone. I want us to keep talking until I get there."

He stuffed both briefcases under his arm while re-dialing Emily one-handed on his cellular. She picked up immediately.

"Keith, I'm going to feel so silly if you come home and I'm not really in labor."

He left his office and stood talking to her in the front office. "Emily, call the doctor, tell him what's happening and see what he says."

"I tried. He's already at the hospital delivering someone else's baby."

"Wouldn't they call him for you?"

"I didn't ask them. If he was delivering my baby, I wouldn't want him to stop to take someone else's call."

"You must be in labor," he said, moving to the door. "For the first time since I've known you, you're being completely irrational. Ask the hospital to page him and have him call you!"

"I can't," she said.

He came to a halt again. "Why?" he demanded.

"Because *you're* on the line."

"I'll hang up," he said with great patience, "and you call me on the cell phone the minute you've finished with the doctor's office. 'Call waiting' will alert us if he tries to get back to us."

"OK. Keith?"

"Yeah?"

She heaved a ragged sigh. "I'm glad I'm having your baby."

Everything inside him melted. "Yes," he replied softly. "So am I. Now phone the doctor!"

He pressed the "end" button and pocketed the phone, then glanced back to see Penny watching him, eyes wide. "Baby's coming?" she asked.

"Seems to be," he said. "Call my parents, would you? Tell them to stand by."

"Will do." She picked up the phone as he strode out into the lobby.

EMILY OPENED the front door as Keith loped from the car to the guest house.

"Hi," she said. She had a cup of tea in her hand and looked pale but calm. "The doctor said I should come in. Are you OK?"

He gave her a gentle hug, afraid to hurt her. "No, I'm not. I'm a nervous wreck. Are *you* OK?"

"Yes, I think so. I called Vangie. She's going to meet us there."

"Good. Are you packed?"

"Yes." She backed into the house, holding the door for him. "You want a cup of tea?"

"I'm more in mind of a double bourbon," he said, "so I'd better skip it. You have a blanket and a pillow?"

She pointed to the mound of things on the sofa. Her jacket lay atop it.

Keith picked up her jacket and held it open for her. "I wish our relationship had been more…" He groped for the right word. "I wish we'd had enough faith in each other to stay together through your pregnancy."

She looked at him in surprise. "But we've been together."

That wasn't what he meant. "But I wasn't there to take Lamaze classes with you. *I* should be coaching you through this, not Vangie."

Emily felt an enormous stab of guilt. This wonderful man was feeling inadequate because of her fiction.

Now would be the time to tell him, she thought. It was tempting to make a clean breast of everything so Rebecca would be born without lies attached.

But Emily realized, if she did tell the truth, Rebecca might very well be born without a father present, and that would be worse.

Genuine love for Keith made her lean against him and wrap her arms around him as far as the swell of her stomach would allow.

He looped his arms around her and she felt secure in the little cocoon they made. Every baby should be born into this warmth, she thought.

"'Course there's an upside to this I'm forgetting," he said, a trace of humor in his voice.

"What's that?" she asked.

"Chances are the amnesia would have made me forget my coaching instructions, anyway."

VANGIE WAS A TYRANT, the nurse was an uncaring monster, and the baby seemed to be having second thoughts about making her debut appearance.

Only Keith remained constant. Emily sat propped against his chest, both of them soaked in her perspiration. He spoke words of encouragement in her ear, fed her ice chips and bathed her face and arms with a damp washcloth.

In the dark clutches of the most horrible pain she could imagine, she found comfort in the knowledge that when all was said and done, this was Keith's baby. Blood, genes, DNA—none of that counted because Keith was the one who'd assumed responsibility, who'd made the decision to love. Rebecca was his.

Love wasn't what, in her lonely young womanhood, she'd imagined it to be. It was much bigger, much deeper. It was composed of one small deed after another, one little kindness piled atop one ignored inconvenience, atop one curbed annoyance. It was making the choice to give.

And in the course of those endless hours of labor, Emily came to a decision of her own. She was Keith's, too.

Rebecca finally made her appearance at ten-twenty that night. She had a puckered red face, a full head of dark hair and lungs that screeched her displeasure at the big cold world.

Emily opened her arms for her daughter, and Keith wrapped his arms around both of them. As she studied the squalling baby with the puffy eyes and indignant expression, felt the embrace into which she and the baby were pressed, she thought she'd never known a more wonderful moment in her entire life.

"Look at that," Keith whispered in wonderment. "We made this beautiful perfect baby."

Emily was too ecstatic to allow even a suggestion of guilt to form. Without a second thought, she leaned into him, saying firmly, "Yes, we did. I don't think anyone anywhere could have done a better job."

Vangie studied Rebecca. "You know," she said, "I'd go a little easy on the self-congratulations if I were you. I think you've given birth to a funnel with arms and legs. Or possibly some strange-looking alarm system, judging by the sound."

Emily reached over Keith's arm to swat at her friend. "You'll be sorry you said that when she's winning beautiful-baby contests."

"Uh-huh." Vangie was clearly doubtful.

"Leave Vangie alone," Keith said, catching Emily's hand and bringing it back into their circle. "She was a great coach."

Emily smiled wearily at her. "Yes, you were. Thank you very much."

"OK, folks." The nurse reached into their warm little nest to reclaim the baby. "I'm sorry to do this to you, but I've got to take her away for a minute. We're going to weigh her and measure her and a few other things."

Vangie patted Keith's shoulder. "Come on, trooper, I'll buy you a cup of coffee. They're going to want us out of here for a little while, then we can come back for another look at the baby."

Keith extricated himself from behind Emily, replaced the pillows and eased her against them. His eyes were both adoring and self-satisfied. "I'll see you as soon as they let me back in."

She pulled him down and held her cheek to his,

feeling as connected to him as if the story she'd told him about Rebecca's conception had really happened.

The nurse watched him turn to look at Emily before he left the room. He didn't wave or blow a kiss, but his eyes said everything.

"Aren't you the lucky one?" the nurse said as the doctor and another nurse put the still-screaming Rebecca on the scale.

Emily wanted to tell her that she didn't know the half of it.

NEIL AND BARBARA accompanied Keith when he returned. Vangie had gone home.

Barbara presented the now sleeping baby with a small white teddy bear that played a Brahms lullaby, and Neil handed his son a white envelope.

"To start her education fund," he said, leaning over the baby and making absurd and completely uninhibited nonsense noises. Barbara watched him fondly, and Emily was struck anew by the bonus of her baby having loving grandparents.

It took her a moment to notice that Keith was staring at the envelope, a frown on his forehead she now identified as the signal that he'd remembered something.

She waited anxiously, wondering what it was.

Then her eyes fell to the envelope again and she had a horrible revelation of her own. A check! Greg had once offered her a check that he'd said Keith had written to buy her out of Greg's life! Was he remembering that? *Oh, God, please don't let him remember that!*

She prayed, knowing nothing that she'd done in the past couple of weeks made her worthy of an answer, but she hoped God would take into consideration the innocent man and baby.

Keith looked up and she met his eyes, not wanting to see accusation there, but unable to look away until she knew.

What was he thinking? He looked confused, but he was also staring at her. Had he tied her to a memory somehow? Connected her to another check?

He shook his head as though to clear it.

Barbara noticed his distraction and put a hand on his arm. "Did you remember something, Keith?"

He tucked the check into the pocket of his shirt. "Not really. Just a fragment of something."

"What?" Neil asked.

"Another check, I think," he said. "I can see myself giving it to someone. I don't know why, but it seems important."

"You write and distribute checks all the time," Neil said. "Hard to know what that could mean."

Keith nodded, then gave his father a hug. "And it doesn't really matter right now. Thank you for the gift for Rebecca."

"Is it too early to call my contacts at Bryn Mawr?" Barbara teased. "Have you decided on a middle name? One of the girls in housekeeping is working on a cross-stitch birthdate plaque."

Emily, with an effort, forced herself to think about

the kindness of these people, instead of her own precarious position.

She smiled at Keith. "What about Barbara?"

He gave her a loving grateful glance and hugged his mother. "Barbara it is."

EMILY TOOK HER BABY home to Keith, feeling like Wonder Woman. Every time she looked into Rebecca's red puckered face she saw a pink and perfect cherub that made her feel she had unique and remarkable superpowers.

But when she looked in the mirror at her own reflection, she was horrified. Her eyes were bloodshot and black and blue, and there were bruises on her cheeks.

And where she'd once been fat with pregnancy, she was now simply fat.

Keith came up behind her while Rebecca slept.

"I look as though I've been on the women's boxing circuit," she said, putting her fingertips to one of the bruises on her face.

He wrapped his arms around her and kissed her cheek. "So, I'll be the first husband whose wife holds a championship belt. The doctor said the bruises will go away in a couple of days. You just put so much effort into producing Rebecca that you broke a few blood vessels."

Emily studied herself in dismay. "Who'd have thought childbirth could make you look like you've been...brawling." She added the last word absently as the impact of what he'd said hit her.

He'd be the first *husband*... She looked in the mirror at his reflection.

"Yes, I meant it," he said, reading her mind. "I have my baby. Now I want my wife."

And she wanted to *be* his wife more than anything. At this point she was as committed to this relationship for herself as much as she'd ever been for her baby.

"You don't want to wait until you start remembering?"

He squeezed her tighter. "I *am* starting to remember."

Her bruised eyes widened. "You are?"

"Well, you know. The flashes. The feelings, the faces, the envelope. Nothing that's coming together yet, but that'll happen. When we started this, I thought I didn't want to commit you to marriage because I wasn't sure what kind of man I'd been, and I wanted to save you from marrying a jerk." He straightened and rubbed his hands gently up and down her arms. His expression was grave. "Now I can't be that noble. I love you, Emmie."

"Oh, Keith." She turned to face him. "I love you, too. I love you. I love you."

All the other truths that she'd forced into a tight little guilty ball that now lived in the pit of her stomach clamored to be heard. *I've lied to you, you don't even* know *me, much less love me, and Rebecca isn't yours—at least not biologically. I fell in love with you when you came to my cabin and declared you wanted us, and I let you believe we were yours because I wanted you for myself every bit as much as I wanted you for the baby.*

Those truths tried to rise again, the words clogging her throat, but she couldn't say them now. If the physical and emotional trauma of his accident was keeping the door to his memory closed, then telling him such hurtful truths might lock and bar the door.

And in the insidious way love had of making a savage out of a gentle woman, she now felt about Keith as she did about her baby. She would protect both of them to her last breath—even from herself.

Keith held her as she clung to him, hoping that her tears meant she was happy. They seemed a little violent for happiness, but then she did everything wholeheartedly.

He lifted her face to his and tried to read her eyes. But what he saw there floored him. How could such happiness be entangled with such genuine pain?

He lifted her in his arms, deciding the pain must be physical. Three short days after giving birth and she was up the instant Rebecca made a sound, trying to do all the things she normally did, despite his protests.

He carried her out of his room so as not to wake Rebecca and placed her on the bed in her old room. She hadn't used it since the night of his father's birthday party.

"What do you need?" he asked anxiously. "A hot shower? An aspirin? A cup of tea?"

She wrapped her arms around his neck and drew him to her. "Just…you," she said, holding on to him.

He went boneless with relief. "You have me," he assured her, crushing her to him. "You have me."

CHAPTER EIGHT

"THIS IS YOUR IDEA of a *small* wedding?" Vangie whispered to Emily a week later as they stood in the church vestibule waiting for the opening bars of "The Wedding March."

The small Beaver Bay community church was filled almost to capacity with Neil and Barbara's friends, as well as hotel employees and their families.

"It was such short notice," Emily replied, her stomach churning with anticipation and anxiety, "that we just sort of put out a general notice at the hotel, and Barbara called her friends and...this is what happened." Emily made a helpless gesture with her cluster of stargazer lilies.

David Ambrosio burst into the vestibule looking out of character but very handsome in a navy blue three-piece suit. Emily snatched up his boutonniere and tucked it into his lapel.

"Where've you been?" she demanded. "I thought I'd have to walk down the aisle with Vangie!"

David heaved a great sigh. "My dear Emily, when your stand-in father is also your caterer, you have to cut him a little slack. Everything's safely delivered from the kitchen to the ballroom for your reception— and I supervised it myself."

"The ballroom? I thought we were going to use the small banquet room."

He indicated the crowded church. "That was the plan, but apparently you and Keith are more popular than we'd anticipated. Barbara called me last night to tell me she thought *everyone* was coming. And it looks like she was right. Where's the baby?"

"Neil has her," Vangie said. "And I don't think he intends to relinquish her anytime soon. How do I look?"

She did a quick turn in a long-sleeved tea-length dress of lilac wool. Her blond hair was caught into a complicated knot around which she'd placed baby's breath.

"Ravishing," David declared, then turned to Emily, who wore an ivory wool dress in an A-line style that hid any evidence of her recent delivery. "And so do you." He smiled affectionately, and for an instant there was something else in his eyes, something…knowing. Then it was gone. "You're going to be very happy," he said, taking her right hand and placing it in the crook of his arm.

"The Wedding March" began and Vangie blew Emily a kiss, then turned to begin her walk down the aisle.

Emily and David followed thirty feet behind. Everyone turned in their pews to watch their approach, and Emily, harboring guilt, as well as happiness, watched for any evidence of suspicion or recrimination in their faces. For any suggestion they questioned the cart-before-the-horse nature of this wedding.

But she didn't find it. Only fondness and good wishes.

When they reached the altar where Keith waited with Jack beside him and David put her arm into Keith's, she had a sense of unreality. This was so much more than she'd ever imagined she would have and, in truth, so much more than she deserved.

But her baby deserved it, and looking at Keith's welcoming smile, she accepted the greed and selfishness within herself that would fight to keep it, no matter what.

The service was warm, touching and brief. When the minister told Keith he could kiss the bride, Rebecca began to screech. Amused laughter filled the church.

As she and Keith walked down the aisle to triumphant organ chords, it occurred to Emily that while this would be the happy ending in most love stories, it was just the beginning of hers. Now came the hard part. If she was to be able to hold on to Keith when he regained his memory, she would have to make herself so necessary to him that he would be able to overlook lies, deceit and trickery and decide he loved her, anyway.

That, she recognized, would be a task at least as difficult as childbirth.

As Keith and Emily paused just outside the church, Neil thrust the wailing Rebecca at Emily. She couldn't help but think about what a wonderful job she'd done producing her. She, Emily, was a veteran of the life wars now. She *could* make herself indispensable to Keith.

While everyone gathered in the ballroom, Emily found a quiet corner in an empty office to nurse Rebecca. The baby quieted immediately, and Emily hummed to her, stroking her unruly dark hair. Rebecca wore a little white stretch sleeper with lacy trim that Barbara had bought.

The office door opened and Keith walked in. He came to join her on the sofa. "How're we doing?" he asked, putting an arm around her bare shoulder.

"Good," she replied. "We've got this nursing thing perfected." She smiled into his eyes. "How are you?"

"There isn't a word big enough," he said, leaning over her to watch the contented baby suckle. Then he looked back into her eyes, his gaze locking with hers. "I feel as though I've reclaimed the whole center of my life, and all that's missing are the fringes. And whether they come back or not doesn't seem to matter as much as it used to." A twinge of regret marred the happiness in his face for a moment. "Except for the accident. I'd like to remember whether or not I was driving."

She tilted her face to kiss him gently. "When the time comes and you remember, we'll deal with it together. But let it go for now, Keith. I want so much for you to be happy."

He returned her kiss a little less gently. Then he leaned his forehead against hers and groaned.

"I hope I can live through another month without

making love to you. I already feel as though I'm being stretched on the rack and beaten for good measure."

She prayed that his memory remained hidden that long.

"Actually, if I'm feeling all right," she said, resting her head on his shoulder, "the doctor says we can make love five weeks from Rebecca's delivery, which will be the second Monday in November. You have anything planned for that night?"

He laughed. "Night, hell. I'm taking that day off. You'd better down your vitamins and start building yourself up."

She made a sound of wicked anticipation. "I can hardly wait."

The reception went on until well into the evening. Neil and Barbara finally shooed Keith and Emily and the baby away at dinnertime.

After Emily fed Rebecca, she was too tired to eat herself and lay down for a nap while the baby slept in her crib. She awoke some time later to find Keith wrapped around her, also asleep. She glanced over at the still-peacefully sleeping baby, and concluded that loving and marrying this man and letting him believe Rebecca was his was the smartest thing she'd ever done.

The two weeks that followed continued in pretty much the same pattern. Rebecca slept until she was hungry, screamed when she awoke, ate, looked alert, watched from her carrier as Emily scurried to accomplish small chores and find time to bathe and feed herself. Then the baby's eyes closed drowsily and she went back to sleep to begin the routine all over again.

Keith bought Emily a new Cadillac she seldom got to use. In fact, she felt she was becoming a narcoleptic. She could fall asleep the moment a chair to sit in presented itself. Keith finally talked her into expressing milk for Rebecca so he could occasionally feed her during the night.

"But you have to go to work in the morning," she protested, leaning sleepily against him as they ate dinner on the sofa because she was too tired to sit up at the table.

"I used to party most of the night and still be at work by eight," he said, spearing a bite of chicken with his fork and bringing it to his mouth.

Emily realized what he'd just said and lifted her head, suddenly alert.

"Do you remember that?" she asked, her voice raspy with lack of sleep. "Or are you just presuming you did that?"

Keith chewed and thought about it. He saw himself with a group of friends at a Lakers game. His heart beat a little faster. Remembering the Lakers might be learned memory, but friends were not. He followed that memory and tried to focus on faces, but it vanished as he pursued the thought. The picture was gone.

He rubbed his head in frustration, wishing he could reach in and pull out the memory. *Damn, damn, damn.*

"I almost had something," he said wearily. "I was with some other guys at a basketball game. I saw it just for an instant."

"Did you remember who they were?"

"No."

Emily hooked an arm around him. "Actually you're very lucky," she said.

He fed her a piece of chicken. "Why?"

She chewed, swallowed, then sighed at the effort required. "Because if you'd remembered a woman, you'd be in big trouble."

"Like you're in any shape to do anything that could hurt me."

"Like you're in any shape to fight me off if I tried."

"Good point." He forked himself another bite of chicken. "But a pretty thing like you must have had quite a few admirers before I came along, and you don't hear me threatening you."

Admirers. She'd had many friends, but not that many admirers until Greg. And he'd been just an illusion, a man who'd charmed her into believing that she was something more than a temporary diversion.

But he'd fathered her baby. And he'd been Keith's brother.

When she remained silent, Keith kissed her forehead. "Did you go to sleep on me?" he asked.

As he tipped his head to look into her face, she took the coward's way out and closed her eyes, pretending that she had.

FALL WAS A BUSY TIME at the hotel; it wasn't unusual to schedule three or four conventions simultaneously and seat several hundred people at dinner night after night. And the resolution of the attendant problems generally fell to Keith.

Still, he was functioning well, his skills at diplomacy and arbitration still apparently in good form.

How he functioned physically, he wasn't sure. He hadn't slept more than four or five hours a night since he and Emily had brought Rebecca home. Emily nearly always got up with the baby, but he was usually aware of her absence and got up with her in sympathy. Besides, he loved the sight of her nursing their baby. He encouraged her to do it in bed so that he could hold both of them and feel as though, at least for those moments, he controlled the safety and security of his family.

But at the office, the invoices from his old briefcase were troubling him. His investigation into them, done only in spare moments, seemed to be taking forever. He had the invoices organized in stacks on his desk and found that each one had been dutifully recorded. Now he asked the computer to list the accounts payable in order of descending amounts.

The Grayson Hotel Supplies invoice, in the high six figures, was listed first. He frowned. Neither the Northwest nor the California Eden used the company, only the Atlantic Eden.

Though many of the hotel's supplies were bought in common and shared among them, it wasn't unusual for the individual hotels to seek out regional price breaks and bargains and purchase some things on their own. But the Grayson Hotel Supplies account was particularly large.

He checked the payables for the other two hotels to see if they'd used Grayson at any time. They hadn't.

He checked over the invoices again and found that Grayson supplied a broad range of products, many of them big-ticket items. He called the telephone number listed on the Grayson invoice and got a recording, asking him to leave a message and telling him that a sales rep would be in touch with him.

He frowned again. It seemed like bad form for a supplier to allow a customer to reach a recording rather than a rep eager to take an order.

There was a knock on his door. He dropped the stacks of invoices into his briefcase and turned off his monitor.

"Come in!" he called.

Marie Antoinette and Batman walked into his office.

"Ah, don't tell me," he said in mild astonishment as the couple approached him. He pointed to Batman. "You're looking for a room where you can hang by your toes, and you—" he turned his attention to Marie Antoinette "—are about to lose your head over something?"

The French queen removed her stemmed mask and revealed the identity he'd suspected—his cousin Janice. She frowned at him and pointed her folded fan at his attire. "You're coming to the Chamber of Commerce Halloween party as an overworked executive?"

He shook his head. "I'm going as a ghost. I'll be invisible."

"You mean you're not coming?"

"You're so smart. No wonder you're a queen."

Janice turned to Jack. "Talk to him. You're the one with special powers."

"Come with us," Jack demanded, "or I'll...I'll walk up the side of your house."

Janice beaned him with her mask. "That's Spiderman. Is that the best you can do?"

"Keith has a new baby, Jannie," Jack said, sitting on the edge of his cousin's desk. "What are you still doing here, anyway? It's after six. Even your dad's gone home."

"I'm just wrapping up a few things."

"When are you going to bring Rebecca in?" Janice asked. She wandered across his office, her wide skirts brushing a plant off a low stand and most of the magazines off his coffee table.

"Oh!" she said in dismay, turning back and knocking the stand over and the last magazine off the table. She bent to pick them up, and the swing of her skirts struck Jack, who'd come to help.

"Forget it," Jack said as he pulled her toward the door. "We'll get out of here, Keith, before she does any more damage. If you're not coming to the party, then go home."

"I'm sorry," Janice said as her brother maneuvered her sideways through the narrow doorway. "I guess these skirts weren't meant for today's offices!" She had to shout the last two words as Jack hauled her away.

Keith laughed, then shut down his computer, replaced the magazines and set the plant and stand up again. He also retrieved several chunks of dirt and vermiculite from the carpet. At last he called home to tell Emily he was on his way. He got the answering machine. That was odd, he thought, hanging up. Where was she? She never went anywhere, except for a brief walk with Vangie and the baby, and that was usually in the morning.

Of course the baby's routine was settling down a little. It was possible she'd run an errand. But she always told him when she was going out.

He called again from the cell phone on the drive home, but there was still no answer.

When he arrived at the guest house, there was no evidence she'd started dinner. He changed into old cords and a sweater, telling himself that she was fine, that she was a competent adult who could function perfectly well without him even though he'd grown accustomed to the reassurance of having her within the reach of his arm or the sound of his voice.

But he realized as he stood alone in the middle of the quiet empty living room, worrying despite his reassurances to himself, how essential Emily had become to his well-being. And this had nothing to do with her tie to his memory and his past. This was more immediate than that. She was his present, his *now*.

He liked coming home and sitting in his chair by the fire with Rebecca while Emily put dinner on the table. The baby reacted to him now, her eyes focusing on his face while hers formed expressions he was sure were an attempt to communicate.

He heard the clock tick, the refrigerator hum, the furnace come on, sounds he never heard over music, conversation and the sneezes, gasps, grunts, wheezes and hiccups from the baby that had terrified him at first but were now the comfortable sounds of his life.

God. He'd become a family man.

It was almost seven-thirty and he had the phone in his hand to dial Vangie when he heard a key in the lock. Emily burst into the room with the baby in the carrier. She deposited it on the floor, glanced up and acknowledged his presence with a quick "Hi!," then went back out again and returned with two large bags of groceries, which she dumped on the counter.

"You must be starving!" she exclaimed, running back to close the door and peeling off her coat. When she faced him, her cheeks were pink and glowing, her eyes bright. "I'm sorry I'm so late. I was right behind an accident on the bri—"

She stopped abruptly, pushing up the sleeves of a soft blue sweatshirt. The shade enhanced her coloring, but he was in no mood to admire that.

"What?" she demanded. "What happened?"

He glanced at the kitchen clock. "You're the one who's been gone for God knows how long. I thought *you* could tell *me*. In fact, if you made a point of warning me in the future when you intend to disappear for hours, it would ease my mind considerably!"

He'd begun his little diatribe quietly, but he was shouting by the time he'd finished. It was weird, he thought in a still-calm portion of his brain, that relief should cause anger. It seemed paradoxical, but he was too furious to analyze it further.

He saw her take a breath as though in an effort to

keep her temper. "I started to say that I was right behind an accident on the bridge. It took an eternity for the tow truck to get there and clear it away. I'm sorry. I had no control over the situation."

"You didn't tell me you were going out." That sounded ridiculously autocratic even to his own ears, but he didn't care.

"Keith, I went for groceries," she said reasonably. "It's Halloween and we have no candy for treats and no pumpkin. It was supposed to be a half-hour trip."

"You had all day to go for groceries!" he shouted. "Why wait until dark?"

"The car has headlights!" she shouted back. "It doesn't matter if it's dark! And I'll schedule my own day, thank you very much!"

Rebecca began to scream.

"Good work, Roper," Emily said with a condemning glance at him as she turned to the carrier. "Now you've upset the baby, too."

"I'll take her while you fix dinner," he said, pushing Emily's hands aside to reach for Rebecca himself.

"No." She stood between him and the carrier, her eyes blazing. "I don't want you touching her while you're in a temper."

Keith picked Emily up under her arms and moved her over several feet. "I'm mad at you, not at my daughter." He scooped Rebecca out of the carrier, stopped at the refrigerator for a bottle of expressed breast milk and started upstairs for the bedroom.

"You have to heat the milk to room temperature

first," Emily hollered after him. "And you can fix your own dinner!"

Keith returned to the kitchen with Rebecca, put the bottle in the microwave, waited a few moments, then removed it and headed back to the stairs and up to the bedroom.

Rebecca didn't like milk out of a bottle as much as she liked her mother, but she was learning to tolerate it. She ate halfheartedly, then burped with gusto. Propped against Keith's knees, she participated in one of their conversations where her replies were mimed.

"You know, you and your mom scared me to death," he said.

She studied him, wide-eyed.

"I'm sorry I frightened you by shouting. I was just so glad to see both of you safe and sound. I know that doesn't make sense, but a lot of things don't. It seems to be a fact of life."

She kicked him in the stomach.

"OK, maybe I had that coming. I'm the dad. I'm supposed to keep a cool head, but that's hard when your wife and daughter are your whole life."

She stuck her tongue out at him.

"Well, all right. If you're not going to be reasonable about it, you can just go to sleep."

He pulled her against his shoulder where she snuggled into his neck and soon fell asleep. Placing her in the crib on her back, he swaddled her in one blanket and covered her with another, then moved quietly out of the room.

When he went into the kitchen, Keith found dinner

on the table, after all. Emily was standing on a step stool, putting groceries away.

Emily felt him come and stand beside her while she shuffled boxed goods around to make room for a package of crackers. His head was level with her breasts.

He put a gentle hand to the back of her thigh. Despite her annoyance with him, her body reacted.

"Hi," he said cautiously.

She smacked him on the head with the box of crackers. "Touch me and you risk severe bodily harm."

"Go ahead," he said, his hand curling around her thigh. "You already stopped my heart when I thought something had happened to you and Rebecca."

She shoved the crackers into place and looked down at him in exasperation. "I told you—"

"I know," he said, now holding both her thighs as she faced him. "There was an accident on the bridge. You were powerless to change anything. You have the right to go shopping whenever the hell you want. But you've got to allow me the right to get rattled when I don't know where you are."

Her anger had been spent long ago, but the tension that had risen like a geyser to meet his still held sway. "I don't like to be yelled at," she said calmly.

His thumbs stroked her bottom. "You respond in kind pretty well."

She fought a smile and rested her hands on his shoulders. "With a baby in the house," she said, "we shouldn't deal with each other that way."

"I agree."

"She took the bottle?"

"Yes. She burped, we talked, then she got bored and went to sleep."

Emily allowed herself a smile. "Thank you."

"It's my job. I thought you weren't going to fix dinner."

"I didn't." She pointed to a box of tea on the counter, and he handed it up to her. "I bought fried chicken at the deli, and I had leftover pasta salad from last night."

"You bought chicken at the deli? Isn't that against some chef's code or something?"

Now she pointed to a bar of baking chocolate. He sniffed it, then passed it up.

"It is. Consider it a rebellion against healthy eating habits brought on by too many months of considering every bite that went into my stomach." She closed the cupboard doors. "I also ate half a bag of bite-size Snickers bars on my way home. I'm going to hate myself in the morning."

He wrapped his arms around her hips and lifted her off the stool. "It won't matter because I'll still love you."

He let her slide down his body, his hands cupping her bottom, stopping her before her feet touched the floor. And every inch of her body screamed with the torture of knowing it was at least another week before they could make love.

He gave her a greedy openmouthed kiss, then held her to him with a ragged sigh. "Is this making you as crazy as it's making me?"

She clung to his neck, thinking if she never had to

move, it would be fine with her. "Why do you think I ate the Snickers?"

"Why do you think I yelled at you?"

"Because you're a despotic male and a control freak with a temper."

He lowered her to her feet and frowned. "Is that what I was before?"

She pulled his head down to her and kissed him, wanting him with a desperation fueled in part by the same possessiveness he'd displayed. "No. It's what you were tonight. We'll hope it was just a temporary aberration."

She ran the toe of her running shoe down the calf of his leg. "You know," she whispered, "it's eight days..."

He became still under her hands, letting her cover his eyes and his jaw with kisses. "Eight days... Not sure I'll last."

"How much difference can eight days make?" she asked breathlessly. "Why don't we just...?"

"No." He removed her arms from around his neck and kissed her hand in apology. "No," he said again. "The doctor said five weeks. We can wait—maybe not gracefully, but we can wait. Have another Snickers."

She pulled herself together and turned him toward the table. "OK, OK. So eat up. You're going to need your strength to carve the pumpkin. It took two bag boys to carry it out to the car."

CHAPTER NINE

KEITH SAW HIMSELF behind the wheel of a car. It was a dream and he knew it, but it had the bite of reality—of memory.

He was talking with a person sitting in the passenger seat. That person was laughing—a deep laugh that sounded rich to his ear as observer, but that he knew enraged him as the man taking part in the action.

The anger was powerful. The observer felt it now with alarm. And the other man's laugh worked on it like a bellows on flame.

Keith willed himself to turn his head, to look at the man in the passenger seat.

His gaze swung slowly over the top of the steering wheel, the dry desert scene visible through the windshield, the sun visor pulled down on the passenger side, to thick dark hair, blue eyes, a laughing face. The same face in the graduation photo at his parents' house. Greg's face.

Keith came awake with a cry, the anguish in it still ringing in his ears as he sat up, gasping for breath. He'd been the one driving the day of the accident.

He'd killed Greg.

Emily sat up beside him. The pale autumn dawn

was just beginning to light the darkness. She put her arms around him and asked, "What is it? A nightmare?"

Yes, it was. "Memory," he replied, leaning an elbow on his knee and dropping his head into his hand. "I was driving. I remember I was driving."

"Keith," she said quietly, "it was a dream. A dream isn't memory."

"This one was," he said with certainty. "I was driving. We were talking. He was laughing. I was angry."

"Keith, that isn't enough to tell you anything."

"It tells me I was driving."

Emily felt the pain emanating from him, knew herself powerless to take it away. Then something occurred to her.

"You drove over or you drove back?" she asked.

He was silent for a moment, then dropped his hand and turned to her. "What do you mean?"

"According to the news reports," she said, sitting up on her knees and facing him, "you and Greg were staying at the Airport Sheraton, a twenty-minute drive from the site. The Realtor met you at the site and showed you over the property. So that means you got there in one piece. If you saw yourself driving, it could have been on the trip *to* the site."

"If I drove there—" he shook his head slowly "—I probably drove back."

"Not necessarily," she said. "It wasn't your car— it was rented. And two drivers often share driving duties. If you drove over, Greg might well have been driving on the way back.''

"But I was angry…''

She took his face in her hands. "Keith, even if you were angry, I know you wouldn't have allowed it to distract you from driving safely. Don't assume guilt for *any*thing until you remember *every*thing.''

He shook his head. "I think the dream means—''

"The dream means there's still a fifty-fifty chance you were the driver. The same chance as before the dream. It doesn't change anything.''

She saw the skepticism in his eyes and wished she could shake it out of him. She knew he had to deal with his loss of memory in his own way, but she hated being so unable to help him.

He pushed her gently onto the pillows and pulled the covers over her. "Go back to sleep,'' he said softly. "I'm going to take a shower and have a cup of coffee.''

She tried to resist. "I'll make breakfast.''

He pushed her back down again. "It's too early. Go back to sleep.''

Emily watched him peer into the crib, reach out a hand to touch the sleeping baby, then head for the bathroom in the gray light of early morning.

KEITH STOOD under the hot shower and let it beat on his face until it cleared the remnants of the dream from his brain. Then he turned and let the water beat on his neck and shoulders in the vain hope it'd make him relax.

The doctor had warned him that he would have many such flashes of memory, and that it might be some time before he could tie them together into a cohesive past. He had to be patient. He had to mellow out—if that was possible when the next flash of memory might prove he'd killed his brother.

You're losing your grip, he told himself, turning the water off. *This isn't like you.* Then he wondered if he knew that or was just presuming that he was made of stronger stuff.

No. He felt strong, determined, focused. It was just that he was bedeviled by things he couldn't control or even really affect. And he didn't like that. He felt sure his reaction applied to the past, as well as the present.

Coffee, then work, he thought, reaching an arm outside the shower for a towel. *Spend some time checking on Grayson Hotel Supplies. Where's the damn towel?*

He pushed the door open, knowing he'd put one there minutes before.

And there was Emily, the towel thrown over her shoulder like one-fifth of a toga. The other four-fifths was missing, and her bare skin was like ivory in the misty room.

There was a dangerous look in her eye.

She held up an end of the towel. ''This what you're after?''

''Yes,'' he said, reaching for it.

She took a step backward and challenged, ''Well, come and get it.''

''Emmie...'' he warned.

She whipped the towel off her shoulder and held it

up before her, peering at him over it. "It comes with a qualified operator."

He took a step toward her, assessing the situation. He knew what she had in mind. He'd sort of lost his sense of time and place when the dream had woken him—but this was the second Monday in November. The day they'd been awaiting with wild impatience.

But the dream had changed things this morning, and when he and Emily finally did come together, he intended to see that it was perfect. And he couldn't do that now.

She took a step toward him, but he put a hand out to stop her. If he let her touch him, he'd be lost.

"I know what you're doing," he said.

"Good." She ignored his stop sign and used his arm to turn him around. "Because I didn't think I was being particularly subtle." She began to dry his back. "You know what day this is?"

"I know what day this is," he replied, trying to turn and confront her, but she simply moved with him and worked her way down his spine. "What about if I see if Mom and Dad can watch Rebecca tonight…"

"Not tonight," she said, as she came around in front of him. She looked into his eyes. "Now."

"Not now," he said firmly, thinking how difficult it was to wield authority while naked and being dried with a towel. "The dream put me at a disadvantage, Emily."

She smiled. "I see indications to the contrary."

Out of patience, he wrested the towel from her, then caught her by the shoulders and held her firmly in place. "I said no. Right now I'm still thinking about myself, and when we do make love, I want all my attention on you. I'll call my parents, and tonight..."

She wrapped her arms around his neck and pressed her body tightly against his. The "evidence to the contrary" was now irrefutable. "From the day you walked into my life," she said, looking into his eyes, love shining from hers, "our lives have been all about what you can do for me and Rebecca. So this morning won't be any different."

"I will not—"

"Oh, yes, you will, and do you know why?" She took his hand and pulled him toward the door.

He drew a breath. "Why?"

"Because right this minute what I want most in the world is to make love to you with all the artistry at my command." She arched a seductive eyebrow. "And you won't deny me."

This wasn't the way he wanted it to be for her. "Emily," he pleaded on a whisper, "you're not listening to me."

She kissed him. "Then, Keith, why don't you stop talking?" She ran a gentle hand down his chest. "We're doing this *my* way."

He swept her up in his arms, all arguments lost.

"No." She kicked and pushed at his chest. "You're not taking over. Put me down."

He continued to hold her. "*You'll* carry *me* in?"

She gave his shoulder a punch. "No. But if you carry *me* in, you'll be having things *your* way. *I'm* taking charge this morning."

He looked dubious. "Shouldn't we be mutually involved in this?"

"Of course, we'll be mutually involved, but I'll be in charge. You love it when I take charge."

Shifting his weight, he looked into her blandly innocent expression and became suspicious when she looked away. "So, we've done this before—you taking charge."

She seemed to find the shower stall fascinating. "Often. All the time."

"You're lying."

She turned to look into his eyes, her own challenging. "I'm lying. You always have to be the one responsible for the outcome of everything—at work and at home. Well, this time I want you to see what it's like when you don't have to be responsible for anything but taking."

He kissed her soundly. "The problem is, that's precisely the kind of lovemaking I want to give you."

She ran her index fingertip over his bottom lip. "Why is that a problem? We'll do it my way, then we'll do it yours."

"Twice?" he asked. "On your first time since the baby?"

"I imagine how comfortable I am will be determined by how cooperative you are."

He accepted defeat—if it could be called that. "All right, but I'm carrying you in," he said stubbornly.

"And we have to be quiet," she whispered as he placed her in the middle of the bed and climbed in beside her, "so we don't wake Rebecca."

He leaned over her on his elbow. "Are you a screamer?" he asked with a grin.

"No," she said, putting her hands on his shoulders and pushing so that he landed on his back. Then she leaned over him. "But you like to make that Tarzan cry."

"I do not."

"Do you remember?"

"No, but—"

"There's probably a vine hanging from the ceiling in your bedroom in California."

He began to circle her breast with a fingertip. "You know, you're very close to having to relinquish control of this situation."

She moved astride him, took both his wrists in her hands and held them to the pillow. "We'll see," she taunted, "which one of us is forced to give up control."

Physically he could take control in a minute. He was a foot taller than she was, and though her figure had remained nicely rounded since the baby, she was nevertheless slender, almost fragile. So the hands that restrained him succeeded because of his willingness to cooperate rather than their own strength.

But he knew she wasn't threatening him with physical superiority. Her weapon was physical sensation and emotional need all wound up in and enhanced by long weeks of lying with her in his arms and being unable to do anything but hold her.

He couldn't remember the past, but as she kissed his throat and began to string a line of kisses across his shoulders, all his life, past and future, seemed to pull into his present.

She lifted her head and smiled. Then she tucked each of his hands under his pillow. "Don't move those," she said with a kiss to his lips.

"Emily, this..." he began to protest, but she was now working her kisses down his body, and the words caught in his throat.

"Just relax," she said in the same tone of voice she used with the baby. "Leave it to me."

He had complex thoughts. Love was about sharing. While he loved being made love to, it couldn't compare with a mutual...a mutual...

It was all too complicated and he was losing the threads of his argument as her fingers followed her kisses.

And she was proving him wrong, anyway. What could be more exquisite than this?

Her hands and her lips were all over him, up his sides, down his legs, up his arms, down his chest, past his waist, over his stomach, lower...

Only the fear of waking the baby and ending this delicious torment before she'd concluded it kept him quiet.

But he was dying with the need to move. As his tension grew, her artful ministrations became more urgent, and she drove him beyond anything he'd ever had to endure before.

Well, he couldn't really remember that, but he doubted that he'd ever willingly restrained himself this long. Every nerve ending in his body screamed.

"Emily, *please*..."

"Yes, darling?" She was looking into his face again, her eyes fathomless.

"If the baby wakes up," he whispered urgently, "before you—"

"She won't as long as you're quiet."

"I promise you I have about ten seconds of quiet left in me. And that might be optimistic. I won't be responsible for—"

"And that's the whole point, isn't it?" she reminded him. "You're not responsible. I am. Give me your hands."

With a soft groan, he reached up to lock fingers with her.

Now he would move. Now he would...but even as he framed the thought she lowered herself onto him. He thrust upward in instinctive response.

Her little gasp of pain made him reach for her hips and try to lift her off him. But she pushed against him, resisting his efforts. "It's all right," she said. "Just a pinch of pain. Are you all right?"

He caressed her thighs from hip to knee. "After what you've done to me?" His voice was strangled with love and desire. "I'll live, but I doubt I'll ever be the same—whatever that was."

"Goodness," she said, reclaiming his hands as she began to move in a slow, deliberate circle. "And I've hardly started."

"Yes. I've been meaning to speak to you about that."

She laughed softly and turned her attention to fulfilling her task with a thoroughness and skill that launched him into a sphere of pleasure and fulfillment he felt certain was beyond anything in his previous experience.

He came down slowly, everything erased from his mind but the woman in his arms.

He reached to the bedside table for the phone and handed it to her. "Call my office."

She thumped him. "Keith Roper, I've just strained every muscle in my body, probably broken most of my blood vessels..."

He took the receiver, punched out the number and handed it back to her. "Tell Penny I'm sick."

She opened her mouth, then realization dawned. She grinned at him as Penny answered the phone.

"Penny, this is Emily Roper. Yes, hi. How are you? Good. Listen, I'm afraid Keith has malaria."

Keith put a hand over his eyes, shaking his head, then heard a loud exclamation on the other end of the line.

"Oh, I know," Emily replied, smiling broadly at him. "I believe it is rare in Oregon, but you know there's an area behind the guest house that's really very...tropical."

Keith groaned.

"Yes. Well. I thought I'd treat him with gin and tonic and keep him home for a day, then see how he is tomorrow."

More conversation on the other end followed by clearly audible laughter. Emily gave him a wry look.

"Thank you, Penny," she said. "I hope you have

a really wonderful day, too.'' She handed Keith the phone. "She saw right through it.''

"Big surprise,'' he said, reaching over to replace the receiver. "Malaria? Tropical area behind the guest house?''

"How would you have explained your sudden illness?''

"I wouldn't have tried,'' he said, pulling her down until she lay on top of him. "That's the advantage of being the boss. People don't question you.'' He kissed her cheek and wrapped his arms around her. "Good morning, Emmie.''

She wrapped her arms around his neck. "Good morning, Keith.''

There was a stirring in the crib. That was soon followed by a hesitant whimper, then a full-blown screech. Rebecca was awake.

Emily dropped her head to Keith's shoulder with a thunk. "Breakfast time,'' she said, and sighed in acceptance.

"You get hers,'' Keith said, "and I'll get ours.''

"You can't cook,'' she reminded him, pulling on a robe and crossing to the crib.

"I can warm leftovers in the microwave.''

She picked up the baby as Keith yanked on his sweats. Rebecca quieted somewhat, convinced now that help was on the way.

"Keith, the leftovers are seafood.''

He leaned over to kiss the top of the baby's head. "Yeah. Doesn't that sound great? And we have leftover salad.''

Seafood did sound great. After all, today the world was her oyster.

They ate breakfast with Rebecca sitting on Keith's knee, her eyes watching his every move. She kicked, made her funny faces and stuck her tongue out at him.

When she went down for another nap, so did they. This time Keith made love to Emily on a comforter spread in front of the fireplace. He was slow and deliberate, his every kiss and touch filled with love.

When Rebecca was awake again a few hours later, Keith put her in a front pack and the three of them went for a walk. The ash and vine maple were turning gold and crimson, and the air had a bite that made Emily cling close to Keith. He had his arm around her as she nuzzled the baby, who was making sounds of excitement.

The next time when Rebecca was put down for a nap, it was midafternoon. They made love again and afterward curled up on the sofa to watch television.

"Psychiatrists who've had nervous breakdowns," Emily read from the television schedule, "and the mates they've driven to alcoholism."

"No." Keith channel surfed while she checked the schedule. "Oh, look. Hockey!"

Emily swatted him with the paper, then studied it again. "Christmas projects you can make with Velcro and stitchery glue."

"Pass."

"Keith! *Sleepless in Seattle* is on HBO!"

"Hey—football."

Emily leaned over to take the remote control from him. He held it beyond her reach.

"Watch it," he said, his expression fierce. "I'll let you take control in bed, but the clicker's mine."

"You can't watch football when you have malaria," she said.

"Why not?"

"Because…because seeing all those people sitting under stadium blankets would have a psychological effect on your chills and fever."

He leaned sideways as she strained to reach the remote. They were body to body, nose to chin. "But I don't have malaria. And *Sleepless in Seattle* gives me hives."

"How do you know? Do you remember having seen it?"

"Yes," he lied. "You made me watch it every time it was on."

She collapsed against him, laughing, wishing desperately that that was true. Guilt prodded her, but she ignored it, not willing to let truth intrude on this wonderful magical day.

"You watch what you want," she said, getting to her feet. "I'll make some fudge."

He caught her to him. "Don't bother. I'll just nibble on you. And you're just the way I like it."

"Really?" she asked, kissing his chin. "Delicious?"

He shook his head. "Nutty."

She made a face at him just as Rebecca announced that she was awake.

Keith went for the baby and gave her a bottle while Emily made the fudge. With Rebecca sucking greedily on her bottle, he peered over Emily's shoulder. "Mmm," he said. "Penuche."

There was a light rap at the door, and Keith, still holding Rebecca, went to answer it. David stood there in apron and chef's hat holding a covered casserole in a towel-lined box.

He walked into the kitchen, Keith at his heels. "You look pretty good for a man with beriberi," he said to him. "Hi, Em."

"It was malaria," Keith corrected. "It so happens that my recovery is due to excellent nursing."

Keith gestured at the pot Emily was stirring. "Penuche. The accepted treatment for malaria."

Emily dipped a dessert spoon into the thickening mixture and offered it to David. "Not that we aren't delighted to see you, but what are you doing here?"

"Your in-laws sent me." He placed the box on the counter and sampled the spoonful of penuche. As he swallowed, he gave Emily and Keith a knowing look. Then he went to Keith and took the baby from him, tickling her lip with his finger. Her arms and legs flailed excitedly. "They heard about your disease and suggested that Emily might be too busy nursing you to prepare dinner. So I am here to the rescue with the finest manicotti you've ever tasted."

Emily put an arm around his shoulders. "Bless you, David."

"It was my pleasure." He made silly faces for the

baby. Rebecca watched in admiration. "After all, the two of you are going to make me rich."

"How's that?" Keith asked.

David grinned at him. "My date in the Ropers' second-baby pool is nine months from today."

Emily smacked his shoulder. "There is no second-baby pool!"

"There is, too," he insisted. "Penny posted it this morning in the staff lounge."

Emily put her hands over her face and went to Keith, who laughed and wrapped her in his arms.

David crossed to the kitchen door. "Well, my work here is done. Enjoy the manicotti—and each other."

"Ah, David?" Keith said.

David turned, an eyebrow raised. "Yeah?"

Keith pointed to the bundle in David's arms. "The baby."

David smiled in feigned embarrassment. "Oh. You wanted her back?"

"Nice try, Ambrosio," Keith said as he took her from him and walked him to the front door. "You've got your own daughters."

David rolled his eyes. "But they're growing up, Keith. They talk back." He pointed to Rebecca. "That's the perfect age."

Keith ushered him through the open door. "Thanks, David."

"Yeah, yeah."

"I COULD CALL IN for you tomorrow," Emily suggested lazily. Keith aimed the remote at the television as "The Tonight Show" credits rolled and pressed "off." "I could say your malaria mutated into something communicable. Then you could stay home with us forever."

He sat in a corner of the sofa, and she lay with her head and shoulders propped against his raised knee, their arms entangled. They'd done their utmost to stretch the day to its limits.

He leaned over to kiss her forehead. "I will stay with you forever, but I have to have a break once in a while to go to work."

"How pedestrian."

Emily made a face, only to find that Keith wasn't looking at her. He was staring at the blank television screen, his eyes unfocused. He'd been withdrawing over the past hour, she'd noticed, and though his fingers still toyed absently with her hair, she knew their cozy delicious day was over.

Something had intruded on their serenity.

"Keith," she said gently, sitting up. "Did you remember something?"

"No." He pulled her into his arms. "I was just thinking. I found something in my briefcase—the one that was in the car at the time of the accident. It was returned just before Rebecca was born."

She wasn't sure if anything he found could present a problem for her, but her guilty conscience made it seem entirely possible.

"What is it?"

He turned sideways on the sofa to face her directly.

"Did I ever mention to you before the accident that I had concerns about the Atlantic Eden's books?"

"What kind of concerns?"

"About anything relating to...embezzlement."

His words took her completely by surprise. "Ah, no." She was on dangerous ground here. It was probably the kind of thing he *would* have discussed with her if they'd had the kind of relationship he thought they had. "We...you didn't like to talk business when we were together."

He accepted that without question. "And that's a good policy," he said, kissing her lightly. "Come on. Let's go to bed."

"Wait." She put her hands on his shoulders, preventing him from standing. "I never agreed with it," she said. "What was in the briefcase?"

"Invoices. And there's a large number of them for a supplier none of the other Edens uses."

She frowned. "What does that mean?"

"I don't know. Maybe nothing." He smoothed her hair back and shook his head thoughtfully. "But it was apparently something that bothered me at the time if I went to the actual files and removed the invoices to look over. Now, I can sometimes verify things on the computer, but I wonder if I ever before felt the need to verify that what was put into the computer was accurate."

Emily, listening to what he said, wasn't sure whether or not to get excited. "Keith, this probably isn't the time, but think about what you just said— that you 'can sometimes verify things on the computer.' That means you must remember doing that in the past.''

He smiled, got to his feet and pulled her to hers. "I know. But is that a learned memory, or something that's come back to me? With the business being all wrapped up with family, it's hard for me to tell. Generally I don't remember the people, but I remember the work. So, why don't I remember why I brought home the invoices?''

"Because it involves...people." The possibilities frightened her.

"Yes," he agreed gravely. "I think so."

"You suspected that someone was embezzling."

"Yes."

"Oh, God."

"Yeah." He turned her toward the bedroom, turning off the table lamp as they passed. "So keep this to yourself until I understand what it's all about."

"Of course," she said. "But shouldn't you at least tell your father? Or Jack? I mean, whoever did it is probably still around, and if he realizes you're looking into it..."

"I know," he said. "I'm being very careful. Don't worry."

"Keith, I'll worry if I want to! Please tell your dad."

"Emmie—" he lowered his voice as they approached their room where Rebecca slept "—tell him what? I don't know anything, and I don't want to trouble him with the suggestion of embezzlement until I can either prove myself wrong or tell him the whole story and build a case where we bring in the police.''

She wrapped her arms around his waist and shuddered. The embezzler could be a dangerous person. ''We're hiring you a bodyguard,'' she said, only half joking.

He laughed and began to peel off her clothes. ''How about a tall bosomy blonde dressed in black with sunglasses and a wrist radio?''

She burrowed her hands under his sweater. ''Then you'd need protection from *me*.''

He caught her hair in a gentle fist and pulled her head back, his mouth a millimeter from hers. ''No, I wouldn't. I've decided that I like it when you take charge. Want to do it again?''

Then he kissed her and she leaned helplessly against him, thinking that if anything ever happened to him, she would die.

CHAPTER TEN

KEITH STUDIED the address for Grayson Hotel Supplies, a post-office box in Charlotte, North Carolina. The state was the home of hardwood forests and fine textiles, and much of the furniture manufactured in the United States was made there.

So far, so good. He'd called the Atlantic Eden and asked for a copy of Grayson's catalog; he'd received it in the mail this morning. It offered many of the products listed on the invoices.

What the catalog didn't show was the folksy photo of their plant and warehouse that usually graced the front or back of such catalogs. There was no photo illustrating how expertly the furniture was made, no photo of embarrassed-looking employees gathered in the parking lot for the group shot.

There was no credit line on the back of the brochure to show who'd printed it, either. It might have been done on a sophisticated home computer.

What he was trying *not* to think about was that Jack was in charge of purchasing for all the Edens. But regional items purchased for a specific hotel were the province of the local manager—and the Atlantic Eden's had been Greg. So there was a distinct possibility that either Jack or Greg had been involved in some clever bookkeeping. Or guilty of gross negligence—one or the other.

There was a light rap on his office door, immediately followed by his father's entrance. Keith turned off his monitor and rose to greet him with a handshake and a smile.

"How's the malaria?" Neil asked.

"I've made a recovery that's stunned medical science."

Neil smiled at him and went to the window. "It tends to come back on you, you know."

Keith chuckled, then poured another cup of coffee, picked up his own and carried both to the window, handing the fresh one to his father.

"Thank you." Neil took a sip and made a sound of approval. "Trust you to get the secretary who makes good coffee. Mine usually tastes like it came from the bottom of an oil drum."

"You assigned Penny to me."

"Yes. And she seems to be happy in her work. So do you." Neil turned to look at him directly. "You function remarkably well for a man without a memory."

Keith dismissed the praise with a shrug. "I remember the work stuff. The doctor told us I would."

Neil nodded, looking him over. "You have all the skill and style you ever had, but with a certain...I don't know, heart, I guess, that you didn't have before."

Keith winced. "I was heartless?"

Neil shook his head. "No. You seemed to have a knack from the beginning to know how to deal with employees and to really enjoy the guests. And they all seemed to love you even though you held yourself a bit apart from them."

Keith listened with a sense of mild alarm. "And why do you think I held myself apart?"

Neil smiled. "It worried your mother more than it worried me," he said, leaning a hip on the windowsill. "She thought it was because you were always so responsible, so principled, and a little distance kept you focused on the facts rather than the people, which meant you could reach a fair solution when there was a problem. She was afraid it would prevent you from ever being serious about a woman, because love requires you to get right in there and feel rather than think." He grinned. "Since Emily, she's stopped worrying—at least about that. Now she worries about your memory and your health."

"My health is fine."

Neil gave him a sly glance. "At least for a man with malaria."

Silence fell between them, then Keith asked, "And what was *your* theory about my behavior?"

"Greg," Neil replied.

Keith lowered his coffee mug. "My brother?"

Neil nodded, looking him in the eye as though appraising his ability to accept what had to be said. "Do you remember him at all?" he asked.

Keith returned his father's look. Would Neil want to hear what he remembered?

"Tell me."

"It isn't much, really," Keith admitted, sloshing the coffee in his mug. "But it...bothers me."

Neil grasped Keith's shoulder, and Keith felt deprived that he couldn't remember the loving father Neil must have been. He decided to be grateful that he could remember the past two months.

"I had a dream the other night about...being in the car with Greg," Keith said. "He was laughing and I was angry. Very angry. I didn't like the way I felt."

"But a dream..."

Keith shook his head. "I don't think it was a dream as much as a memory that simply came to me when I was asleep." He sighed, frowning. "If I was so responsible and principled—" he repeated his father's words "—was I also a pain in the butt? Did I resent Greg because he was fun-loving?"

"No. You felt about Greg like we all did. He had some good qualities—he could be warm and witty and was great with guests—but he resisted any part of the job that was difficult or that he didn't like. He exasperated the hell out of all of us, and there were times when we should have turned him out to find his own meal ticket, but—" Neil shrugged, his eyes brimming suddenly with tears "—he was our son. We kept hoping he would have an epiphany and turn into you. But it didn't happen, so we did the cowardly thing and just let him be who he was."

That was so honest that Keith half expected memories to flood in on him. But nothing happened.

"You aren't still worried about whether or not you were driving?" Neil demanded with sudden severity.

Keith didn't answer quickly enough.

"Well, stop it," Neil said. "I can tell you with complete conviction that if you were driving, whatever happened was something you couldn't have avoided."

"Dad," Keith said, "it was a single-car accident."

"Doesn't matter. I know you. And I know that even if you and Greg were arguing and you *were* angry, you didn't do anything careless or deliberate. I know this. Trust me."

Keith saw the unwavering confidence in his father's eyes and couldn't help but ask, "You're really sure you know me that well?"

"You've worked with me for more than fifteen years," Neil said, "and before that your mother and I supervised your homework, went to all your football games, knew all your friends, how you dealt with money and life. Yes, I know you." He smiled. "The only thing I didn't know about was Emily and the baby. But you were always private about your relationships with women."

Keith nodded. "So Emily said."

"Actually I came in here—" Neil paused to take another sip of coffee "—to see if you were feeling comfortable enough with the status quo for your mother and I to take off for a week."

Excellent timing, Keith thought. He was thinking about going to the source of the Grayson catalog and preferred to do that when his father wasn't around. And the staff was more than competent enough to handle things for the couple of days he'd be gone. "Sure. I'm fine. Where are you going?"

"You probably don't remember this." Neil looked around as though in fear of being overheard. Then he leaned closer to Keith and said quietly, "In fact, I might not have remembered, either, except that my secretary, who makes coffee that tastes like motor oil, does have a good mind for dates. She reminded me. It's our fortieth anniversary on the fifteenth."

Keith smiled, trying to imagine what he and Emily would be like by their own fortieth anniversary, and whether or not Rebecca would be in the family business.

"Great! But we should have a big blowout for you here."

"No. Everyone went out of their way for my birthday. I thought we'd get away for our anniversary. Do something romantic."

"I highly recommend malaria," Keith said.

Neil elbowed him. "I was thinking I'd take her to Paris for a week. The city of lights and lovers."

"*Ooh-la-la!*"

"*Oui.* Well, that's my entire mastery of the French language. We can get a flight out of Portland tomorrow afternoon, but I wanted to check with you before I confirm and spring it on your mother. We'll stop by and see you before we go."

"Great."

"One more thing." Neil pointed at Keith's tie. "I don't remember your neckwear being anything but dark and conservative."

Keith grinned and walked with his father to the door. "Emily gave it to me. And the design is by Henri Matisse. If you're going to Paris, you'd better be more appreciative of his work."

Neil hung his head. "I stand corrected."

When his father stepped out, they saw a cluster of men and women gathered in the reception area.

The group turned, everyone smiling guiltily, then breaking up and returning to work. Emily, with Rebecca, and Penny remained.

Emily looked casual but wonderful in pencil-slim jeans and a baggy yellow sweatshirt with flowers embroidered across it. The baby's head and shoulders rose from a nest of white blankets. She looked alert and happy.

As Keith approached with his father and she and the baby looked his way, he saw a vision of motherhood and sweetness and promise. He could have dissolved with the pleasure of knowing they were his.

"Hi, Emily!" his father said heartily. "Let me see that baby." As he took Rebecca and held her up to his face, she gave him a big gummy smile. He laughed and cuddled her close. "Can I go show her off?" he asked Emily.

"Of course," she said, taking out a clean diaper and draping it over the shoulder of his Armani suit. "Just in case she spits up on you."

Penny went to her desk and began to shuffle papers.

"Everything all right?" Keith asked, pulling Emily into his office.

"Fine," she said, looking around her with interest.

"Rebecca and I thought we'd see if you were busy for lunch."

"You've never done that before," he said. He perched on the corner of his desk and watched her, thinking he saw something subtly different about her today. He couldn't decide what it was.

She came over to him and wrapped her arms around his neck. "I know. After yesterday, it was hard to be without you all day. Meeting you for lunch was Rebecca's suggestion." She smiled into his eyes and he was sure he must have imagined a difference in her.

Love rose in him and he kissed her. When he pulled away and looked into her face again, what he saw there startled him. He'd been right the first time. Something was different. The love in her eyes was still bright, the wanting him very much alive, but under it was a mist of...sadness?

Before he could ask her about it, his father rapped on the door and burst in with the baby, his eyes alight with the pleasures of grandfatherhood.

Neil invited himself along for lunch and spent much of the time telling Emily where he intended to take Barbara on their Parisian trip.

And when Keith got home that night, Emily met him at the door in a black negligee he'd never seen before. She served him champagne and pâté, and before he knew what had happened, he was taking the negligee off her and forgetting everything but her silken embrace.

EMILY WALKED with Vangie along the beach, Rebecca bundled up against the November wind and fast asleep in her front pack. The sky was a bright blue after several days of rain, and the day had a painful beauty about it, like the calm before a storm.

And Emily knew one was coming.

"What are you talking about?" Vangie demanded, a white beret pulled down over her blond hair. She huddled into her lined denim jacket. "Nothing's going to happen. You've shown no indications of clairvoyance before—we have no reason to believe you have the gift now."

"He's going to start remembering," Emily predicted grimly. "I feel it. Little things are coming back to him, things so subtle I almost miss them. Yesterday he wired flowers to his parents in Paris because it's their anniversary, and he asked the florist to make sure the bouquet included mimosa because his mother loved them."

Even Vangie seemed dutifully stricken with that information. "Well, it doesn't matter," she said, putting an arm around Emily's shoulders. "We knew he'd remember eventually. And while I was skeptical about this whole thing at first, I've seen what it's done for you and for him. He's so in love with you every woman on staff is green with envy. Even when he remembers, he won't be able to live without you. You might have some tall explaining to do, but you'll be fine."

Emily did her best to believe that.

To keep her mind off the worrisome detail of just how she would explain what she'd done, she concentrated on trying to solve the mystery of the Atlantic

Eden invoices without letting Keith know what she was up to. Something about those invoices scared her.

She tried to pump Keith for information while pushing a cart through the grocery store in Beaver Bay. Keith carried Rebecca, absently patting her back as he kept pace with Emily.

"I haven't had time to do much investigating," he told her as they passed a display of canned nuts. "With my parents gone, any crisis in any department in any one of the Edens lands on my desk." He grabbed a tin of cashews.

"Do you have any idea how much fat there is in those?" she asked, watching with horror as he dropped the tin in the cart.

"Don't care," he said.

"That's because you're not trying to regain your figure."

He winked at her. "You look perfect. But you can get yourself something bland and fibrous and leave the nuts for me."

She sighed. "I don't have that kind of willpower."

"I'll hide them."

"I'll find them. I have a highly developed nose for fat-inducing edibles." She took down a jar of pickled vegetables. "Your dad likes these, doesn't he? I saw him working on the relish tray the night of his birthday party."

Keith shrugged. "I didn't notice. Why? What's all this stuff for?" He pointed to the gourmet goodies in the cart.

"I thought we'd have your mom and dad over for

Thanksgiving. And Jack and Janice, if they're not doing anything.'' He picked a bag of nut-and-candy mix off the shelf. She took it from him and replaced it. ''Are you listening to me?''

''Mom and Dad,'' he repeated. ''Jack and Janice. Right. Sounds like fun. But can we get six people around our table?''

''I thought David and Maria and the girls, too.''

''We'll have to rent a hall!''

She laughed, then nuzzled Rebecca when the baby responded to the sound of her voice. ''I'll borrow another table from the hotel dining room. It isn't a family dinner unless people are climbing all over each other and bumping elbows while they eat.''

He raised an eyebrow. ''How do you know that? I thought it was just you and your mom.''

She hunched a shoulder, remembering the bleakness of those days, brightened only occasionally by an invitation to someone else's home. Like that one Thanksgiving dinner at a neighbor's she was remembering now. The family were Irish, and there'd been twenty people around a Ping-Pong table that had been brought up from the basement and covered with a sheet.

Her mother had left early, but Emily had pleaded to be allowed to stay. The conversation had been confusing and deafening. Children laughed and played, adults argued in loud and opinionated voices, then they, too, had laughed. To Emily it had sounded like music.

"It usually was just the two of us," she admitted. "But I know what Thanksgiving *should* be like."

He put a hand to the nape of her neck and rubbed gently. "Then we'll do our best to make it that way."

"Did you find out anything about that Grayson company?" she asked, trying to make the question sound casual as she pushed the cart around a corner and studied several shelves of rice. "Should we have wild-rice dressing in the turkey?"

"Sure. David makes something with fruit and nuts in it that's—" He stopped, realizing what he'd said.

She looked up at him in pleased surprise. "He does! He was featured in *Oregon* magazine because of it! You remembered!" It occurred to her that she shouldn't be so thrilled. Slowly but surely the curtain on his past was rising. But she couldn't help the happiness she felt for him. "Keith, that was definitely episodic memory—isn't that what the doctor calls it?"

He nodded, not nearly as delighted as she was. "Yeah. It's coming. I just hoped it'd return in a flood rather than a trickle." He reached up for the bag of wild rice she pointed to. "And no, I haven't had time to find out much of anything about Grayson. I may just go out there one day."

"Out where?" she asked, stopping in her tracks.

"To North Carolina, where the plant is."

"Well...why?"

He seemed puzzled by the question. "To see it for myself, Emmie. If we are genuinely doing that much business with them, they should be glad to see me."

"And if we aren't and it's something else?"

He kissed her temple. "I won't do anything foolish, I promise. And I seem to be in pretty good shape. I could probably beat somebody up if I needed to."

She stared at him. "You are not going to North Carolina by yourself."

He met her exasperated gaze, his own gaze half amused, half dismayed. "Emily," he said, lowering his voice as a pair of older women came up the aisle. "I will do what I have to do."

He put a warning hand on her arm and she slapped it away. "Don't shush me!" But she lowered her voice, anyway. "I hate being shushed!"

The women cast them disapproving glances before disappearing around the end of the aisle.

"Then calm down," he suggested in a firm, quiet tone, "or you'll upset Rebecca and get us thrown out."

Emily angled her chin and pushed the cart at breakneck speed up the aisle, leaving him in her dust. Rounding the corner toward produce, she crashed headlong into another cart.

Jack Roper was pushing it. He looked at Emily, his glasses askew from the impact. Then he rubbed his stomach where his cart handle must have struck him.

"Jack!" she gasped. "I am so sorry! I was in a hurry..." Microwavable dinners were tossed all over the bottom of his cart, and apricots were scattered like balls on a pool table. "Are you OK?"

"Uh..." He made a production of testing his arms for fractures. Then he felt his stomach again. "Nothing broken, except maybe my ulcer, and I was getting

tired of it, anyway.'' He looked past her and smiled.
"Hi, Rebecca! Hey, Keith, you didn't tell me you'd
married a woman with demolition-derby experience.''
He came around his cart for a closer look at the baby,
who stared back at him with interest.

"I heard the crash,'' Keith said. "You all right?
Your stuff?''

Jack laughed, patting Emily's back. "Sure. Everything's fine. Heard from your folks?''

Keith shook his head. "I presume that means
they're having a great time.''

"Good. Well—'' Jack grabbed his cart and began
to push it toward the checkout stand ''—you two have
a nice evening.''

"Wait!'' Emily caught his arm, embarrassed by the
incident and eager to make amends. "Do you and Janice have plans for Thanksgiving? Keith and I were
just talking about asking you to join us. Neil and Barbara will be back, and you know David Ambrosio and
his family....''

Jack looked pleased. "I don't know if Janice has
plans, but I'd love to come. What can I bring?''

"Nothing. I'll call you about the time.''

"Terrific.'' He waved and began to head for the
checkout again, then turned back and pointed to her
cart, "Get a horn for that thing.''

Emily didn't speak to Keith as she finished her
shopping, nor when a pretty young box girl pushed
their cart out to the car and helped them pack the
trunk. The girl smiled shyly at Keith, then hurried back
to the store, the strings of her apron flying.

Keith put Rebecca into the infant seat as Emily waited silently.

"How long are you going to pout?" he asked mildly.

"I'm not pouting," she said. "You want to go pry into something the police should be involved in, but it appears you don't consider it any of my business. I'm just your wife and the mother of your child." OK, that was a lie, but she was too upset about his plan to go to North Carolina to let it bother her. "Could we go, please? Rebecca's already overdue for dinner."

As though Rebecca had heard and understood, she screamed all the way home.

Nerves frazzled, Emily left Keith to unpack the car while she took the baby into the bedroom to feed her. Then she brought her back to the kitchen and handed her to Keith.

"Will you keep Rebecca entertained while I fix dinner?" she asked.

Keith looked at her suspiciously. She guessed he'd expected her to remain silent and withdrawn, but she had a more sophisticated strategy in mind.

While Keith lay on his back on the sofa, raising and lowering Rebecca until she was all gummy smiles, Emily prepared steaks, baked potatoes and asparagus, which had cost almost as much as an average hourly wage.

As she was setting the table, Keith carried a sleeping Rebecca into the bedroom.

He returned as she put their food-laden plates down. He stared, then sat across from her with a raised eyebrow. "All my favorite things," he said. "Is there a strategy at work here?"

She looked up at him, wide-eyed and ingenuous. "You enjoy steak and asparagus, so I prepared them for you. That's love, darling, not strategy. Eat up before it gets cold."

"My conducting this investigation over your objections does not mean that I don't love you."

She smiled at him. "Of course it doesn't."

He was silent a moment. "It means," he said finally, "that I have a responsibility to my family and to the company to find out what's going on. As soon as I have any proof, I'll bring someone else into it."

She nodded and smiled again. "I understand."

He dropped his fork with a clatter. "Emily, do you think you could find a reaction somewhere between volcano and robot?"

She pretended surprise. "Darling, if you want a reasoned reaction, then you'll have to deal with a woman who isn't in love with you."

"If you call me darling one more time..." His threat remained unfinished.

She met his angry glare. "Keith, it's an endearment."

"With no passion behind it, it's a four-letter word."

"It has seven—"

His hand slammed on the table, and she and all the crockery and silver jumped. "You know what I mean!" he shouted. "I will do what I have to do, and you will not give me that vacant iceberg look because it isn't what *you* want me to do."

She put her fork down. "Goodness. Volcano, robot and iceberg. You think a lot of me, don't you." She slapped her napkin onto the table. "Excuse me."

He pushed his chair back and caught her wrist before she could escape. "Emmie, I don't remember much about our past," he said, pulling her toward him. "But this isn't the way to conduct an argument, is it? By walking away?"

"In an argument," she said hotly, her bottom lip quivering, "both sides are heard. This is nothing more than a revelation of what you intend to do." To her utter horror, she was about to cry. "You're not interested in what I have to say, so let me go."

"Emily..."

She began to struggle in earnest, tears coursing down her cheeks. She realized her reaction had as much to do with her anguish over his eventual discovery of the truth as it did with her concern for his safety. This shouting seemed prophetic of what must certainly come.

"All right, all right." He gathered her into his arms, repeating the words over and over, his voice growing more and more gentle. "I promise I won't go to North Carolina alone. I promise."

Filled with guilt as she was, she found his concession even harder to bear than his impatience and anger. The fight went out of her. She stopped struggling and let him hold her, certain the day was coming when she would no longer have that choice.

He carried her to the sofa and lay with her in his arms until she fell asleep.

CHAPTER ELEVEN

KEITH WALKED into the front lobby after lunch the next day and encountered Henry VIII and his lady. After a moment's bafflement, he remembered that the Society for Creative Anachronism was holding its conference at the Northwest Eden.

He greeted the pair with a smile and prepared to circle around them when the king stopped him, jeweled hand extended.

"Lord Roper," he said, "good to see you again. Do you remember that we became acquainted when I held court in California, November last?"

Keith had a vague flash of people in sixteenth-century costume, but he wasn't sure if that was because he wanted to, or because he actually recalled them.

"You remember your queen?" the king asked, indicating the woman beside him.

Keith bowed. "Lady Catherine," he said.

She smiled sweetly. "No, sir."

"Lady Anne?"

"No."

"Lady Jane?"

"Ah...no."

He racked his brain. Henry VIII's fourth wife was Anne of Cleves, Henry's attempt to forge an alliance with Germany. *"Guten Tag, Majestat,"* he said.

Her eyes gleamed with obvious delight and she offered her hand. "You will always be welcome at court, my lord," she declared magnanimously.

He kissed her hand and backed away. *"Danke, Majestat."*

He headed for his office, wondering how the hell it was possible for a man to remember the names of all of Henry VIII's wives and not recall his own past. And where had his knowledge of German come from?

IN KEITH'S OFFICE Emily and Penny engaged in quiet earnest conversation while rifling through the desk drawers.

"I suspected there was something going on," Penny said, sorting carefully through the pages in a folder, "when he spent so much time in his office on the computer. Of course, now that his father's away, he's all over the hotel. And lucky for you, or we wouldn't have been able to schedule this little breaking and entering."

Emily, sitting in Keith's chair, rolled it backward as she opened the shallow middle drawer. She looked up and caught Penny's eye. "I can't stress how important it is that you keep this just between us. Keith doesn't know where the problem is yet, and I'm worried that if whoever did this realizes he's investigating, he'll be in danger."

Penny nodded. "I know, Mrs. Roper. You've explained all that. And I'll keep an eye on him for you, I promise. If I even suspect he's in trouble, I'll call you."

"Good." Emily sorted through the papers in the drawer, which seemed to consist primarily of copies of schedules—employees' schedules, conference-complex schedules. A small compartment contained pens, pencils, paper clips and the like.

She pushed the drawer closed and frowned. "I don't understand it. Keith's old briefcase isn't around—not at home or here. I thought maybe he'd have taken the invoices and filed them somewhere, but we've been all through the file cabinets and his desk. Where could they be?"

Penny closed the folder and replaced it in the desk's left-hand drawer.

"Maybe in his new briefcase," she said. "He has that with him."

Emily shook her head. "I checked that last night while he was sleeping. No invoices."

Penny sighed and sank into a chair. "Mrs. Roper, why is it so important for you to find the invoices? I mean, *he* knows where they are."

"Because I want to get to the bottom of this before something happens to him. With his father gone, he hasn't had much chance to continue his investigation."

"And the senior Ropers are having such a good time in Paris they're staying an extra week."

"Precisely." Emily looked around the office, trying to imagine where Keith could have put the invoices.

"He'll be swamped for another week. So I'm going to finish this investigation for him." Her eyes fell on the door halfway along the wall on the right-hand side. "What's through that door?"

"Nothing," Penny replied, crossing the room to open it. "I mean, it's not a connecting door, it's a closet."

Emily was up in an instant. "What's in it?"

"Changes of clothes for when he works long hours, towels and toiletries, that kind of thing."

Emily looked through the suits and shirts, then between the towels and stationery supplies on a wall of shelves to her left. Nothing.

Suddenly there was the sound of someone trying the office door.

Emily and Penny turned to each other in alarm.

"I thought you said he was going to be gone all afternoon!" Emily whispered.

"He told me to block it off on his calendar!" she replied.

The knob was fiddled with again.

Emily imagined Keith divorcing her for snooping through his office before he even discovered that she'd tricked her way into his life.

Penny pushed her into the closet and closed the door.

Oh, this was good, Emily thought. He would either come to hang something up and discover her, or spend all afternoon sitting at his desk, precluding her escape until he left for the day.

And if it was the latter, she would have to explain

why she wasn't there when he got home. She prayed that Vangie, who was watching Rebecca, wouldn't call Keith when she didn't show up at the agreed-upon hour.

Emily pressed herself into the corner, straining to hear Penny's rationale for being locked in the boss's office.

She heard Penny's cheerful voice. "Hi, Mr. Roper! I didn't think you'd be back today."

"Neither did I, but my meeting was postponed," he replied. "What's going on? You have a man in here?"

"Yes, he's in the closet. Don't wake him, though. I'm afraid I was too much for him."

"Why are the windows open?"

"Same reason the door was locked. I thought I'd take advantage of your being gone to air out the office, but I didn't want to freeze the reception area. Sorry."

No one spoke for a moment. Emily imagined Penny walking across to close the windows she must have opened before she admitted Keith.

"Have you had lunch?" Penny asked. "Can I get you anything?"

"I've eaten, thanks."

"Sorry about the windows."

"Penny?"

"Yes?"

"Why were *you* locked in here with the windows open?"

Good question. Emily held her breath.

"Well..." Penny sounded guilty. Emily squeezed her eyes shut, sure the secretary was about to confess.

"I don't really have a man in the closet, but...I do have one in maintenance. I called him to see if we were still on for tonight, and I didn't want anyone in the reception area to hear me. I'm sorry. I thought you weren't coming back. I promise you I didn't sit in your chair and I didn't make any executive decisions."

There was silence again. Emily wondered if Penny's excuse sounded as flimsy to Keith as it had to her.

"All right," he said finally. "Get me some fresh coffee and all is forgiven."

"Right."

"Did my wife call?"

"Ah, no. No, she didn't."

"Thank you."

The office door closed. Emily tried to make herself invisible, certain Keith would open the closet door at any moment to hang up his suit coat.

But he didn't. A long loud silence filled the darkness.

Something was digging into her leg and she reached a hand back carefully to figure out if it could be moved. She encountered what felt like rigid leather, then let her fingers explore its angular form. When she realized what it was, she felt a jolt of excitement. A briefcase. Not the one Keith carried, because that one was soft-sided. This must be the one that had been returned to him. The one that had originally contained the invoices.

She probed for the clasps. They didn't work. Of course, it was locked.

Well, no matter. Now at least she knew where the briefcase was.

She huddled in the corner of the closet, resigning herself to waiting out the afternoon in darkness. But it was only about five minutes later when she heard Keith's voice. He'd apparently picked up the phone in response to a buzz from Penny.

"Sure," he said. "I'll be there in a moment."

Emily perked up as she heard small indistinguishable sounds, then the opening and closing of the office door.

Dare she believe it? Reprieve! Penny must have managed to find some crisis for him to attend to. Good old Penny!

Emily waited several minutes to make sure, then, afraid of waiting too long, pushed the closet door slightly open and peered through the narrow slit. His chair was empty.

With a sigh of relief, she pushed her way out and ran for the office door.

"Just a minute." The calm and heart-stoppingly familiar voice froze her hand to the doorknob. Turning, she saw Keith standing near the windows, arms folded. Beside him stood Penny, looking both guilty and defensive.

"Lock the door," he said stiffly to Emily.

She complied, then followed his pointing finger to the small sofa. She sat and Penny joined her.

Keith picked up his phone, told the switchboard that he and Penny were temporarily out of the office and asked them to take his calls. Then he returned to sit on the edge of the windowsill and regarded first Emily, then Penny, coldly.

"How did you know?" Emily asked, determined not to behave like a penitent.

"You left your purse under my desk," he replied, apparently not pleased with her lack of remorse. "You want to tell me what the two of you were doing locked in my office and going through my desk? And please, Penny, something more believable than the airing-the-office story and the call to the guy in maintenance. Everybody knows you're seeing Steve Binford in security."

Penny looked up at him in surprise. "I didn't know *you* knew."

"I'm the boss. I know everything. So?"

Penny studied her folded hands, her thumbs pushing against each other. "No, Mr. Roper," she said finally. "I don't want to explain."

"You're aware this is cause for dismissal?"

"Oh, stop it!" Emily jumped to her feet. "He's not going to fire you, Penny," she reassured her cohort. "He would never do something so unfair. I put her up to it. It's all my fault. If you want to take it out on somebody, I'm your man...woman...whatever."

"I'm going to get to that," he said. "Until then, sit down and be quiet. Penny?"

Penny sighed, an air of grim acceptance about her, and shook her head. "No, sir."

"Penny," he said reasonably, "who do you work for? Who deserves your loyalty?"

Her cheeks were pink, her manner apologetic but

firm. "Your wife does, because I know what's behind this. And I have to agree with her."

He raised his arms in exasperation. "Then for the grace of God, tell *me* what's behind this!"

Penny silently refused.

"May I speak now?" Emily asked, mustering her dignity. "I can answer all the questions Penny won't."

Heaving a sigh, he folded his arms. "Then please, do."

She told him about her plan to find the invoices and about enlisting Penny to help her. She left out the part about asking his secretary to spy on him. Though this scheme had failed, she might still make use of that one in the future.

"I told you I was handling the problem," he said.

"Yes, you did. But with your parents staying away an extra week, you'll be busier and your investigation will go even more slowly, and I...I thought I could help."

He studied her with a mixture of alarm and impatience. "Let me make sure I understand this. You react like a wild woman because I—a big strong man—am conducting an investigation you conclude is dangerous to my health. So *you* decide to handle it? You? A woman half my size and weight? And *I* am expected to take that with equanimity?"

"No," she replied simply. "You weren't supposed to take it at all. You weren't supposed to know about it."

"Well," he said, his expression firming, "now I do, and if you so much as make one inquiry into this by

computer, by phone, in person, in any way, I will..."
He couldn't think of a threat horrible enough to deter
her. Except one. "I will fire Penny."

"You wouldn't!" she gasped.

"You're welcome to try me." He turned to Penny.
"You are the best secretary this company has, and
whether I stay here or whether I go back to California
when my memory returns, I'd like you to continue to
work with me. You're smart and hardworking and
pleasant company. But I swear if you butt into this,
I'll see that you live out your Eden career in the laundry. Is that clear?"

Penny swallowed. "Yes," she replied in a small
voice. "Very clear."

"All right." He got up and opened the door. "Excuse us for a few minutes, Penny."

The secretary hurried out, casting him a quick apologetic glance as she passed him. He closed the door
behind her and locked it again.

Emily watched him, her eyes uncertain. The last reaction he wanted from her was fear, but if that was
what it took to keep her out of this, so be it. The more
he looked into this Grayson business, the more money
he guessed was involved and the more desperate he
imagined the perpetrator to be. He would not have
Emily in the middle of it.

"Where's the baby?" he asked.

Emily huffed at him defensively. "Don't ask me
that as though I've shuffled her off so I can enjoy a
lark. Vangie has her. Rebecca's fine."

"Your career as an investigator is over," he said

with all the severity he could manage. "Do you understand me?"

She didn't seem intimidated. "Of course I do. You're being protective and predictably male. And while I often appreciate that in you, this time I don't."

"I'm not asking you to appreciate it, just to comply with it. Or Penny goes."

She looked into his eyes, searching, he was sure, for the chink in his resolve that would allow her to believe he didn't mean it. He made sure it wasn't there.

She finally sighed and stood, her dark eyes angry. "Fine. But I'm really mad at you."

He acknowledged that with a nod. "I'm not really pleased with you, either." He took her arm. "Come on. I'll walk you out."

"I can find my way," she said, trying to pull her arm free.

But he held on and gave her a shake. "Do you have any idea what would become of me if anything happened to you or Rebecca?" She stared at him, her eyes vaguely repentant now. "I would die," he said without waiting for her to reply. "No question. It might not be physical death, but all the life you restored in me when I walked into that kitchen and remembered you would be snuffed out like a bug under a shoe. Don't do that to me," he pleaded.

Her face took on that look from the other night when she'd sobbed in his arms, and he knew he'd won. Everything she did was guided by love for their family. He just had to make her understand that the same thing guided him.

AND THAT WAS HOW Keith found himself sitting next to David Ambrosio in a Charlotte taxicab when he'd told Emily they were meeting with a conference planner in Denver.

He was working on the assumption that what she didn't know wouldn't hurt her, and salved his conscience by keeping his promise not to travel to North Carolina unaccompanied.

What protection or even assistance David could be in a crunch was doubtful, but he was a trusted friend and good company.

"Wonderful cooks in Charlotte," David said, watching the passing scenery and pointing out restaurants. "Old Southern traditions. She-crab soup. Shrimp and corn pie. Where is this Grayson place, anyway?"

The taxi had crossed town and was now in a run-down industrial area the driver had warned them was no place to linger.

As it turned out, there wasn't a reason to stop, anyway. The address didn't exist. Keith checked it over and handed it to David to verify.

Keith asked the driver if the street picked up somewhere else. The driver said it didn't, then consulted his map and showed it to Keith. "Either your address is wrong, suh," he said, "or someone's pullin' your leg."

Keith asked him to take them to their hotel.

"What do we do now?" David asked.

"Tomorrow we wait to see who picks up mail at the post-office box," Keith said. "I'm sure whoever's behind this has hired someone to collect the checks paid to Grayson."

David frowned. "But that's once a month."

"Right. And what time of the month is this?"

David consulted his watch. "Ah. We paid all accounts yesterday, so if the mail is dependable, the check should be there in the morning."

"Very good."

"And what if it isn't?"

"We'll wait one more day."

WITH DAVID totally engrossed in his dessert of sherry-and-Madeira syllabub, Keith's mind drifted to Emily and Rebecca.

He and Emily had recovered seamlessly from their confrontation in his office. They'd made love that night and it seemed as though nothing had changed. But he'd seen that subtle difference in her eyes again the following morning.

She was afraid of something.

And it was more than the fear she felt for him over this investigation. He couldn't help but wonder if she was afraid their relationship might change when his memory returned. From what she'd told him about their past, they were managing together much more smoothly now than they ever had. Perhaps it was because of the baby, but he didn't think so.

He adored Emily, and what he'd told her that day

in his office had been the absolute truth. He'd die without her. Hadn't he always felt that way? Love for her seemed to live in his soul, to occupy the marrow of his bones, his every cell. He couldn't imagine he'd ever felt any different.

He looked up to see his friend patting his lips with a linen napkin, his dessert dish empty. "David," he said, "what was my relationship with Emily like before the accident?"

David's brow furrowed in thought. "Well…I didn't know you had one. But you were like that, very private with your ladies."

"Ladies? Plural?"

"Yes. You were quite the ladies' man, but as far as most of us observed, you'd never had anyone special since Celine. And anyway, you were in California except for the occasional trip to the Northwest."

"But Emily was here. She never talked about us?"

David shook his head. "When she arrived here from the Atlantic, she was already pregnant, and all she told us was that the father wasn't in the picture. She never identified him."

It hurt Keith to hear those words. "I can't believe I was the kind of man who'd have walked out on her."

"You weren't," David said. "I imagine you made some kind of arrangement, and she had the class not to share it with us, because she was protecting your identity. Your image as our beloved employer might have been shaken if everyone had known you'd fathered an employee's baby. Everyone always thought of you as…a cut above us."

Keith made a scornful sound.

David grinned. "But I nobly kept the secret that *I* didn't think so."

"I appreciate that."

David refilled their wineglasses and his expression grew somber. "Who do you think is responsible for the phony Grayson Hotel Supplies checks?"

Keith picked up his glass and replied evasively, "I don't have enough evidence to know for sure."

David allowed that with a nod of his head. "But you have enough evidence to make a good guess." When Keith failed to take the opportunity to do that, David did it for him. "It looks like Jack did it," he said. "It certainly couldn't have been done without his knowledge. He approves all purchases."

Keith nodded. Many things pointed to Jack, but Keith had difficulty believing it. Jack was always friendly and open, and though he, Keith, didn't remember their past as children, he did remember the past two months when Jack had done his best to help him fit into the routine of the Northwest Eden, when he'd helped him remember who worked where and identified the most reliable sources for getting things done.

He didn't want to believe it was Jack. "He doesn't pay the bills and make the entries."

"I have to verify the kitchen's budget every month," David said. "Doesn't he have to do the same for purchasing?"

"Yes, he does."

"Then?"

"I'm not placing blame until I'm sure."

"So maybe you are a cut above the rest of us. I'm willing to jump in and blame Jack."

KEITH AND DAVID had been pretending to study the contents of an envelope at a high glass-topped table in a corner of a small regional post office for more than an hour.

David glanced at his watch. "Nine-thirty and I'm already bored to tears. That's why I became a chef and not a cop."

"Really." Keith watched the door as a young man with a backpack slung over his shoulder ambled in. "I didn't know you'd ever considered police work."

"In my youth I weighed the macho appeal of it against cooking in the interest of meeting women."

He paused as the young man with the pack went directly to the box they'd been watching. The man opened the box, removed an envelope whose Eden logo Keith could identify even from the table and dropped his pack to put the envelope inside.

Keith and David pretended to pore over a brochure about Charlotte they'd picked up that morning at the hotel—then trailed the backpacker out of the building and watched him climb into a red Toyota pickup.

They hurried to their rental car and followed.

David craned his neck to keep the truck in sight as Keith maneuvered through the heavy morning traffic.

David pointed up a side street. "He turned right at the light!"

Keith turned on a yellow light while David swore and braced his hand on the dashboard.

"There he is!" David pointed triumphantly. "Ahead of that Cadillac."

Keith had just located the Toyota about four vehicles ahead when another pickup carrying bags of cement pulled out in front of him. He slammed on the brakes and looked in his rearview, certain he was about to be rear-ended.

"Something red turned left up ahead," David said. "I'm not sure if it was him. I couldn't see."

Keith made a left at the next corner and found himself in a busy commercial area.

"Got him," he said. The red pickup was visible a block ahead. It was pulling into a parking spot.

Keith pulled over to the curb about half a block farther on and watched through the rear window as the man carried his backpack into the Interstate Bank of Charlotte.

"Come on," he said to David.

"Where?" David asked, jumping out of the car to follow him. "We're going to confront him in the bank?"

"He'll be less likely to rabbit with other people around."

David hurried to keep up with him. "Rabbit?"

"Run." Keith reached the bank and opened the door. "If you'd chosen to become a cop," he said with a grin, "you'd have known that. There he is at the table. We'll flank him. You do know what that is? We're not going to hit him with a steak, we're—"

"Oh, shut up."

Concentrating on filling out a deposit slip, it took the young man a minute to realize he had company. He raised his head slowly and turned to his left. David smiled at him.

The young man turned to his right, obviously prepared to run. He collided with Keith.

"Take it easy," Keith advised, edging him back toward David. He indicated the armed guard across the bank. "We don't want to get the attention of anyone with a badge, do we? My friend and I just want to see what you're doing."

"I'm...I'm making a deposit," the young man said, his voice tremulous. "What's it to you?"

Keith decided the young man was too nervous to be a career criminal. He had to be someone hired simply to pick up the checks and make the deposit.

Keith turned the check on the table toward him. It was the standard Eden corporate check made out on the computer to Grayson Hotel Supplies.

"You own this company?" Keith asked.

"No!" the young man said instantly, loudly.

"Keep your voice down," Keith said mildly. "Who does?"

The young man considered a moment, then went on the offensive. "Who the hell are you?" he demanded. "I don't think I want to answer your questions, so get out of my way."

He tried to ram Keith with his shoulder. Keith didn't know what kind of training had prepared him to expect the move, but he had. He remained steady on his feet, and when the guard looked up at the slight commotion, Keith put an arm around the young man and smiled at the guard to indicate that everything was all right.

He tapped an index finger on the check's logo. "This is who I am. President of Roper Hotels. And this is my—" he consulted the check "—thirty-seven thousand, two hundred and fifty dollars you're about to deposit into the account of a supply company that doesn't exist."

"It does exist," the young man insisted, now visibly trembling.

"We investigated," Keith told him. "There's no such address."

"But I put money in their account every month! I pick up the checks at the post office and I deposit them here." His cheeks were now the color of marshmallows.

"Who hired you to do this?" Keith asked.

"I don't know. Somebody knew somebody who knew somebody." The young man looked at Keith, his eyes fear-filled. "They promised me I'd get my two thousand dollars a month and I wouldn't get busted. Come on, man! If I don't deposit this check, I'm in trouble, big time. That's what they told me when I was hired."

Keith glanced at David, an idea forming. He turned back to the kid and did his best to look dangerous. "Well, if you don't do exactly what I say, you won't have to worry about *them* hurting you because I'll do it myself."

CHAPTER TWELVE

"So our purchasing records reveal that the Atlantic Eden was being doubly supplied," Emily said. She was huddled with Penny in Keith's office going over the information they'd collected in the past day and a half, while Keith and David had been in Denver. "By the companies we all use and by this Grayson place. But when we actually do an inventory, the things from Grayson don't show up."

Penny nodded, her eyes bright with excitement. Then she frowned. "But Mr. Roper knows all this. So what have we accomplished, besides possibly getting me fired?"

"Oh, Penny, Keith wouldn't fire you no matter what he threatened. And we haven't accomplished anything yet. But he's not due back until tomorrow. Maybe I can solve this before he gets home."

"By yourself?" Penny, her stalwart companion, looked horrified.

But Emily was determined. She'd been thinking about her situation for a day and a half, and she knew it was just a matter of time before Keith remembered that they didn't have a common past, after all.

Well, she'd do anything to save her marriage, and

maybe solving the Grayson mystery and stopping the financial drain on the Atlantic Eden would help.

It wouldn't matter that Keith had insisted she not get involved. She felt sure he'd feel differently if she produced the culprit—with proof.

"The next thing to do," Emily said, "is find out where Grayson deposits its money and who signs on it. 'Course we can get the bank and account number from the backs of our canceled checks, but if these people are smart, the endorsement's just a rubber stamp."

Penny waved one of the checks they'd retrieved from the files, then studied it. "Yep." She frowned and reached for the phone. "I have a friend who works for an independent auditing company. She might be able to look into this for us."

"Is it legal?" Emily asked.

Penny stilled. "Does it matter to us?"

Emily didn't have to think about it. "Grayson obviously isn't concerned with what's legal. Why should we be?"

Penny punched out the number. "Yes, good afternoon," she said after a moment. "Gloria Milton, please."

Emily listened as Penny explained that she was helping the company she worked for with an audit of their books, and that they'd found a discrepancy in the invoices from a company named Grayson Hotel Supplies. She gave her friend the name of Grayson's bank and their account number.

"Right," she said. "We're sure money's being siphoned off into that account. We're trying to find out whose name is on the account so we can try solving it in-house first without involving the police. Do you think you can help?''

Penny listened a moment. "Yes, well, if that happens, I'll get you a job here." She made a face at Emily. "You're a pal, Gloria. Do you think we can have an answer by end of business today?" She gave Emily a thumbs-up. "Great. Thanks. I owe you big."

While Penny stayed by the phone, Emily ran to the hotel kitchen for sandwiches.

"Emily! Hi!" The sound of Jack's voice behind her made Emily jump.

She hadn't spoken the words aloud, but she suspected Jack was involved in the embezzlement. He was responsible for the purchasing department, and because he was a member of the family, she was fairly sure nothing he did was monitored.

But Keith's safety was at stake here, so she turned to Jack with a bright smile. "Hi, Jack. You coming to charm the kitchen staff out of a ham sandwich, too?"

He shook his head. "No." He held up a gym bag. "I was just on my way to the pool when I saw you. Are you back to work now?"

"Not yet," she replied. "I'm just spiffing up Keith's office while he's gone."

"Spiffing up? We do have a housekeeping crew that takes care of administrative offices, as well."

"Right. I just brought in a few touches. A photo of Rebecca for his desk, copies of some of the old pictures we had blown up for Neil's party to hang on his wall, that sort of thing.''

Jack studied her, and though she looked for it, she could find no hint of suspicion in his eyes. He smiled. "Well, don't work too hard. We want you in good shape to fix Thanksgiving dinner. Janice says she'd love to come.''

"Oh, good.''

He headed off for the pool with a wave.

Emily chatted with friends in the kitchen while they prepared sandwiches for Penny and her, answering their teasing questions about marrying the boss by claiming it had been part of her plan all along. As she expected, they laughed.

She felt a burning pain in her stomach.

She hurried back to the office to find the phone ringing. Emily locked the office door behind her and ran to stand over Penny, whose pen was poised over a piece of Eden stationery.

After a moment, she wrote, "J. B. Roper.''

Emily sank into a chair.

Penny thanked Gloria profusely, then hung up the phone. "Keith's cousin!'' she exclaimed in a whisper. "But which one? Jack or Janice?''

Emily's appetite had vanished. Finding proof did not bring the satisfaction she'd hoped it would. Worse, she and Keith had been arguing about his investigation of the Grayson account in the market the day she'd collided with Jack in the grocery store. Jack might have overheard. If he was J.B., Keith could be in trouble right now.

"How can we check this," Penny asked, "without going to personnel?"

Emily and Penny stared morosely at each other, then Penny said, "I know. The annual report!"

She went to a file drawer, pulled out the report and brought it to the desk.

They leafed through it, finding a page of photos and bios of Keith, Greg, Neil and Barbara. Jack and Janice were on the same page—John Barton Roper and Janice Beverly Roper.

Penny gasped. "It can't be!"

But it was. Emily groaned in frustration. She wanted this issue to be a fait accompli when Keith got home. No more having to worry about the perpetrator learning of Keith's investigation and harming him in some way. She wanted it over—certain the time was coming soon when she would have to give her full attention to keeping her position as his wife.

The telephone rang.

Penny answered it. "Keith Roper's office. Oh, yes, Mrs. Roper. Are you calling from—?" The smile on her face evaporated and she turned to Emily in alarm. "Yes, she's here. Hold on, Mrs. Roper."

Penny put her hand over the mouthpiece as she passed the receiver to Emily. "Mr. Roper's had a mild heart attack!"

Emily's heart rose to her throat. "Barbara?" she said, getting to her feet, "What's happened? How's Neil?"

"I think he's going to be fine," Barbara replied, her voice thinned by fear and the transatlantic connection.

"It happened last night and I rushed him right to the hospital. The doctor said there was minimal damage, but he needs to rest. So we're coming home a few days early. I was hoping Keith would be able to pick us up in Portland. The flight arrives at ten in the morning."

It would delay her investigation of the cousins, but Neil's good health and comfort was what was important now. "Keith's been out of town for a few days, Barbara, and he's due back tomorrow, but not until the afternoon. Rebecca and I will come pick you up. Got a flight number?"

Emily wrote it down. "You're sure Neil's all right?"

"I'm sure. We had a wonderful time until last night, but now he's anxious to get home."

"We'll use the limo so he can lie down in comfort on the ride home."

"Bless you, Emily."

Penny shook her head as Emily hung up the phone. "Could anything else go wrong?"

She'd just posed the question when a shrill bell rang, indicating the elevator was stuck. "I had to ask," Penny said dryly. "You go home. If I get any brilliant ideas, I'll call you."

NEIL LOOKED WELL but tired, and was happy to curl up under a blanket on the seat right behind the driver's. The back seat was reserved for Rebecca's car seat. Emily and Barbara joined her, talking quietly while Neil slept.

"He's such a rock," Barbara said softly. "But he's a man from the old school. He was always kind and wonderful with the boys, but he protected us from everything." She sighed, the stress of the past couple of days showing on her face.

Emily took her hand.

"Keith fought it," Barbara went on, "wanting to deal with things himself. Greg was just the opposite. He seemed to find it easy to let everyone do for him, shield him, clean up after him." She shook her head. "If you worked at the Atlantic Eden, you must have known him."

Emily's heart thumped. "Yes, a little."

"On the surface he was warm and charming, but it usually only took a little while to realize that he was selfish and his own top priority. Neil tried everything to turn him around, unable to believe that the same genes that had created Keith could have made Greg. He was sure the problem with Greg was one he could fix if he could just identify it."

"I'm sorry." Emily put an arm around Barbara's shoulders, feeling like a fraud listening and pretending that she'd barely known him. "But try not to worry anymore. We've invited David and Maria to join us at the guest house for Thanksgiving. I thought you'd be tired from your trip and would just as soon not have to think about dinner."

"Oh, that'd be wonderful," Barbara said. Then she added, as though afraid to burden her, "We usually have Jack and Janice, too."

Emily nodded—thinking wryly to herself that her

world was suddenly filled with things that were difficult to discuss under the circumstances. "Yes, I've already invited them."

Barbara sighed again, leaning back and closing her eyes. "It'll be wonderful to have a real family Thanksgiving. It's been so long. Haven't done it since the boys were small."

The limo delivered Neil and Barbara to their doorstep, where their housekeeper was waiting to welcome them.

Emily promised to check on them when Keith arrived home.

She went to the guest house for her own car, then stopped at Vangie's to see if her friend could watch Rebecca.

"Sure," Vangie said, placing the sleeping baby on the sofa. "More investigative stuff?"

"Yes." Emily consulted her watch. "I have three hours before Keith gets back." She gave Vangie a quick hug. "Thanks. You're a doll."

"Just see that I get a promotion!" Vangie called after her.

First Emily had to see if the cousins were in. If they were, she intended to confront them, counting on the innocent one to support her against the other. She hurried to Keith's office, hoping to get Penny to check for her.

She came to an abrupt halt when she found herself looking at the face of a complete stranger—a beautiful brunette with an elegant chignon.

"Hello," the woman said in a professional tone.

"May I help you?" Then her gaze narrowed. "Mrs. Roper?"

"Yes," Emily said, glancing around as though that would make Penny magically appear. "Where's Penny?"

"She had a fender bender on the way in this morning," the young woman said. "Knocked her out for a minute. Steve Binford was with her, and he called an ambulance. He phoned us from the hospital and said she seems fine, but they wanted to keep her for observation to make sure."

Emily gasped, wondering if it had really been an accident. "Did anyone see it happen?"

Penny's replacement seemed to consider that a strange question. "Yes. Steve Binford—"

"Of course. You said that." Emily forced herself to think straight. Why wouldn't it have been an accident? No one knew she and Penny had been looking into Grayson Hotel Supplies.

"Mrs. Roper, I'm Wendy Hartford. I'm usually on the front desk. Is there something I can help you with?"

All right. It was now or never. "Yes, thank you. Would you check to see if Jack Roper and Janice Roper are in their offices?"

"No," Wendy replied. "I mean, no, they're not in their offices. They're with Mr. Roper—Mr. Keith. Your husband." She laughed. "All these Roper names get hard to handle."

Emily felt a jolt of fear. "My husband," she made

herself say calmly, "hasn't returned from the airport yet."

Wendy frowned. "Yes, he has, Mrs. Roper. He and Mr. Ambrosio chartered a flight all the way to the airport in Lincoln City. They drove in half an hour ago."

"Where are they?" Emily choked out.

"I believe they went to the roof garden."

The roof garden. Eight stories up. Oh, God.

"Call security!" she shouted as she ran to the stairs. Although it was a bit of a climb, the stairs were faster than the elevator. "And tell them to meet me there!"

KEITH STEPPED OFF the elevator with his cousins, wishing he could remember his past, so that he could determine how events had come to this.

He and David had waited at the young man's apartment the previous day, and the boy had been right. When the embezzler saw that the check hadn't been deposited...she called. Listening, Keith had recognized Janice's voice immediately. The boy, on his instructions, told Janice that the Charlotte police had confiscated the check.

Then Keith and David had chartered a flight home.

He'd felt certain that would be enough either to make Janice run or force a confrontation.

It was the latter. Ostensibly his cousin had invited him to the roof garden to look it over with an eye to buying new furniture to go with the canopy. A spring fashion show had already been booked for it.

But he knew better. In November the roof garden

would be deserted. Either Janice wanted a private place to talk or... He preferred not to think about what, but he remained alert.

Janice was carrying on cheerfully about umbrellaed tables as they stepped off the elevator, only to be met by a blast of chilling wind straight from the ocean.

Janice turned away from the view and walked toward the part of the roof garden where the wrought-iron railing was being reconstructed. A double line of rope completed the half-finished railing. Keith followed her.

"I'd like to put potted flowers all along the fence," she was saying as she walked fearlessly close to the rope. "Nasturtiums that would cascade over the side would look wonderful from below, too. What do you think? And umbrellas and chair cushions in yellow and orange to match the flowers."

Keith joined her, looking down and nodding. "Sounds good. Your decorator's sense has always served us well." He turned to Jack, who remained a good twenty feet away, his face pale, his expression panicky. "What do you think, Jack?"

Jack watched him, his eyes wary.

As Keith swung back to Janice, a curious thing happened. His gaze swept over treetops, sky, a tall pine.... The images ran together in his mind, blurring into one another.

And suddenly his mind created another image of trees and sky, this one zooming past him at lightning speed as the car he was in missed a curve and went over an embankment. He'd taken off his seat belt. To reach for something? Greg's laughter rang in his ears. Then Greg had lost control....

He remembered flying through the air and thinking with a kind of detached astonishment that his landing was not going to be pleasant.

And then it struck him.

He hadn't been driving. Greg's death was not his fault!

He felt as if a rope that had been holding him down had been suddenly cut and he was free. He rose and rose, the sensation remarkably similar to what he'd experienced when he'd been thrown from the car.

But death wasn't threatening him this time. He was alive. And he hadn't killed Greg!

He heard his own laughter ring across the rooftop and only absently noticed Janice's shock.

Janice.

The present came back to him and he stood quietly for a moment, letting it settle into place. When he looked up again, Janice had a gun trained on him.

He felt no sense of panic. And another piece of the memory puzzle fitted into place. He had parents who loved him and who'd been there every time he'd needed them. He'd had an aunt and an uncle who'd been kind and gentle. But more important to the moment, he had a smart funny cousin he'd always loved. A more serious timid cousin he'd also always loved.

WITHOUT THOUGHT for stealth or even caution, Emily burst onto the roof, afraid for one awful moment when it appeared to be empty.

Then she heard voices to her left, surprisingly quiet voices, considering what she thought she'd find—accusations, denials, threats, counterthreats.

But there Keith and Janice were with only a few feet between them, Jack off to one side. She wondered briefly if she'd somehow misinterpreted the situation—if the cousins had *not* chosen the highest, most remote part of the complex because they meant Keith harm.

She started toward them, then Janice shifted slightly and Emily saw the gun in her hand.

Keith was half a foot from the edge of the roof and the unfinished railing. A scream rose in Emily's throat, but she controlled it by clenching her teeth.

"Janice, for God's sake!" Jack said, moving toward his sister.

There was a small clicking sound. A sound that on a television cop show usually preceded the firing of a gun.

"Jack, stay out of it or I'll shoot him!" Janice said. There was a note of absolute certainty in her voice.

"No," Jack told her, taking another step forward. "You're not going to shoot anybody."

There was an explosion of sound, and the Caution sign near Keith's foot fell over.

This time Emily screamed.

Janice glanced at her, then refocused on Keith. "Stay back, Emily," she warned.

"Jack," Keith said quietly, "get Emily out of here."

"Why don't we all get out of here?" Emily said,

forcing the words out of a throat so tight and painful she was surprised she could make a sound. "Please, Janice..."

Janice shook her head. "No. There's no getting out unless Keith does exactly what I ask."

"Help me remember what happened, Janice," Keith said calmly. "I'm starting to pull it together, but I don't quite have it. You and Jack were embezzling, and Greg discovered it, but rather than stopping you, he took money to stay quiet?"

"No," she corrected, equally calm. "Greg was embezzling, and I discovered it when your mom and I went to the Atlantic to see about redecorating the ballroom. I checked the computer for the source of a chair I wanted and in the process happened upon the Grayson account. It seemed to be a large payable with nothing to show for it. Jack never knew the account existed until I pointed it out to him. Then he kept quiet about it because Greg had bought me off, and Jack didn't want to rat on me, though he was always on me to stop it."

"Were you in debt?" Keith asked.

"No," she replied easily. "Greg was. He said your father wouldn't increase his yearly income, so he'd found another way to pay for girls and gambling." She shook her head wearily. "God, I was just so tired of you and Greg always getting everything. *You* may have deserved it, but Greg didn't, because he never gave a rip. But Jack and I did. Jack's always been stuck in purchasing because he would never push hard enough to convince anyone that he'd be good anywhere else.''

She smiled apologetically at her brother. ''And no one ever paid attention to me because I was always just your cousin—and a female. I wanted the job managing the Atlantic, but Greg—who was never on time, never informed, never cared—got it instead. So I decided—'' she sighed heavily ''—if I couldn't have the prestige of a title, I'd take the money. When I threatened to expose Greg, he made me a signatory on the account, and when he died, it was easy for me to keep it going.''

''And that made you happy?'' Keith asked.

She shook her head. ''When your own family doesn't notice how much you give, how hard you try, then nothing makes you happy. So you settle for other things.''

''Jannie...'' Keith's voice was gentle with affection and sadness.

Emily saw Janice's eyes brim with tears. ''Anyway, it's too late now.'' Janice leveled the gun at him. ''What I need from you is the promise that I can get out of here with a good head start or—I swear to God—if I'm going to lose it all, so are you.''

Keith took several steps toward her. Emily gasped.

Janice held the gun in both hands, firming her stance. ''Keith...'' she warned.

''I remember something else,'' he said, his voice even more gentle. ''I remember the four of us, you and Jack and Greg and me on the beach in Florida when the first Eden went up. Remember? The four of us used to fish off the pier.''

Janice looked a little confused and her eyes seemed to shift focus. Then she shook her head. ''That was a long time ago, Keith.''

''Yes. But the four of us were inseparable. And you were always mad at us boys because you could never catch any fish.''

She held out against the memory for a moment, then smiled fractionally. ''Because you guys took all the bait. Well, Jack and Greg did. You always shared yours with me.''

Keith nodded. ''Because you always shared those awful coconut things in your lunch. What were they called?''

''Snowballs,'' she answered, then repeated more slowly, ''Yeah. Snowballs.'' Some indefinable expression crossed her face, then she stiffened and shook her head. ''Keith, we're talking half a million dollars here. It outweighs the bait.''

He was silent a moment, then nodded. ''OK.''

Emily saw Jack's head come up and Janice's surprised stare.

''What?'' Jack asked.

Keith, arms folded, shrugged off the half a million dollars. ''To Janice it outweighs the bait,'' he said with a smile. ''But to me, it doesn't outweigh the snowballs. Go. I'll see that you're not followed.''

Janice stared at him for what seemed an eternity, her expression evolving from disbelief to scorn, then regret and back to disbelief.

"You'd let me go?" she said. It wasn't really a question, but a statement made in wonder.

"I don't want to," he said. "We've already lost Greg. Then it'd be just Jack and me left to console each other." He put an arm out to Jack and Jack walked into it, tears welling in his eyes.

They stood arm in arm, facing Janice. "Do you *want* to leave us? Or can we just stop this here and make it right?"

She looked heavenward, her lips trembling. Then she turned back to Keith. "It can't be made right."

"Yes, it can. Greg started it—you didn't. What did you do with the money?"

She bit her lip, tossed her hair, took a deep breath. "Nothing," she replied unsteadily. "I just...took it."

"OK. So we put back what's left in the account and call it square. You don't need Grayson Supplies anymore."

She didn't seem able to comprehend what he offered. "It can't be that easy," she said.

He held firm. "It can be. It is. Just say the word."

Jack put an arm out to her. "Come on, Jannie. Please."

Emily watched Janice think it over for what seemed an eternity and finally lower the gun. Then Bill Dodge from security, whom Emily hadn't even noticed arrive, took the gun from her hand.

Janice flew into Keith and Jack's embrace, overcome with racking sobs.

Emily crossed to Dodge and took his arm. Gesturing at the man who'd come with him, she said, "I think everything's all right now. Thanks for coming.'' She turned and saw David standing by the elevator. She didn't question her friend's presence, just went into his arms for a hug, then got on the elevator with him and the security guards.

She waited for Keith in his office. Her heart was beating fast, her throat was dry and her hands were shaking. It was love, she realized. Not the blinding rush a woman felt when her man emerged safe from danger, but the deep-down altering of her reality that took place when she finally understood what her man was made of. When he not only survived danger, but killed it with his bare hands. Or in this case, his big heart.

CHAPTER THIRTEEN

EMILY WAS STARING out the window at the darkening sky when she heard the door to Keith's office open. She turned to find him standing there, looking remarkably unaffected by the events of the afternoon.

If she'd felt guilt before about what she'd allowed Keith to believe, it was nothing compared to what she experienced now that she *really* knew him.

But that didn't prevent her from walking into his arms, determined to savor however long was left in their relationship.

His references on the roof to his childhood had to mean he'd retrieved at least some of his memory. And as she drew her head back to look into his face, she saw something changed there, some new element to his smile.

But he wound his fingers in her hair and brought her mouth to his in an eager hungry kiss. "God, I missed you," he said against her lips. "I know it was only two days, but it felt like forever. How's Rebecca?"

"Wonderful," she said. "But…how are you? I'm still shaking."

He sank into a chair and drew her into his lap, then

leaned back as though exhausted. "I took Janice home. Jack's going to stay with her tonight."

Emily settled comfortably against him, finding a place for her head on his shoulder. "I personally thought you were toast," she said, playing with his tie. "How did you know she wouldn't shoot you? There was a lot of money at stake."

"Yeah, it was weird," he said, his voice reflecting a kind of awe. "All I did was turn my head and I had this impression of things speeding by me just like I had during the accident with Greg. And it brought it all back to me. I forgot to be afraid, and I remembered that Janice and I had a warm loving past. I knew she wouldn't hurt me."

"You have your memory back?" she asked. Certainly not all of it, or he wouldn't be holding her in his arms right now.

"Of the accident," he said. "I remembered being in the car—on the passenger side."

She threw her arms around his neck, relieved that he could now put that worry aside.

"I also remembered what went on before. I'd suspected something was going on with the Atlantic Eden's books for a while, and I'd gone there to look things over for myself. I knew when I met Greg in Santa Fe that he was siphoning money, but I wanted to have a clear head when we met with the Realtor, so I didn't bring it up until we drove back to the hotel. Greg denied it, then I produced the invoices for things that weren't part of our inventory, and he finally admitted it. When I asked him how he could steal from his own family, he laughed.'' Keith's voice lowered. "I remember clearly wanting to kill him.''

Keith paused a moment, then drew a breath. "But I didn't. I was still trying to understand how he could steal from our parents when he turned to laugh at me again and missed a bend in the road.''

Emily kissed his cheek, wanting to erase the pain she could feel in him. "Don't think about that any- more,'' she said. "You...you must have remembered your childhood, too.''

"Yes,'' he said, a bright note in his voice. "That's come back. I can see all of us as children. We had a great time together under the eye of a baby-sitter who stayed close but let us do pretty much what we wanted while our parents built and opened the hotel.'' He laughed, almost to himself. "Jack had no adventure quotient even then. And Greg was already showing signs of becoming a jerk. But Janice was great. Un- fortunately my aunt died when Jack and Janice were still in grade school. As a result Janice had little to do with the hotel while my uncle was alive, because he kept trying to turn her into her mother—a chic society lady. My father finally brought her into the company when my uncle passed away. She wanted the Atlantic Eden manager's job, but Dad was convinced that more responsibility would shape Greg up, so he gave the position to him, instead. She wanted to get even...but I guess you heard that part.''

Emily nestled against him, listening. If he'd remem- bered his childhood, certainly other memories would follow soon.

"I can't remember much else about Greg, though," he said, rubbing his forehead with his hand. "I can remember us as children and I can remember just before the accident, but all the rest...I don't know. I try to think and it's as though my mind bounces off those other memories, doesn't want to touch them. And it hurts. Physically."

Emily could hear the pain in his voice. Her own relief almost choked her. She ran her fingers through his hair and rubbed gently. "Then don't force things. Let your memories come when they're ready to come."

They sat wrapped in each other's arms for a long time, then he said lazily, "You heard from the folks?"

She froze, having forgotten in all the excitement that he didn't know about his father.

"What?" he asked anxiously.

She squeezed his shoulder. "Nothing awful. Your dad's fine, but he suffered a mild heart attack in Paris, so they flew home early. I picked them up at the airport this morning."

He gasped and sat up straighter in his chair.

"He's fine, believe me," she said, reaching for the phone. "I left them at their place after Dr. Miller got there, then came right back to the hotel because I knew Jack and Janice were behind Grayson, and I wanted to—"

She stopped abruptly, realizing her mistake.

He took the receiver from her, a frown settling over his features. "How did you know that?"

She grabbed the receiver back, punched out his parents' number, then returned it to him. "We can talk about it after you've checked with them."

Emily went into the outer office to ask Wendy if anyone had heard from Penny.

"She's fine," Wendy reported. "The hospital sent her home, after all, but the doctor thought she should stay home today. She asked you to call her when you have the chance." Wendy smiled. "I told her you were in with Mr. Roper and I wasn't sure I should disturb you."

Emily thanked her and returned Penny's call from Wendy's phone.

"Wendy said Mr. Keith was back already!" Penny said worriedly. "What happened? Did you get the Grayson thing taken care of?"

Emily explained what had happened and told her briefly about the scene on the roof.

Penny was quiet for a long moment. "He's just going to forget it?"

"Apparently."

"Wow."

"Yes."

"How's Mr. Neil?" Penny asked. "They got in all right?"

"He looks tired, but I think he's going to be fine if he takes it easy for a while."

"Uh-oh. Mr. Keith doing double duty again."

"At least the Grayson business is off his mind."

Penny promised to be in bright and early the following morning. Emily hung up, asked Wendy to send her flowers, then peeked inside Keith's office.

He stood at his desk, still talking to his father. "OK, look. If you're feeling up to it, I'll drop by just to say hi. Want me to bring you anything?" Keith listened, then shook his head. He noticed Emily and waved her in. "No, I'm not bringing work home for you. I took care of everything while you were gone, and I can do it for a while longer. I meant, did you want something to eat? Maybe a couple of David's brioches?"

Keith listened again, grinned, then his expression softened. "Yes, I've remembered a few things—such as that brioches are your passion. Mom want anything? OK, brioches and a cup of David's red-and-white-bean salad. We'll pick those up and be right there."

Keith cleared the line, then dialed again, sitting on the edge of his desk and pointing Emily to his chair. He asked for David, explained about his parents and placed his order. "No, thanks," he said. "We'll come by and pick it up. Yeah, I'm fine. No. We'll have to have a night without our wives sometime and talk about it. Yeah. About ten minutes?"

Keith hung up the phone, and as though their conversation had never been interrupted, he asked again, "How did you know about Jack and Janice?"

Since there was so much she couldn't tell him, she decided to come clean about this. "Penny has a friend in an auditing company, so we called her and asked her to find out who signed on the account."

He looked heavenward. "Emily, that's illegal."

"Yes, I know."

He took her calm admission with a raised eyebrow.

"So that's why Penny isn't here today? You fired her to save me the trouble?"

She pulled a face. "You know you wouldn't do that. She had a small fender bender on her way in to work this morning. Nothing serious, but she bumped her head, and the doctor suggested she stay home for a day."

He stood, took several steps away from her, then turned back, his blue eyes turbulent. "You know, if we're going to live out the rest of our lives together, you're going to have to stop thinking that I don't mean what I say. I told you before I left for Charlotte..."

She stood and put her arms around him to stop his pacing. He kept his hands in his pockets, obviously trying not to react to her.

"You told me you would fire Penny if I looked into the Grayson business," she said, "but that would be unfair." She lowered her voice. "Of course, you could fire *me*—" What he'd said suddenly registered. "Before you went *where?*" she demanded.

He sighed. "To Charlotte. North Carolina."

"You told me you were going to Denver!"

"I know." He managed to look apologetic without looking penitent. "I didn't want you to worry."

She gasped, her entire being bristling. "You actually *went* there and you're grumping at me because I did some checking on the computer?"

"You could have been caught nosing around," he said. "This is just one workstation in a connected system. And I was gone."

"Yes. And if I'd tried to reach you in Denver, I'd

have been out of luck, wouldn't I?'' It was ridiculous to make an issue over the fact that he'd lied to her in view of the lies she'd told him, but a part of her couldn't quite recover from the sight of a gun trained on him.

"David's wife knew where we were," he said.

"You're not married to Maria," she reminded him.

He tried another tack. "You asked me not to go alone and I didn't. I took David."

"Oh, yes." She spread her arms. "Commando-trained Call-Me-Van-Damme Ambrosio."

He broke into a smile, then caught her to him and kissed her. "I was on the boxing team in college. And in the German club."

"And how would the German club have helped you?"

He kissed her again. "It wouldn't. I just happened to remember that detail. And don't knock my friends. David backed me up. He even wanted to wait with me for Janice to make her move, but I took him home before I came in."

"Yeah, well, he was on the roof backing you up again," she said. "I suppose you'll want to yell at him, too."

"I think neither of us is in a position to gripe about the other," he conceded. "Shall we declare a truce and go see my parents?"

"WE'RE NOT GOING to mention the Grayson business," Keith said before ringing his parents' doorbell. "I never mentioned any of it to Dad, so we're clean.

And I've sworn the security people to secrecy. So as of this moment, it never happened, all right?"

"Of course," she replied.

Frances, the Ropers' housekeeper, led them to the sitting room where Neil was ensconced amid a stack of pillows on the sofa.

Barbara sprang up to greet them and smiled at Keith. "You've remembered something? Your father said you remembered about him loving..."

Before she could say the word, he produced the box of brioches.

Frances came to claim them. "I'll put these on a plate," she said. Emily handed her the bean salad.

Keith explained his sudden return of memory by telling his parents he'd gone to the roof garden to check the progress on the railing. Then he told a modified version of the story he'd told Emily.

They talked for an hour, reminiscences building one upon another until everyone was laughing, although Barbara also sniffled a little.

Emily got the picture of a warm and loving family who'd endured the typical struggles, but who were held together by a sturdy selfless love and a common passion for the business they shared.

Except for Greg.

"Sometimes I think his death was a form of natural selection," Neil said, his voice heavy, his gaze focused on a memory of his younger son. "We talk about survival of the fittest, but I think there's also a survival of the useful. If you're not productive, if you don't care about your fellow man, then you pull against life's purpose. And ultimately—like Greg did—you destroy yourself.''

Keith raised his hand to his forehead, a pain thumping there. ''That's something I can't remember,'' he said. ''I see our childhood clearly and I see that last day, but I can't remember Greg as an adult.''

''Maybe that's enough for now.'' Barbara stood. ''Please don't think I'm throwing you out, but your father has to get some rest, and you two have to go pick up Rebecca from Vangie's.''

Keith leaned down to embrace his father. ''You stay home for a couple of days at least.''

''I thought maybe I'd come in to check my mail tomorrow afternoon.''

''No,'' Keith said. ''I'll bring it to you.''

''I'll just sit in the office and—''

''No.''

Neil frowned at him, but there was grudging affection in his eyes. ''You're back, all right. You may be president of the company, but I'm chairman of the board.''

''I know, but as of now you're on sick leave, so don't try to throw your weight around. I'll stop by on my way home every night to give you a rundown on what's going on—but only if you promise to stay here and relax and don't give Mom any trouble.''

Neil caught Emily's eye. ''How do you put up with this?''

She heaved a long-suffering sigh. ''Every day's a struggle. But in this instance he's right. Do as he says.

Bye.'' Emily hugged him while Keith embraced his mother.

Barbara walked them to the door. "Have I ever told you," she asked Emily, "how pleased I am that you married my son?"

"She was the only thing I didn't forget," Keith said, looking lovingly into her eyes. "The moment I saw her, I knew her."

Barbara kissed both of them, then stepped back with a smile of satisfaction. "That's love. It's alive in us even when other supposedly more sophisticated parts don't function. Good night, kids. See you tomorrow, Keith."

KEITH PLAYED with Rebecca on a blanket on the floor in the living room while Emily prepared dinner. Rebecca's favorite toy was a soft block with different colors and figures on each side and a rattle inside.

Keith dangled the toy over her while she gurgled and cooed and flailed her arms and legs. Propped on an elbow, he seemed fascinated by her reactions.

Emily peered out of the kitchen to watch them, her heart so full she thought it might break. She had to tell him. She *had* to.

But he was just getting his memory back. Thinking about his brother physically hurt him, and his father was not in the best of health.

Honesty now might do more harm than good.

She realized that sounded like rationalization, but it was a decision she went with, anyway.

Rebecca sat in her carrier on the table while they ate. She was still wide-awake.

"Am I hearing things," Keith asked, making faces at Rebecca while she smiled at him, "or is she saying vowels?"

Emily laughed. "It does sound like that. Maybe your mother should make that call to her connections at Bryn Mawr."

Keith pushed his empty plate aside, one hand playing with the baby's fingers as though he couldn't get enough of her now that he was home again. He picked up his wineglass and finished the last mouthful.

"When my childhood came back to me on the roof," he said, frowning into the empty glass, "I felt this rush of warmth and love. And suddenly I remembered every detail about my mother and father. All the kindness, all the support, all the attention, all the unqualified love. It made me feel as though I was...standing on a mountain with everything in the world I would ever need."

Emily listened greedily. That was how *his* love made her feel. But unlike him, she hadn't the security of knowing it was hers forever, no matter what.

That was the feeling she'd missed as a child. And it was bigger and ran deeper than she'd ever imagined.

"That's why it was so easy for you to understand and forgive your cousin," she said.

He caught one of Rebecca's bootied feet in his hand. "Yes, and it's what I want Rebecca to know."

So did Emily, but had she made that impossible?

When Rebecca went to sleep, Keith stoked the fire

and they lay in the flame-lit darkness, clothes in a pile beside them.

Emily kissed him with a desperation that raised an echoing desperation in him. But her tenderness and her need reached him. He felt her in his heart. And he waited for her, teased her into catching up, then made her wait for him, and wait and wait.

Emily clung to him afterward. But he felt the desperation and the need still alive in her.

He pulled her into the crook of his arm. "Emmie, what's the matter?"

"Nothing," she said into his shoulder. "It's just been such a long day."

He kissed her cheek. "The bad part is over. Let's just put it away." He brushed the hair back from her face. "And anyway, I thought you'd have a welcome-home planned."

She smiled. "I thought I just welcomed you home."

"Well...I was hoping for a cheerleader outfit and chocolate mousse and maybe a peacock feather."

She giggled. "That sounds like something worth filming."

"Yeah," he said, "that, too."

She held him tightly. "Maybe I could just be a chef madly in love with her hotelier husband. Want to try it?"

"I'm all yours."

Her embrace tightened around him, and he ran a hand over her hip, beginning to love her again even as a part of him wondered about the urgency in her touch.

OVER THE NEXT FEW DAYS, Emily was able to live her childhood dream. She had a husband who loved her and who was there every time she turned to him. She had a baby who was plump-cheeked and perfect and too beautiful for words. She had in-laws who were like parents, and Neil seemed to be growing stronger every day.

Rain had come to the Oregon coast with a vengeance, but it didn't matter to Emily or Keith. The little guest house was a warm and cozy haven from the elements and from the daily pressures Keith faced at the hotel.

They sat on the sofa one evening, Emily leaning against Keith's chest, as they watched *Gone with the Wind.* She was drowsy with contentment.

During a commercial break he picked up the remote and muted the sound.

"You know," he began reluctantly, almost apologetically, "I hate to bring up anything unpleasant, but we have to start thinking about leaving here."

Emily, a bowl of popcorn balanced on her lap, sat up abruptly, her mellow mood shattered. Keith reached out to save the bowl as she turned toward him.

She'd expected to see the threat coming, to have time to prepare, to mount a resistance. "Leave?" she said. "Why?"

He leaned around her to place the bowl on the coffee table. "Em, I run the California Eden. I've got to get back to it. The holiday period is quiet, but I've been looking over the bookings and we have three big conferences in January. I should be there." He wrapped both arms around her protectively. "I know you love it here. I do, too. And my parents are going to miss you and Rebecca, but I have to think of the business."

"Yes. Of course." Panic subsided as Emily understood. He was beginning to plan the rest of their lives.

They'd finished the trying-it-out period when they'd gotten married, but even then their relationship had had a temporary quality. Keith hadn't yet regained his memory, and he'd been struggling with the Grayson issue. The present had been so all-consuming that they hadn't given much thought to the future.

Now it was time.

"But should you go back," she asked, cautious, "before you remember...everything?"

He kissed her cheek. "That could take a while, and we have to get on with our lives. Do you like L.A.? I can't seem to remember that. I can see you in my arms and in my nights—" he squeezed her affectionately "—but not really in my world. I suppose I kept you out of it and all to myself."

Fear clutched her heart with icy fingers. It was beginning. One day soon it would occur to him that he was reclaiming no memory of her because he hadn't any, because she'd never *been* in his world.

Time was running out.

The commercial break over, Keith clicked off the mute and Rhett Butler expressed surprise at finding Scarlett in an intoxicated state in her hotel room.

Emily sympathized with Scarlett. Love could drive

a woman to drink—particularly a woman who connived for her own purposes.

Later that night as she lay in Keith's arms, the even rise and fall of his chest a movement that seemed to stabilize her whole world, she knew she had to put her fears aside and tell him the truth.

Neil was doing well, Keith adored Rebecca wholeheartedly, and he was as kind and loving a husband as any woman could hope for.

She had no more excuses.

Except Thanksgiving. She would tell him right after the holiday.

CHAPTER FOURTEEN

ON WEDNESDAY MORNING Emily prepared cheese omelettes while Keith showered. Her heart was thudding and her hands were damp. Now that she'd decided to tell Keith the truth, she felt like 110 pounds of guilt.

She couldn't tell him for two more days, but her body seemed to want to get it over with, to say it. And the face her mirror had reflected this morning looked like that of a woman on death row.

She heard the shower stop. That meant Keith would be dressing and coming down within five minutes.

She folded the omelettes and put bread in the toaster. She had to calm down, sit on her revelation for two more days. She could do it.

And when the time came, Keith would listen to her and he would understand. He loved Rebecca and he loved her. He would understand. He would.

Breakfast was ready and she heard his footsteps on the stairs when the doorbell rang.

She rushed to the door, wondering if something had happened to Neil.

It was Janice. She stood on the doorstep in a long mohair coat, her loose blond hair billowing about her face. Her blue eyes still looked as stunned as they had that afternoon on the roof.

"Janice, hi." Emily pulled her inside. "You're just in time for breakfast."

"Oh, thanks." Janice smiled a little uncertainly. "But I can't stay. I just have…something for Keith. I was hoping to catch him before he left."

"Good timing, Jannie." Keith walked into the room, buttoning the cuff of a crisp white shirt, his suit coat over his arm. He tossed it on a chair. "What's up?"

Emily turned to make herself scarce, but Janice caught her arm. "You don't have to leave—I'll just be a minute." She pulled an envelope out of her pocket and handed it to Keith. "This is everything that was in the Grayson account and about half of what I took from Greg."

He nodded. "Good."

"Jack got me in touch with your friend, Ben Gordon, and I put the condo up for sale."

"I told you not to do that," Keith said gently.

"I know. But I have to. I slipped into this out of…what? A loss of self-respect? Self-importance? I just know I'm not going to get it back until *you* get everything back. Jack invited me to move in with him for a while." Her composure began to crack. "He wanted to come in here with me, but I made him wait in the car. I had to do this alone."

Keith took her hand. "Steady. It's not as big as it seems right now. It'll be all right."

She swallowed and sniffed. "Yeah. Thanks to you.

Anyway—'' she delved into a small paper bag she held ''—I brought you something else.''

She pulled out a plastic-wrapped package that had once held two coconut-covered cupcakes, one with white frosting and one with pink. Snowballs. Only the white one remained.

She handed him the package. "You always refused the pink one," she said.

Emily bit a trembling lip.

Keith grinned. "Does this mean I have to give you worms, or will you settle for— What's for breakfast, Emmie?"

"Ah, cheese omelettes," she replied, pulling herself together and taking Janice's coat. "Go get Jack and I'll whip up a couple more."

Janice and Jack played with Rebecca while Emily cooked and Keith brewed another pot of coffee and made toast.

Over breakfast they talked about the company's future. Keith said that he'd just finalized the deal to purchase the property in Santa Fe, and that they were going ahead with the plans for a Southwest Eden. Construction would start in the spring.

"Before that," he said, leaning back in his chair and tapping his finger on the rim of his coffee cup, "I think the four of us and David should go down there and do some research on regional decorating style and cuisine." He looked around the table. "What do you think?"

Emily smiled, finding it easy to imagine all of them touring the area and sampling the food. She chose not to concentrate on how quickly that offer might be re-scinded—at least to her.

Janice, still seeming to have difficulty with the idea that all was forgiven, looked at him in surprise. Hope seemed to shimmer in her eyes for a minute, then she reached for the jam. "I don't think so."

Jack's eyes met Keith's across the table. There was a plea in them.

"Why not?" Keith asked.

She put the jam spoon down and turned to look at him directly. "Because while I appreciate what you're trying to do, I can't believe you'll be able to forget—"

"Janice," Keith interrupted, "I can forget if you can. Put it aside and let's move on. The rest of us are going into this project as a team. And this will be your last duty as interior designer for Roper Hotels."

Janice paled. Jack straightened in alarm, his gaze swinging from his sister to his cousin. Emily waited.

"When you take over the Atlantic Eden," Keith said, snatching the jam from Janice's hand, "you won't have time for that."

Janice's cheeks flushed as she stared at Keith. "What?" she asked.

He handed the jam to Jack, who was now grinning. "Family's going to have to pull its weight. My father stays here, I'll be in California, that leaves you to take care of the Atlantic. You can take Jack with you if you think that'll help. Maybe we can even cultivate a taste for management in him so that when the South-west is ready, he'll be ready, too. What do you think?"

Janice closed her eyes a moment, drew a deep

breath, then opened them and smiled at Keith, then at Jack. "I think we can do anything!"

"All *right*," Keith said. "There's an attitude I can live with. Now..."

They continued to make plans, then headed off to the hotel together, Keith pausing just long enough to give Emily, then Rebecca, a kiss.

Emily spent Rebecca's naps cleaning the house, and her periods awake working in the kitchen with the baby on the counter beside her, watching her with interest.

She fought a guilty conscience and a bad headache.

But preparing food had always been a kind of therapy. She baked pumpkin and mince pies, and made an apple cranberry relish.

She moved the furniture out of the way to make room for the table in the living room. The small kitchen alcove where it now stood would not accommodate ten people—eleven if Vangie came.

She put Rebecca in her car seat and drove to the hotel, where she borrowed a tablecloth and linen napkins from the kitchen.

"It'll be a treat to be cooked for," David said as he prepared chicken breasts for the approaching dinner period. "Is there anything we can contribute?"

Emily smiled. "How about those cheese-wrapped olives you do? Or the water chestnuts in bacon? Vangie was going to bring hors d'oeuvres but she traded shifts with someone who had a last-minute change of plans."

"You got it." He waved a flour-covered hand at

her as she headed for the door, the table linens in a plastic bag.

Once home, she worked on a centerpiece for the table using small gourds into which she made holes for candles. Then she filled a little pumpkin with wheat stalks and colorful leaves she'd gathered on her walks with Vangie.

After preparing an easy pasta dish for dinner that night, she was standing at the counter slicing cucumbers for a salad when she heard Keith's car pull into the driveway.

She drew a deep breath, forcing herself to relax; it was almost more than she could do to swallow the truth for one more day.

But this Thanksgiving dinner was, in a way, a thank-you to Keith's family and to David and Maria for all the love and kindness they'd shown her. She didn't want anything to spoil it.

So she and Keith would have another long evening together and she would cherish every moment. Her happy home might be a thing of the past come Friday.

KEITH TURNED his key in the lock, grateful to be home and looking forward to the long weekend. The day had been filled with a score of small crises, none of which amounted to much, but all of which diverted his attention from the wisps of memory that seemed to be stirring in his mind.

He hadn't been able to put them together yet. It had something to do with Greg, and what they'd shared as brothers. He remembered the anger he'd felt with him the day of the accident, but except for their childhood, that was all he remembered.

He wanted to believe they'd had more. He wanted to *remember*. But so far that period had remained closed until the stirs and flashes today.

He was hoping that this weekend at home would bring it all back.

He locked the door behind him and stood and stared at the living room. Chairs, tables, even the sofa had been moved to the farthest edges of the room, and a large table took up all the space in the middle. Kitchen chairs had been pulled around it, as well as odd chairs from other parts of the house.

Keith tossed his briefcase onto the sofa and his coat after it, unknotting his tie as he maneuvered between the sofa and an end table and headed for the kitchen.

"Emily," he said, "did you shift the furniture all by your—" He stopped abruptly as everything before his eyes began to waver, like a picture seen through old glass. The one clear image was Emily.

She'd turned away from the counter to look at him as he walked into the kitchen. She wore a shapeless white apron over a white blouse, and suddenly this image of her was superimposed by another image of her, looking very much the same, only in a different setting. She was in the hotel kitchen, talking to the chef.

He stood there as the scene ran through his mind like a videotape.

He felt anger at his brother when he looked at Emily. It was the same visceral fury he'd felt in the car the day of the accident.

And he could tell she was pregnant. Her eyes and her complexion glowed as if magical forces were at work in her.

But then she raised her eyes to him and the laughter in her face died.

He shook his head, confused. Why would Emily have looked at him that way?

With a downward rush of icy dread, he realized that this wasn't the face of a woman who loved him. It wasn't even the face of a woman who *knew* him. He'd seen recognition in her eyes, but only after the chef had said his name. Then the recognition was replaced with scorn, as though she'd analyzed him, decided that he fit some unfavorable preconception, that he wasn't worth her time.

Suddenly, as though the old glass had been shattered, he remembered what he'd thought at that moment.

Greg has no doubt been telling her about his cruel older brother.

As though the old wavy glass had been a floodgate, memory came at him in a rush.

He hadn't been Emily's lover—Greg had. Greg had told him she was pregnant and asked him to buy her out of his life. That was why he'd felt anger when he'd seen her in the hotel kitchen.

He'd told Greg he would provide the money, but if Greg wanted her out of his life, he would have to send her on her way himself.

Keith looked at Emily, whose eyes were now wide and horrified, and tried to understand his mistake.

What had happened? What had made him recognize Emily as his? Her baby as his?

He couldn't imagine.

Then all the thoughts he'd had about her when he'd first seen her came back to him. He remembered thinking how different she was from his ex-wife, how she seemed to have the passion he'd longed for. Then— and this was probably it—he recalled thinking about what he'd do if she was his. He would love her, spoil her, protect her.

It seemed that his poor scrambled mind had somehow shaken all that up and reconstructed it with a little creative license. A *lot* of creative license.

Then it occurred to him that while he'd suffered from a mangled memory, Emily had not. He felt as if he'd fallen off a high precipice.

His mind apprised him of the situation in plain and simple words, apparently on the chance that he wasn't absorbing the importance of the facts yet.

Emily let you believe that you'd been lovers—that Rebecca was your baby!

And that was when his tenuous self-control began to disintegrate. The past was clear. Now it was the present that was falling apart.

Emily knew what had happened without Keith having to say a word. She'd seen it all play out on his face—the sudden loss of focus in his eyes, the confusion followed by a glimpse of understanding, followed by realization and anger—and now his expression was so tormented she could barely look at it.

She was almost afraid to touch him, but he'd gone pale and was holding his stomach. He looked as though he might collapse if she didn't help him to a chair.

"Keith," she said softly, putting her hand on his arm.

He yanked himself away. "Why did you do it?" he demanded.

"Keith..." She tried to touch him again, feeling an urgent need to grab him and hold on, knowing that a chasm had just opened between them that might be impossible to bridge. He jerked away again, one finger pointed at her in warning. The man who'd been the epitome of tenderness and consideration was suddenly all dark anger.

She didn't blame him, but she wanted to explain how innocent it had all been in the beginning, how she'd done it for the baby and then for him, and how it had all come to mean so much to her personally that not even a guilty conscience had been able to pull the truth out of her.

When she stumbled over an answer, he demanded again, "Why? Wasn't a hundred thousand dollars enough?"

For a minute she didn't know what he meant. Then she remembered the check she'd torn up in Greg's face. She hadn't even noticed the amount, only known she didn't want it. And while that might have felt satisfying then, she had a feeling it wouldn't stand her in very good stead now. Had Greg taped it together and cashed it, letting Keith believe she'd taken it?

She gathered her dignity around her and tried to feel as though she had some right to it. "Do you really want to know what happened?"

"I *know* what happened," he said in a thunderous voice. "I remember now. You were Greg's, not mine. Rebecca is..." His voice broke, then he tried again. "Rebecca is Greg's, not mine."

"Neither of us was ever his!" she screamed at him. "I was lonely, he was charming and funny, and I was a fool. I thought he was sincere when he said he loved me. I thought I could trust him when he said he was going to fight you so that we could be married."

The need to continue screaming at him was almost overwhelming, but she struggled to calm herself. It was so important that he understand.

"He told me you were insisting on a prenuptial agreement," she said, her voice high and anxious, "or he would be financially cut off. And he used that as an excuse to back out, saying that if that happened, our baby wouldn't have anything. Then he offered me the check, which I tore up."

"It was cashed," Keith said stiffly.

"Not by me," she returned. "I tore it up."

"Wanting to prove that your love was real?" he asked with sarcasm.

"To prove that I couldn't be bought," she corrected. "Then I transferred to the Northwest Eden. I'd have left the company altogether, but I needed my health insurance."

He jammed his hands in his pockets and turned as though he needed to pace. But the living room was impassable, so he stayed in the kitchen, going to the far window and looking out at the darkness.

"And you needed another Roper," he said grimly, "since the first one didn't come through?"

Emily felt as though her heart had stopped beating, as though life itself had stalled within her.

"I wasn't after a Roper," she said, struggling to breathe, to speak. "Greg approached me shortly after I started working at the Atlantic. He was charming and attentive and I fell for it. I'm ashamed for having been so stupid, but I have Rebecca, and that makes it hard to regret anything."

She'd said the words in all honesty, with no intention of hurting him, but she saw him press his stomach again as he continued to stare out at the night.

"When you did that tour of the kitchen here," she said, coming to stand behind him, "then came to my place afterward, so sure we'd been lovers, I tried a couple of times to correct you, but you were convinced. And you showed all the qualities I'd prayed to see in Greg but never did after I told him I was pregnant. And then you begged me to stay with you because you thought you remembered me!"

She drew a shaky breath. The burden of his pain and her own weighed on her like an anvil on her chest.

Keith turned away from the window, his expression unreadable.

"So there was never really any love for me involved," he said coolly. "It was either pity or convenience. You were either sorry for me and wanted to help, or I was just the brother who could do for you what the other couldn't.''

She felt as though she were sinking in quicksand.

"No," she said, forcing herself to keep talking. "I loved you because you *wanted* to love me. No one in my life ever had. But there you were, being everything I'd ever dreamed about—perfect husband, loving father.'' She made herself look into his eyes. "And every day I loved you more."

"And hoped, I imagine," he said, "that my memory never came back."

She squared her shoulders, prepared to admit the truth. "There were times in the beginning when I selfishly thought that. But the more I knew you and loved you, the more I wanted you to be able to reclaim your life."

"And that's why you let me believe that I loved you, and that your baby was my baby."

"Examine what you felt when you walked in the door five minutes ago," she challenged, her voice strained, "and deny either of those facts to me."

He glared at her a moment, then walked past her to the other end of the kitchen and turned to her.

"I can't deny," he said finally, "I've loved Rebecca since before I ever saw her, and I always will."

She tried to take comfort in that.

"But what I feel for you right now is too clouded in anger and a sense of treachery for me to understand what it is. I just know that it's no longer at all what it was—or at least, what I thought it was."

And that was as clean a stab to the heart as she'd ever experienced.

She raised her head and asked calmly, "Do you want me to go?"

"Yes," he said without hesitating even a heartbeat.

Emily felt the floor fall away from under her. Over. Done. Finished.

"But unlike you," he said, "I can't make major decisions based solely on what I want when there's a baby involved, and an old man whose health is shaky and who worships the ground you walk on."

She felt an instant's relief, then realized that staying might very well hurt as much as having to leave him.

"Then what do you want?" she asked.

He closed his eyes and shook his head. "Right now I don't know—" he opened his eyes with obvious reluctance, as though the sight of her was painful "—except that I don't want my parents upset tomorrow. Somehow we're going to have to pretend that everything's fine between us."

She couldn't imagine how she would do that, but she would. She loved his parents, too.

He went to the sofa for his coat. "I'm going out."

He headed for the door and left. A moment later there was the sound of a revving engine, then a tire-squealing exit from the driveway.

Emily stood in the small kitchen, thinking that somehow she'd come full circle. Here she was again, all alone. And she knew she had no one to blame but herself. She'd wanted too much; that had always been her problem.

A cry came from the bedroom. Emily went to get Rebecca, comforted by the knowledge that she had her baby, even if she was on the brink of losing everything else. But she wouldn't be the only loser here. If she and Keith couldn't find a solution, Rebecca would grow up without a father, because Emily knew she would never love another man the way she loved him.

And suddenly Emily saw her mother in a completely different light. Maybe she'd loved Emily's father the same way Emily loved Keith, and no other man could ever take his place.

A new understanding settled inside her. And a renewed sense of determination. If there was any way to make things up to Keith, to weather this so that they could stay together, she would find it.

Exhausted, both emotionally and physically, she fell asleep shortly after midnight. Keith hadn't come home.

SHE HEARD the baby cry and pulled herself awake. The memory of the earlier scene between Keith and her played out in her mind, flooding her with misery. She slowly swung her legs over the side of the bed, and stumbled through the darkness to the crib.

It was empty.

Her heart almost stopped. And then she realized that she could still hear baby sounds. She followed them halfway down the stairs and stopped when she saw a light on in the kitchen and heard Keith's quiet voice.

She sank onto a step and watched him with Rebecca

at his shoulder. He'd gotten a bottle out of the refrigerator and was putting it in the microwave.

He still wore his suit pants, but his sleeves were rolled up, his tie was gone, and he was in his stocking feet.

"What do you say we run away together?" he said to Rebecca as the microwave hummed. "My name's on your birth certificate, so it shouldn't be a problem for anybody. Your mom pulled a fast one on us there, but really, in every way that counts, you're mine...and I'm yours."

The microwave dinged. Emily shrank into the shadows as he wandered out of the kitchen and into the living room, holding both baby and bottle.

"God, what a mess this room is," he said. "Nothing's where it should be, and you have to move like a snake to get around. Want to go upstairs, Rebecca?"

Emily scrambled silently to her feet and ran up the steps, wanting desperately to get back into bed before he saw her.

But she forgot about the small side table she'd put in the hallway. She collided with it and couldn't stifle her cry of pain.

Keith was just climbing the stairs when he heard the crash. Even the baby stopped sucking on the bottle, her eyes wide.

He ran up and flipped on the light to see Emily righting the same little table *he'd* collided with when he'd heard the baby cry and gone to get her.

There was a look of fear on Emily's face. Had she overheard what he'd said to Rebecca about running away? He hoped so, though he wasn't entirely pleased with himself that he did. Still, he was in no mood to be judgmental about it. He wasn't the one who'd lied.

"Uh, I was on my way to the bathroom," she said, rubbing her knee. "I forgot I'd moved the table." She looked at the baby, who gave her a gummy smile. With a wary glance at Keith, she came closer and kissed Rebecca's cheek.

He caught a whiff of the floral scent of her hair and sensed the warmth of her body even though she didn't touch him.

"Thank you for getting up with her," she said, taking the nipple of the bottle and guiding it back to Rebecca's mouth. The baby settled against him again, sucking like a little machine.

"It's my job," he said, his words a threat. "Says so on the birth certificate."

A suggestion of anger flashed in her eyes, but it was supplanted instantly by love and pain and a trust that undercut his efforts to frighten her. "And you do it very well. Good night, Keith," she said, and went into the bathroom and closed the door.

He returned to the room she'd occupied when he'd first moved her into the guest house. Then he propped the pillows up against the headboard and lay in the dark with Rebecca. Trust. Ha. That was something he'd never extend to her again.

CHAPTER FIFTEEN

THE GUEST HOUSE was in a state of pandemonium. The women were crowded in the kitchen, David's daughters sat together in a large chair, one holding Rebecca, the other feeding her her bottle, and the men shouted to one another across the table that took up the center of the living room. They were watching football, their loyalties split between the two teams.

There was something wonderful about it, Keith thought. Or there would be if the sky hadn't fallen. Still, he was doing his best to behave as though all was well, and Emily seemed to be doing the same.

In fact, he rather resented her acting ability. She treated his parents with warm respect and everyone else to a friendly harassment they seemed to enjoy.

She came out of the kitchen with a platter of hors d'oeuvres and put them in the middle of the table, inviting the men to help themselves. "There'll be real food in about an hour," she promised. She patted Neil's shoulder affectionately as she went by.

Keith, in the act of passing a plate of hors d'oeuvres to his father, happened to catch Emily's eye. He saw pain there and realized that her warm hospitality was not coming easily at all.

He made sure his own face was blank. The pain in her eyes seemed to deepen and she turned back to the kitchen and the company of the hardworking laughing women.

David's wife dominated the conversation through dinner with stories about David that had even Keith laughing hysterically. Maria Ambrosio was a small woman with a dramatic delivery.

"And there I am, clinging to the shower rod, naked as a jaybird, with hot water spewing up the faucet, instead of down!" Everyone gasped and choked with laughter. "And here's David trying to reach the tap behind the tub with the handle of a plunger and yelling for the girls to get Mr. Walley next door. He's a plumber," she explained.

"And that," she added with an affectionate pat on David's cheek, "was the last time I ever let him fix anything that isn't food."

David gave her a reproachful look, then kissed her palm.

"Have you ever noticed," Jack said, helping himself to seconds of everything and passing platters around, "that no one ever has stories about Keith?"

"That's because nothing outrageous ever happens to people in control of the situation," Neil said. "Right, Keith?"

Janice dropped a dollop of cranberry sauce on a slice of turkey. "Emily must have stories," she said, passing the cut-glass bowl on to her. "The rumor is that he spirited you to the California Eden all the time for assignations. You must have something incriminating you can share with us.''

It occurred to Keith how sad it was that that wasn't true. Before his memory had returned, he'd filled the gaps with imaginings about those times Emily had said he'd sent for her. He created an elegant setting in his mind and placed her there with him, imagining quiet evenings by the fire, midnight raids on the refrigerator, long sunny mornings of lovemaking.

Now the knowledge that he hadn't even known Emily then was a blow to his heart. Still, he wouldn't have liked to be the butt of some story or be made to look ridiculous. He wasn't sure he had David's ability to laugh at himself—at least not right now. Right now nothing about him and Emily seemed very funny.

So he was shocked when Emily put her fork down and nodded her head. ''OK,'' she said, darting a warning glance in his direction, ''let me think.''

Everyone grinned at him, apparently thrilled at the prospect of hearing how he'd made a fool of himself. Then they turned to Emily, waiting expectantly.

He glowered at her from across the table, an expression he was sure everyone around the table presumed to be playful. But she would know better.

She met the look, held it with one that had that same strange combination of anger and love he'd seen in her eyes the night before, then turned away from him and smiled at her audience.

''I've got it,'' she said.

Everyone leaned closer.

"There was the time Keith tried to cook and the fire department came."

This was complete fiction, but a ripple of laughter and anticipation ran through her audience. "He was cooking bacon," she went on, "and thought he'd turned the heat off under the pan when he'd actually turned it up. In his condo, when the sprinkler system goes off, it alerts the fire department—so there I am in my nightgown, drenched to the bone and trying to explain to a group of firemen who've just been called out at six in the morning that it was all a mistake. As I recall," Emily said, the taunting smile she gave him really a dare, "you told me it was all *my* fault."

He looked into her eyes, accepting the dare. "No, it *was* your fault," he said. He turned to their guests. "Everything that's happened to me since I met her has been her fault."

There were loud groans of protest.

"Now how can you blame her," his father asked, "when *you* burned the bacon?"

"Because she distracted me while I was cooking it."

More groans and the taking of sides, and then Barbara launched into a story about Neil that involved their old cabin cruiser and a Coast Guard rescue.

Emily tallied takers for pumpkin pie and mince pie and carried a stack of plates into the kitchen.

Janice and Barbara followed with more dishes, and Maria brought in the leftovers.

Emily carried her pies to the far corner of the

kitchen and fumbled in an overhead cupboard for a set of fancy dessert plates that were just beyond her reach.

"You do have an active imagination," Keith said under his breath as he stood behind her and brought down the plates. "Bacon? Sprinkler systems? Angry firemen?"

"You wanted the day to go well," she replied without turning to him. She could feel his body against her, smell his herbal cologne. "So I made up a past for us. I thought I went really easy on you."

She was now so accustomed to his nearness that she could tell a change of mood without even looking at him.

"Not from where I'm standing," he said. It was clear they were no longer talking about the story she'd made up—at least not the one about the bacon.

The guests stayed late and had sandwiches. They'd moved the dining-room table back and replaced the furniture, and everyone ate off their laps. The conversation was more subdued now, nostalgic rather than funny. Jack sat in a chair with Rebecca asleep in his arms, and Janice sat on the floor with David's girls, looking through a movie magazine one of them had brought.

Emily came in with a bottle of brandy and glasses, and hot chocolate for the girls. When she'd finished passing them around, she looked for a place to sit.

Barbara and Neil had the love seat. David and Maria were curled up on one end of the sofa. Keith sat at the other end, knees relaxed and apart, taking up the extra room. So Emily turned to get one of the kitchen chairs.

Keith wasn't ready to make the concession, but his mother had been watching him surreptitiously for the past few hours, and he didn't want to do anything to feed what he was sure was already a suspicion.

"Come here, Em," he said, moving closer to the corner of the sofa and making room for her.

She turned back at the kitchen doorway, looked at the space he'd made, then at him, and he could see what she was thinking. *No, thank you.*

But he patted the cushion invitingly for the benefit of everyone watching, then firmed his expression, indicating she'd better accept his invitation.

She finally did, not sitting stiffly beside him as he'd expected, but leaning into the curve he'd made of his body and taking the arm he'd placed on the back of the sofa and bringing it over her shoulder. Then she even entwined her fingers in his.

Damn her, he thought. She always went too far. He'd wanted the day to be warm and welcoming for his parents, his cousins and his friends, and she had to go and make it wonderful, even memorable. She had to join in the storytelling by making up a crazy tale about him. And then, when all he wanted was for her to cooperate and sit beside him, she had to move into his personal space and make him sharply aware of how much he missed this sort of intimacy with her.

It was almost impossible, he realized, to have his arm around her and not respond. But he tried. He wanted to make it look to everyone else as though everything was fine without touching Emily in any way she could interpret as forgiveness.

Then he realized she was doing the same thing. She'd cuddled against him, but her body was stiff, the hand holding his, cold.

He got the bleakly amusing picture in his mind of two penguins on an ice floe.

"Well," his father said, "this has been the greatest Thanksgiving Day I can remember in years." He squeezed Barbara's shoulder. "Don't you think, Babs?"

"Yes. Very definitely." She was leaning against Neil's shoulder and she straightened with a smile. "I'd been afraid the holidays would be awful this year, but..." Her voice faltered. When Neil patted her arm reassuringly, she went on. "But instead, I think they're going to be wonderful. I'm really looking forward to Christmas. We'll have to do it at our house to have room for the presents we're already collecting for Rebecca. What do you say?"

She looked around the group, and the nods were enthusiastic and unanimous, although Keith's and Emily's were forcedly so.

"We've had a wonderful time, too," Maria said, smiling at Emily. "David and I both come from big Italian families, and today reminded me of being with them. Thank you."

Janice, too, smiled up at Emily, then at Keith. "Jack and I were talking about it," she said, "and if we didn't already belong to this family, we'd probably apply for membership."

"And I'd like to apply for one of these," Jack said in a very soft voice, indicating the cherubic baby asleep in his arms.

"They're not available by application, Jack." David laughed. "You have to make your own."

Jack grinned. "Not another one of those do-it-yourself things that comes with foreign instructions."

David laughed again. "There are often lots of instructions involved, though mine weren't foreign. Ow!"

That last was a response to an elbow in the side from Maria. "I really hate to break this up," she said, "but we should get the girls home."

Both were sound asleep on the floor.

David got his older daughter to her feet and led her out to the car while Keith carried the younger girl.

The group stood around to wave the Ambrosios off and that seemed to create an exodus. Janice hugged everyone and Jack reluctantly handed the baby to Emily.

"Thank you," he said. "This has been a great day."

"Save us Christmas," Barbara reminded him.

"Of course we will." He and Janice climbed into his truck and drove off with a beep of the horn.

"I'll walk you guys down the lane," Keith said. "I'll be right back," he told Emily.

She smiled. "I'll be waiting," she said for his parents' benefit. She ignored his grim glance and hurried inside.

It was a cold crisp night, and the moon lit their way

up the long drive toward the big house. Barbara turned suddenly to Keith. "What's the problem?" she asked.

Keith's sound of surprise wasn't entirely forced. "What do you mean? There's no problem."

"She told you about the baby, didn't she?" Neil said.

Keith stopped. "What?"

Barbara took his hand and drew him gently toward the house. Neil hooked an arm around his shoulder.

"We've known from the beginning," Barbara said, her voice serene. There was a gust of wind from the ocean and she huddled closer to him. "And you knew before the accident that Greg had gotten her pregnant. Do you remember that?"

"Yes, I do now." Keith turned to his father in concern. "Are you OK? You shouldn't be getting upset."

"The only thing that upsets me," Neil said, "is that the two of you didn't look happy today. You acted like it, but you didn't fool me or your mother."

"You didn't tell us about Emily and Greg at the time," his mother went on. "I imagine it was because you were trying to protect us. We all went through a lot with Greg." She sighed as though she'd accepted that was over. "But—" she squeezed his arm "—a mother's always watching. I went to the Atlantic to help Janice with the ballroom—frustrated decorator that I am—and though Greg never brought Emily to meet me, I saw them together on several occasions. You did spend a few days at the Atlantic around the time she would have gotten pregnant, but I like to think you wouldn't have been so careless, or if you had been, you'd have done something about it. Leaving a pregnant young woman to fend for herself is Greg's style, not yours.''

They'd reached the back door of the house. Neil unlocked it and flipped on the kitchen light.

''After the accident, when we brought you home and you told us you thought you remembered her, you seemed so happy with that knowledge.'' Barbara smiled warmly, holding his hand in her two. ''I thought you were mistaken, but it didn't seem like the time to try to tell you what I thought. And although we didn't really know Emily, David always raved about her, so we thought it wise to just let things be, hoping that allowing you to believe you had this wonderful connection would ultimately be better for you.''

Keith felt a burning in his heart that spread across his chest and into his throat.

Neil squeezed his shoulder, his eyes full of love and pride. ''I know what hurts the most. You're thinking the baby is Greg's and not yours. But genetic makeup isn't responsible for love and spirit, and yet at almost two months old, Rebecca is filled with both. You did that.''

For all his anger at Emily, he couldn't deny her devotion as a mother. ''Emily's with her all the time.''

''Who took Emily into his life and loved her so that she could be safe and happy and make a home for her baby? And in return you got a woman who's made you smile and laugh. You didn't do that very much after Celine.''

That wasn't exactly how Keith saw it, but he didn't

want to argue about it now. He'd loved Emily and invited her to share his home with him because he'd thought they had a past. Because he'd thought she was carrying his child.

It seemed reasonable that if his premise was wrong, that negated all the results, like a faulty experiment.

It seemed reasonable—it just didn't *feel* reasonable.

He hugged his mother, then his father. "When your love came back to me," he said, remembering that moment on the roof garden, "I felt strong. And I remembered clearly every time you came through for me—even in little ways. Thank you." He studied his father. "You had a big day. You'd better take it easy tomorrow."

Neil poked a finger at Keith's chest. "You're running the hotel, Keith, but kindly remember that you do not run your father."

"No, you're right. Mom does."

Barbara chuckled, then looked severe. "Neil, you're taking it easy tomorrow." Then she smiled again. "But that'll be no hardship because you'll have football on television and Emily's leftovers."

"Hmm." Neil tried to look disgruntled, but failed. "All right, then." He turned to Keith. "You should do the same thing. You have the weekend off. Try to relax and then think things through. You'll come to the right decision."

As Keith walked back up the lane in the fragrant windy darkness, he decided that his father had more faith in him than he did. Right now he couldn't imagine how things could be made right.

He let himself into the kitchen. The dishwasher was running, the turkey roaster sat in hot sudsy water in the sink, and a choral group on television sang sentimental songs about love and family.

The house felt warm and cozy, wonderful aromas still lingering in the air. It had been precisely the kind of day he'd hoped it would be. Emily had extended herself beyond the call of duty to see that his family and friends were made to feel welcome. Because he was so angry with her, it annoyed him that she'd been the perfect hostess. He wasn't sure that made sense, but didn't think it had to. He was the wronged party. He could feel however the hell he chose.

He found fresh coffee in the pot and poured himself a cup. Then he studied the remaining half of a pumpkin pie wrapped to be returned to the refrigerator, trying to decide if he was actually hungry or simply wanted it.

Before he could make up his mind, he heard light footsteps on the stairs, and Emily walked into the kitchen. She gave him a brief neutral glance, then reached into a cupboard and took out a saucer. "Your parents all right?" she asked.

He leaned back against the counter, crossing one ankle over the other. "They're fine. I think they had a good time."

"I'm glad," she said, pulling the plastic wrap off the pie. She cut a generous wedge and put it on the saucer. "I've really come to love them." She turned and held the saucer out to him.

He straightened to accept it, but his manner remained unyielding. It annoyed him that even when he was angry with her, she could still anticipate his wants and needs. "And yet you've been lying to them for months."

It was a direct attack and probably not fair, considering the day she'd put in, but he had a need to cause her the kind of pain he felt. He just wished there was more pleasure in it.

Her shoulders slumped for an instant, then she covered what was left of the pie and put it in the refrigerator.

"No," she said, her face pale. "You brought me into your family and told them who you thought I was—the woman you loved and who loved you. And I didn't correct you because by that time—" she closed the refrigerator door and stared up at him "—that was who I was."

Her look of fragility made him lose all heart for a quarrel. That annoyed him. It occurred to him that he was annoyed by quite a few things, but again, he considered himself entitled.

Noticing the full trash bag, he put his pie aside and carried the bag out to the can behind the house. He drew in a deep breath of cold air, wondering why he felt moody and tense around Emily when she was the one who'd deceived him.

He went back inside and reclaimed his pie. "Is there anything else I can do?" he asked.

"Thank you," she said, "but I have everything under control."

"Then I'll take my coffee upstairs."

"Good night," she said pleasantly, but didn't turn around.

"Good night," he replied.

Upstairs he stopped in the doorway to his room, noticing instantly that something was missing. The crib.

He put the pie and coffee down on his bedside table and marched down the hall to the room he'd occupied the night before and found that Emily had moved back into it and had brought the baby.

He rolled the crib slowly and carefully out of the room, down the hall and back into his room, putting it against the wall where it had been before. His name was on the birth certificate. Emily could damn well separate herself from him, but she couldn't take Rebecca.

It was more than an hour before he heard her leave the kitchen and start upstairs.

He switched off his bedside lamp and turned his back to the open doorway.

Her footsteps topped the stairs and then moved quietly in the other direction. A light went on. There was a moment's pause, then firm footsteps toward his room.

"She'll have you up at least twice tonight." Her words flew over his head like warning shots. "Maybe three times. By then she's going to want me and not some imitation."

"I adjusted to an imitation," he said coolly. "So will she. Go to bed before you wake her up."

There was another brief pause, then the footsteps marched in the other direction and the door of the bedroom down the hall closed quietly.

CHAPTER SIXTEEN

KEITH STRUGGLED to let go of his anger. He knew he had to. He'd come to the conclusion sometime during the night that he couldn't live without Emily and Rebecca. The rage he'd maintained over how she'd lied to him did not seem to override his need for her and the baby.

It was early afternoon and rain beat relentlessly against the roof and windows. He'd moved the furniture back into the living room that morning, then checked on his father after lunch while Emily tidied up. His father had cajoled him into watching the rest of a football game with him, and his mother asked him on his way out how things were between him and Emily.

"We're working on it," he said noncommittally.

"Well, work harder," his mother admonished, reaching up to kiss his cheek. "I want to see your smile back. Emily's, too."

The guest house was quiet when he walked in. He guessed Emily was upstairs with Rebecca.

He found the baby asleep in her crib in his room, but no sign of Emily. Then he heard the sound of the shower running in Emily's bathroom.

Virulent need and desire warred with his anger. It was no contest. He followed the sound. The baby quilt Emily worked on in the evenings lay on her bed. He went past it into the bathroom.

As he walked in, the shower stopped.

EMILY STOOD for a moment behind the steamy glass doors and concluded that the shower hadn't helped her headache.

She struggled to cope with the fact that her life stood on a knife edge, one way promising everything a woman could hope for herself and her baby, and the other simply repeating the loneliness she already knew so well.

She yanked off her shower cap, ruffled her hair and determined there was nothing to be gained by standing around analyzing it. She pushed open the shower door and reached for her towel. But it wasn't there.

"This what you're looking for?"

She gasped as Keith stepped into view, her towel over his shoulder.

Disbelief battled with hope inside her and the struggle left her breathless.

"Yes," she whispered, reaching out a hand for it.

He took a step backward. "Well, come and get it," he said. His eyes were dark and turbulent with a passion she'd been afraid she'd never see again.

She questioned him with her eyes, afraid to presume.

He came toward her then and wrapped the towel

around her. "It comes with a qualified operator," he said, and pulled her into his arms.

She melted against him, helpless with love, relief, gratitude. She wrapped her arms around his neck and kissed him with all the fervor those emotions fanned in her.

The tension and the enforced emotional separation of the past two days stirred her fervor quickly to flame, and before either said another word she'd lost the towel, Keith was free of his clothes and they were entangled in a swift and wild lovemaking on her bed.

Emily welcomed him into her, whispering words of penance and promise.

Keith took all she offered, thrusting deep inside her, laying claim, staking possession.

It was only then that Emily became aware of the subtle difference in his touch. But it was too late.

He didn't notice the stiffening of her body, only pulled her closer to him as he came.

Her traitorous body responded and she uttered a little cry that was half pleasure, half anguish, as she crested with him.

When he rolled off to lie beside her with his arm around her, she pushed away from him and scrambled to her feet. She went to the closet, yanked her robe off a hook and pulled it on. Walking to the foot of the bed, she said, "That wasn't about love at all, Keith. Why did you do it?"

He looked confused for a moment, then sighed. "Because I thought it was time we—"

"Had sex again," she finished for him.

"No." He got to his feet and tugged on his jeans. "If we're going to stay together, we have to start communicating again."

"Are we staying together?"

He zipped and buttoned the fly, casting her a look of impatience. "I thought you wanted to."

"Oh, I do," she said, "but why do *you* want to?"

Keith grabbed his T-shirt from the floor and pulled it over his head, unwilling to let her see the need she sparked in him, the way it grew greedy and large when he held her.

"Because Rebecca is mine now," he said, tucking his shirt into his jeans. "And we have to start building a life for her."

Some awful emotion was visible in her eyes and it reached out to stab him. She pressed her lips together to stop their trembling, then said, "So Rebecca belongs to you, but in your mind *I'll* always belong to Greg, is that it?"

"No, that isn't it!" he shouted. "But you can't expect me to act as though nothing's changed. I fell in love with you because you lied to me about our life together! You think I'll get over that in two days?"

"Oh, no, you didn't!" she denied hotly. "You loved me because you loved me! And you're holding on to anger because you can't accept your own responsibility for that!"

"*My* responsibility?" he demanded. "What in hell did *I* do?"

"You loved me!" she said again. "And not because

of Rebecca, but because of *me!*'' They stood at the foot of the bed glaring at each other.

"I had no memory! I believed what you told me!"

"I didn't tell you that we'd been lovers," she said. "*You* told me we'd been lovers, and you were so sure that you insisted I move in with you that very night. You pleaded with me to stay with you!"

"And you tried so hard to convince me that I was mistaken," he said with quiet sarcasm.

She had to take blame for that. "You're right. I went along with you because it didn't take me any time to see that you were what I'd been looking for all my life and I didn't want to lose you." She swallowed. "But have you ever considered why you suddenly remembered everything about your past except those few months before the accident?"

He stiffened. "What are you suggesting?"

"I think," she said, gentling her tone, "that somewhere inside you, you knew the truth and you didn't want to deal with it, so you kept it at bay. You used to have a reputation for being ruthless about getting what you wanted, the way you wanted it. I think you became a little selective about what you wanted to remember and what you chose to forget."

He considered that for a moment, then nodded, his expression arrogant. "Well, that's entirely possible— I would've preferred never to have to deal with what you've done. But there's Rebecca."

Emily's dream of a beautiful future disappeared. "And you think I would stay with you," she said coldly, "because I want a father for Rebecca."

He studied her a moment as though her answer had surprised him. Then he planted his hands on his hips. "No," he replied. "I think you'll stay with me because however we came to this, she is now mine."

Emotion clogged her throat and beat like a drum in her ears. "If I didn't love you," she said, her voice little more than a whisper, "I might be able to do that. But I don't ever want my daughter to see what it's like when love isn't returned. We'll leave in the morning." She turned toward the bathroom, desperate to get away.

Keith was lost for an argument. He *did* return her love, and he *did* regret that their lovemaking just now had been about sex rather than communication of that love. But he didn't know how to make her believe him after what they'd just said to each other.

So he straightened his shoulders and threatened loudly, "I won't let you take Rebecca! She's mine."

"Then I'll see you in court!" she sobbed, and closed the bathroom door behind her.

Rebecca began to cry from the other room.

KEITH STAYED downstairs with Rebecca all evening. Emily stayed in her room.

There was a knock on the front door at nine o'clock. It was Janice with Bill Dodge from security, only he was wearing a suit instead of his uniform. Behind them stood Jack and Vangie. The four of them shared two umbrellas.

Janice ran into Keith's arms, her cheeks pink, her eyes bright with excitement. She looked as though she had a new lease on life. The last thing he thought he could cope with at that moment was someone else's happiness.

But there was no avoiding it, and Keith invited all four of them in. "Can I offer you coffee or a drink?" he asked politely, gesturing them into the living room after they'd shed their coats and left their umbrellas outside.

Janice dismissed the niceties with a wave of her hands. "Guess what?" she demanded.

He sighed. "Ah, I give up."

She didn't seem to mind. "I sold the condo! For an absolutely staggering sum because it's been personally decorated by me and because the president of Cosmetech bought it for his summer home. Now I can pay you back the rest of what I owe."

"I told you not to sell your home." Keith turned to Jack for support, but found that he'd picked up Rebecca and was dancing around the living room with her while Bill and Vangie inspected the contents of a candy bowl.

"I know. And I told you I wanted to. So we'll be square." She hugged him again, and this time she didn't let go. "Thank you, Keith, for proving to me that you're never down too low or in too deep that love can't bring you back." She gave him a final squeeze, then asked, "Where's Emily?"

He pointed upstairs. "Catching up on some sleep," he lied. Then he hooked a thumb at her companions. "You and Dodge?" he asked quietly.

She nodded, her eyes serene. "He came to see me

after the...incident and asked me if I wanted to talk. I did. We did. And now—'' she smiled hugely ''—he's coming to the Atlantic with Jack and me. But right now, we're all going dancing. Vangie and Jack have been exchanging greetings for months—every time he walks by the front desk—so he thought it was time he carried things a little farther. I was hoping you and Emily would join us.''

''Sorry,'' he said. ''Maybe next time.''

The group left on a wave of cheer and laughter and he watched jealously as they piled into a small import car and drove away.

Closing the door, he walked back to the sofa and lay down with a now wide-awake Rebecca on his chest, thinking about what Janice had said. *You're never down too low or in too deep that love can't bring you back.*

In his case, he wasn't so sure.

He took Rebecca up to her crib around eleven, then leaned over her for a moment and rubbed her tummy when she fussed at being moved. Soon she was asleep again. He covered her and tiptoed out of the room.

He walked quietly down the hall to Emily's room. Her door was ajar and, sticking his head in, he looked for some sign that she was awake. But she slept like someone exhausted, flat on her back, completely still, one arm hanging over the side of the bed.

He crossed to her and lifted her arm back onto the bed. Her hand was cold, and he held it in his for a moment, then pulled the blanket over her.

He fought an impulse to shake her awake, apologize

for hurting her, tell her he had no intention of ever letting her go.

But she needed her sleep. He would tell her in the morning.

He went back to his room to lie down and close his eyes, certain he wouldn't be able to sleep.

HE AWOKE to the sound of rain on the roof, rain on the windows. Still.

His head ached and he was hot. He'd fallen asleep on top of the covers, fully dressed, and had awakened sometime during the night, frozen to the marrow. He'd changed into sweats and climbed under the blankets.

Now he threw the covers back and sat up as his mind came awake with jarring suddenness. Emily. He was going to apologize to Emily this morning and try to put their lives back together.

Out of habit he looked toward Rebecca's crib and saw that it was empty. Emily must already be up.

He swung his legs over the side of the bed and pulled on his running shoes, his heart tripping at the thought of trying to make her see things his way. It wouldn't be easy.

Not until he was halfway down the stairs did he realize how silent the house was. The rain beat down on everything, of course, but at this time of year in Oregon rain was such a constant that he rarely noticed the sound. But over the past couple of months his ears had become accustomed to the music of domesticity— the rattle and ping of dishes and pans in the kitchen, humming, laughter, baby sounds that were nonsense yet somehow poignantly significant, and Emily's voice pitched to respond to Rebecca.

He heard none of that this morning.

He ran down the last few steps and stopped dead. No Emily. No Rebecca. And then he remembered what Emily had said the night before. *We'll leave in the morning.*

He looked around the empty rooms and saw his life unfold before him—not as it had been, but as it would be without his wife and his daughter. Nothing. Nothing everywhere he turned.

He indulged in one moment of abject terror, of complete despair, of absolute desperation. Then he pulled himself together and glanced at his watch. It was just after seven. She couldn't have gotten far. He ran upstairs for his keys and was in the Lexus in seconds, ripping down the lane toward the road.

He made the corner almost on two wheels, his foot to the floor as he prepared himself to search every road in Oregon if necessary. His heart sank when he saw nothing ahead of him on the long ribbon of road. But he *would* find her. He had to believe that or there was nothing left for him.

He noticed a bright patch of red on the side of the road and then a bright patch of yellow. Walkers, those brave souls who challenged the elements to get their daily cardiovascular workout.

It was only as he sped past, his windshield wipers working frantically, that he noticed that the yellow walker was carrying a front pack and holding an umbrella over herself and her much taller companion. The red walker waved at him.

His father! Emily!

Keith checked his mirror quickly, then screeched to a stop and did a tight U-turn. He pulled up to where they'd stopped to wait for him.

He was a mass of frayed nerves as he got out of the car, but he forced himself to be calm.

"Hey, you're too late!" his father said cheerfully. "We've already done our mile. Want to have breakfast with us?"

Breakfast. He'd spent endless minutes certain his wife had left him, and here his father was talking breakfast.

"What are you two doing?" he asked a little more sharply than he'd intended. He pointed to his father. "*You* are supposed to be taking it easy, and *you*—" he pointed to Emily "—have a baby out in the pouring rain."

Emily gave him a look that reminded him of how angry she'd been the night before. "I woke up really early and decided to bake a coffee cake. I brought some over to your parents and your father was heading out for a walk, so I thought I'd keep him company."

Neil put an arm around her. "Nice girl. She didn't think I should go off on my own. Your mother's still asleep."

Keith pointed to the Lexus. "Get in and I'll drive you back."

"But we're—" his father began.

"Please." Keith's voice held an edge of frustration

that made Emily and his father look at each other and turn to the car.

Barbara met them in the driveway with her umbrella.

"Where *were* you?" she demanded of Neil.

Neil rolled his eyes at Emily and Keith as the three got out of the car. "I was walking with my daughter-in-law and my granddaughter," he said with exaggerated patience. "Is that all right with you?"

Barbara leaned into the car to smile and coo at the baby, then turned to Neil with a ferocious expression. "Well, you might have told me. I've been out of my mind with worry."

"You were asleep," Neil said.

"You could have written a note."

Emily hugged Barbara and explained about delivering the coffee cake just as Neil was leaving on his walk. "I'm sorry we worried you." Then she hugged Neil and grinned conspiratorially. "Next time we decide to get some exercise it seems we'll have to consult our personal trainers first. Enjoy the coffee cake."

Emily and Keith watched as Barbara preceded Neil into the house. "I've already eaten half of it," they heard her say to him. "So there."

Neil swatted her playfully. "You must have really been worried."

Keith smiled, then climbed into the car beside a grim-faced Emily. Neither said anything until they were back in the guest house and she'd put Rebecca in the carrier on the kitchen counter and pulled out a frying pan.

Keith kept his distance, unsure what she intended to do with it.

"Look," she said, dropping the pan onto the stove with a clang. "I'm sorry you were worried, but when I got to your parents and your father was heading out on his own, I was a little concerned. He's been fine, but I didn't think he should go off with nobody around to help if he had a problem. So I went along."

It would have been easy to simply accept her apology, but Keith swallowed his pride and told her the truth.

"I was worried," he said, going to lean on the counter beside the baby, "because last night you said you and Rebecca were leaving this morning."

She went to the refrigerator and came back with eggs and milk and a loaf of bread. Her quick glance at him was wry. "Yeah, well, it was big talk. You said I couldn't do that because she was your daughter, and she is..."

Her face crumpled suddenly. Sobbing, she put both hands to her face.

Keith pulled her into his arms, feeling every one of her sobs as though it was his own.

"Emmie, I'm sorry," he said, holding her close. "I understand what happened. I was just being a rat about it because...I don't know. I guess I wanted someone to suffer with me."

She raised her head from his shoulder, tears streaming down her face. "I don't see how you could understand what I did to you, when even I don't understand it!" She continued to sob, then drew a breath and tried to go on. "You just seemed so...so sure that we belonged to you, and...and even though I barely knew you, you cared so much m-more about the baby than Greg ever did." She fell against him again. "I wasn't strong enough to make you listen to the truth."

He rubbed her back and kissed the top of her head. "It's OK, it's OK. I'm glad you didn't. The truth is, when Greg told me about you and I saw you in the kitchen at the Atlantic, I wished you were mine, instead of his."

She looked up at him again, her eyes pools of midnight. "You did?"

He nodded. "I did. I imagined what I'd do if you *were* mine. I even imagined making love to you." He smiled grimly. "I think that's what caused the short in my brain. I knew Greg had died, and when I saw you here, all I remembered was making love to you. Because I thought it was real. I wanted it to be real."

Her shiny eyes studied him with a love that humbled him. "If I could give something," she said, her voice tight with emotion, "an eye or a limb, *some-*thing, so that I could turn things back and Rebecca could be yours, instead of—"

He kissed her before she could finish. "She *is* mine," he said. "That'll never be in question. And I want you whole because we're going to have one long eventful life together. Tell me that's what you want, too."

Emily closed her eyes and clung to him, saying a fervent prayer of thanks that God was merciful, as well as just. "Yes. Oh, yes."

Rebecca squealed from her carrier. Keith and Emily turned to her to see her give her gummy smile, her arms and legs flailing.

Keith lifted her out of the carrier and held her next to his heart. Emily leaned into him, one hand on the arm that held their baby.

Rain beat on the roof and on the windows, but Emily felt sunshine on her face.

EVER HAD ONE OF THOSE DAYS?

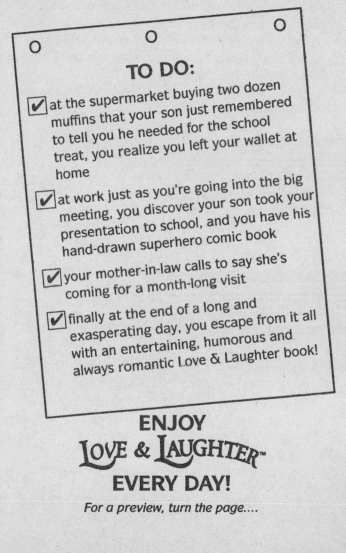

TO DO:

☑ at the supermarket buying two dozen muffins that your son just remembered to tell you he needed for the school treat, you realize you left your wallet at home

☑ at work just as you're going into the big meeting, you discover your son took your presentation to school, and you have his hand-drawn superhero comic book

☑ your mother-in-law calls to say she's coming for a month-long visit

☑ finally at the end of a long and exasperating day, you escape from it all with an entertaining, humorous and always romantic Love & Laughter book!

ENJOY
LOVE & LAUGHTER™
EVERY DAY!

For a preview, turn the page....

*Here's a sneak peek at
Carrie Alexander's THE AMOROUS HEIRESS
Available September 1997...*

"YOU'RE A VERY popular lady," Jed Kelley observed as Augustina closed the door on her suitors.

She waved a hand. "Just two of a dozen." Technically true since her grandmother had put her on the open market. "You're not afraid of a little competition, are you?"

"Competition?" He looked puzzled. "I thought the position was mine."

Augustina shook her head, smiling coyly. "You didn't think Grandmother was the final arbiter of the decision, did you? I say a trial period is in order." No matter that Jed Kelley had miraculously passed Grandmother's muster, Augustina felt the need for a little propriety. But, on the other hand, she could be married before the summer was out and be free as a bird, with the added bonus of a husband it wouldn't be all that difficult to learn to love.

She got up the courage to reach for his hand, and then just like that, she—Miss Gussy Gutless Fairchild—was holding Jed Kelley's hand. He looked down at their linked hands. "Of course, you don't really know what sort of work I can do, do you?"

A funny way to put it, she thought absently, cradling his callused hand between both of her own. "We can get to know each other, and then, if that works out..." she murmured. *Wow.* If she'd known what this arranged marriage thing was all about, she'd have been a supporter of Grandmother's campaign from the start!

"Are you a palm reader?" Jed asked gruffly. His voice was as raspy as sandpaper and it was rubbing her all the right ways, but the question flustered her. She dropped his hand.

"I'm sorry."

"No problem," he said, "as long as I'm hired."

"Hired!" she scoffed. "What a way of putting it!"

Jed folded his arms across his chest. "So we're back to the trial period."

"Yes." Augustina frowned and her gaze dropped to his work boots. Okay, so he wasn't as well off as the majority of her suitors, but really, did he think she was going to *pay* him to marry her?

"Fine, then." He flipped her a wave and, speechless, she watched him leave. She was trembling all over like a malaria victim in a snowstorm, shot with hot charges and cold shivers until her brain was numb. This couldn't be true. Fantasy men didn't happen to nice girls like her.

"Augustina?"

Her grandmother's voice intruded on Gussy's privacy. "Ahh. There you are. I see you met the new gardener?"

Breathtaking romance is predicted in your future with Harlequin's newest collection: Fortune Cookie.

Three of your favorite Harlequin authors, Janice Kaiser, Margaret St. George and M.J. Rodgers will regale you with the romantic adventures of three heroines who are promised fame, fortune, danger and intrigue when they crack open their fortune cookies on a fateful night at a Chinese restaurant.

Join in the adventure with your own personalized fortune, inserted in every book!

Don't miss this exciting new collection!

Available in September
wherever Harlequin books are sold.

HARLEQUIN®

HARLEQUIN SUPERROMANCE®

EMERGENCY!

If you love medical drama and romance on the wards,
then our new medical series by bestselling author
Bobby Hutchinson will bring you to fever pitch....

August 1997—THE BABY DOCTOR (#753)
by Bobby Hutchinson

Dr. Morgan Jacobsen is a skilled obstetrician.
Unfortunately, outside of work she's a klutz. Her
new partner at The Women's Center, Dr. Luke Gilbert,
brings out the worst in her, but Morgan brings out
the best in *him*—and his daughter—until their
children become friends. Then there's more
trouble than even Morgan can handle....

**Look for *The Baby Doctor* in August wherever
Harlequin books are sold.**

HARLEQUIN AND SILHOUETTE
ARE PLEASED TO PRESENT

Born in the USA

Love, marriage—and the pursuit of family!

Check your retail shelves for these upcoming titles:

July 1997
Last Chance Cafe by Curtiss Ann Matlock
The most determined bachelor in Oklahoma is in trouble! A
lovely widow with three daughters has moved next door—and
the girls want a dad! But he wants to know if their mom needs
a husband....

August 1997
Thorne's Wife by Joan Hohl
Pennsylvania. It was only to be a marriage of convenience—
until they fell in love! Now, three years later, tragedy
threatens to separate them forever and Valerie wants only to
be in the strength of her husband's arms. For she has some
very special news for the expectant father...

September 1997
Desperate Measures by Paula Detmer Riggs
New Mexico judge Amanda Wainwright's daughter has been
kidnapped, and the price of her freedom is a verdict in
favor of a notorious crime boss. So enters ex-FBI agent
Devlin Buchanan—ruthless, unstoppable—and soon there is
no risk he will not take for her.

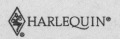

HARLEQUIN®   Silhouette®

Let's Celebrate!

LOVE & LAUGHTER™

invites you to
the party of the season!

Grab your popcorn and be prepared to laugh
as we celebrate with **LOVE & LAUGHTER**.

Harlequin's newest series is going Hollywood!

Let us make you laugh with three months of terrific
books, authors and romance, plus a chance to win a
FREE 15-copy video collection of the best romantic
comedies ever made.

For more details look in the back pages of any
Love & Laughter title, from July to September,
at your favorite retail outlet.

Don't forget the popcorn!

Available wherever
Harlequin books are sold.

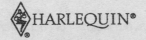

◆ HARLEQUIN®

Look us up on-line at: http://www.romance.net   LLCELEB

HARLEQUIN WOMEN KNOW ROMANCE WHEN THEY SEE IT.

And they'll see it on **ROMANCE CLASSICS**, the new 24-hour TV channel devoted to romantic movies and original programs like the special **Romantically Speaking-Harlequin® Goes Prime Time.**

Romantically Speaking-Harlequin® Goes Prime Time introduces you to many of your favorite romance authors in a program developed exclusively for Harlequin® readers.

Watch for **Romantically Speaking-Harlequin® Goes Prime Time** beginning in the summer of 1997.

If you're not receiving ROMANCE CLASSICS, call your local cable operator or satellite provider and ask for it today!

Escape to the network of your dreams.

ROMANCE CLASSICS